chakravyuh

chakravyuh

THROUGH THE EYES OF THE YOUNG WARRIOR

THE MISFORTUNES OF A FATHER
ARE GIFTS TO HIS SON

ANIKET S SHARMA

AUTHOR'S CHANNEL

http://authorschannel.in/

http://authorschannel.in/

108,1st floor,3rd cross, 3rd stage,
8th Main, Pillana Garden Lingarajapurm,
Bangalore 560045

First Edition 2019.

Second Edition 2020.

ISBN 978-81-936602-8-7

Edited by Suranjan Paul

KARMANYE VADHIKARASTE MA PHALESHU KADACHANA!
MA KARMAPHALAHETURBHURMA TE SANGOSTVAKARMANI!!

(Bhagavad Geeta, Chapter 2, Verse 47)

To Vaani

CONTENTS

INTRODUCTION

LOVE, PASSION, DECEIT, ANGER, loyalty, betrayal, war, peace, luxury and austerity; these experiences are a part of every human life. Our life changes every moment, our thoughts change every second, some succumb to the miseries, and some become immortal. A young boy, born in luxury, descendant to a powerful lineage was separated from his father at the age of three. For thirteen years, he lived with his maternal relatives, learnt the lessons of life, controlled his wrath, and finally, when he met his father, alas, destiny had other plans. He was invited to the cruelest battle of humankind, fought to prevail justice and Dharma. This is the story of a son, a brother, a husband, a fighter, and an intellect. This is story of ABHIMANYU.

Abhimanyu, the son of Subhadra and Arjuna, nephew of Krishna, was born in a palace, was separated from his father, but lived the life of a prince with his maternal uncles. He was a born warrior and was destined to become immortal. The story revolves around the protagonist, Abhimanyu and his presence in the battlefield for thirteen days. He speaks his mind to what he sees in the battlefield. His judgment of the situations is his own and he sees the world through his eyes. Though he follows the commands of his elders, but his vision is aligned with a different world. By the age of sixteen he had seen many folds of life and each fold has taught him many lessons. Thanks to Krishna, he is a learned scholar and a dignified warrior. Although he has spent sixteen years in a palace, his enthusiasm of learning texts, arts and war form added immense value in his upbringing. The knowledge he gained in the abode of Krishna helps him in learning the insights of life on the battlefield. The palette of weapons, when paints the earth red, the lives when convert to a pile of mere dust and bones, the warriors when become just pieces of flesh, a young boy beating in midst of all odds writes a new chapter in the history for the future generations.

He is fearless, he is valiant, but he is young. What he sees in the field, he evaluates as per his knowledge of world and desires.

He is not restricted with the dogmas of Kshatriya dharma; neither is he bound by any vows. He represents a group with the ambition of prevailing justice and his presence in the field is a result of the glory he earned, the skills he cultivated. His eclectic vision evaluates the different episodes on the war field – the formation of the armies, the dependency on Arjuna, the trepidation of Yudhishthira, the anger of Krishna, and the loyalty of Drona. The readers will visualize the thirteen days of war through the eyes of Abhimanyu.

PROLOGUE

INDRAPRASTHA was flourishing with the righteous king Yudhishthira.

Once desolated and far from the sign of human race, Khandava forest was converted to a land of prosperity. Arjuna's celestial weapon had engulfed the forest and fed the hunger of fire. It was no more a no man's land.

After the *Swayamvar* of Draupadi, Arjuna returned as victorious and five brothers became the husbands of the princess of Panchal. They reached Hastinapur with their wife and mother Kunti. Beholding the increasing friction among the two groups, Dhritarashtra, caretaker king of Hastinapur asked the five brothers to redevelop their old capital *Khandavaprastha*. The land was ruled by the ancestors of *Kurus* from *Pururavas* to *Nahusha*, from *Yayati* to *Dushyant* and *Bharat*. It was left desolated when *Hasti*, great grandson of Bharata formed Hastinapur and the capital was shifted from Khandavaprastha to new city. Pandavas converted the ruined place to a land filled with unprecedented wealth. They created a palace decked with exquisite artistry, attractive and sight eluding floors. It was no less than Indra's heaven with all the signs of opulence. They named it Indraprastha, the city of effulgence.

Yudhishthira became the king of Indraprastha and the twin brothers Nakul and Sahadeva extended the dominions of the capital. Nobody dared to attack the land protected by warrior Arjuna and guarded by Bhima. There was no enemy left even in the remotest regions. Either they were defeated or became ally of Indraprastha. Yudhishthira was unopposed emperor. The wealth increased many folds and the denizens got all comfort to grow in that new capital.

After ruling for more than thirty years, the courtiers and gurus of king Yudhishthira suggested to perform Rajsuya Yagna. The invites ware sent to the rulers of different regions. The acquiescing kings would have to attend the sacrifice in token of acknowledgement of Yudhishthira's supremacy. The day was decided, and people gathered in Indraprastha. The entire city was decked with floral unguents, garlands, unique flowers, and jewels. The guests brought exquisite gifts from their respective kingdoms to honor the king of Indraprastha, a heavenly abode like of Indra.

Yudhishthira sent special invites for his uncle Dhritarashtra and honoring the invitation Dhritarashtra sent Duryodhana, Dushasana and his other sons along with Karna, guru Drona, guru Kripa, Ashwatthama, Sisupala, and grandsire Bhishma to witness the success of Yagna.

~~

"Grandsire Bhishma, Guru Drona, kings, courtiers, and countrymen", addressed Yudhishthira.

"I extend my gratitude for accepting the invitation for Rajsuya Yagna. With the blessings of grandsire and my uncle, this city has grown multi fold and many treaties are formed with multiple remote kingdoms. Indraprastha has become the center of this planet with no sign of hunger, poverty, fear, and displeasure. I, eldest of all Pandavas, welcome you with all my regards.", concluded Yudhishthira.

The time came for performing the honors of the occasion. As per the custom, the first honor should be rendered to the guest, worthiest of all and who had taken antecedence over kings and gurus. Yudhishthira turned towards grandsire to take his advice and the later emphatically chose Krishna for the first honors. Yudhishthira and other Pandavas were elated, and many other guests also opined for the honors of Krishna. But there was one man who couldn't tolerate it. Sisupala, king of Chedi kingdom, couldn't accept that a cowherd belonging to non-Kshatriya clan is honored by Kshatriyas.

Sisupala stood up, and ridiculing the decision of Yudhishthira said, "How unjust and unlawful to select a cowherd for the first honor when the kings of different calibers and credentials are gathered here. But I am not surprised as what can one expect from a man who was born illegitimate? There is no doubt in the lunacy of this king who takes advice from a cowherd boor. What to say about the man who was born out from the womb of a woman who killed her other sons? And what shall I say of this honored man! He is fool by birth. Always surrounded by cows and bulls, his intelligence is not yonder cattle."

Demeaning everyone sitting in the courtroom, Sisupala couldn't control his arrogance and continued, "It is unjust to ignore the kings and gurus present in this palace. The king of Indraprastha, today, showed his vulgar partiality for Krishna, whose father was mere servant in the palace of Ugrasena. This Pandu son proved his raw intellect and unworthy wisdom before his own countrymen. O Yudhishthira! You are fooled by this dotard Bhishma who has no business in your country. Why did you follow the advice of this lunatic old man? Why you chose Krishna over your preceptor Drona, your mentor Kripa? If not anyone outside, you could have chosen this insane dotard Bhishma who rendered foolish advice to you, but still he is the oldest man in your own family. But you chose this man of no intelligence."

He was unstoppable and kept on cursing Pandu son in front of all guests. He continued rendering his disrespect for grandsire and his arrogance was getting louder on Krishna. But few kings applauded the words of Sisupala which gave him courage to demean Krishna more.

He turned towards Krishna and said, "O Krishna! What impudence on your part to accept this undeserved honor suggested by foolish Yudhishthira? Have you forgotten your lineage? Or did you forget the tradition of royal honors? Do you not get this farce is nothing but ghastly mockery and disgrace on yourself? You are no different from this senile dotard Bhishma and foolish emperor Yudhishthira who thought to become the ruler of rulers after performing this Yagna?"

He continued cursing and started walking out from the palace hall. Few kings joined him in his procession of opposing Yudhishthira. It was chaotic in the courtroom. Beholding the situation going adverse, king Yudhishthira ran towards the rulers walking out and tried to calm them but in vain. Sisupala's aggressive vanity uprooted the decorum of the palace.

Till then calm Krishna stoop up and raised his voice against the arrogance of Sisupala, "O Sisupala! You crossed the boundaries today. You not only went against the dignity of this courtroom but also demean the pride of Rajsuya Yagna. Your follies have reached the brim of its cauldron. The rogue should be punished." Saying this Krishna released his *Sudarshan* towards Sisupala beheading him before the eyes of all courtiers and guests. Anger was silenced and the rogue was annihilated. Nobody could stand before the angry Krishna.

The rituals were performed the Yagna was celebrated with Yudhishthira recognized as the emperor. *Hail Yudhishthira! Hail Indraprastha!* The slogans filled the courtroom.

~~

Yagna completed and all the princes, kings, priests, and other guests were duly respected, and they left the kingdom.

Duryodhana was observing the entire processions silently. The desires were growing in his mind. He roamed across the palace seeing the exquisiteness and sumptuous belongings of Pandavas. The artwork done by elite artisans were no less than illusions. And in one of those illusions, the eldest Kaurava got trapped. Confused with a pool as a glass floor, he fell down and got drenched. *Drenched in water! Drenched in embarrassment!* He came out of water when Bhima mocked, *"O Son of Dhritarashtra! The floor is other side."* This went as an arrow of disrespect for Duryodhana. He couldn't accept the farce mockery of his cousin and left the place.

Burning with jealousy at the prosperity of Pandavas; and angry with mockery of Bhima, Duryodhana was unable to control his belligerence. The grief of remote kingdoms becoming ally with Yudhishthira was unbearable. The desire of pouncing and robbing everything was then incepted. He was absorbed in grief. Grief of seeing the prosperity of his own brothers. Ironical but true!

He was restless and shared the desire of owning the entire wealth of Pandavas with his uncle Shakuni. He expressed that he wanted to attack Indraprastha and win all the jewels, wealth, and rule over the five brothers. He arrogantly mentioned, "All these Pandavas will be my slave."

Shakuni, the master manipulator of speech said, "Son! If you can win everything without war, then why you want to shed the blood? Your sire will not agree to raid Indraprastha, but I know it's not difficult to drive Yudhishthira out of Indraprastha."

Duryodhana's eyes glittered and he couldn't believe his ears. He incredulously asked for the plans of Shakuni and then Shakuni revealed, "Yudhishthira is addict of dice game with no knowledge of tricks. If we invite him for the game, he would never say no. That will be our opportunity to roll the dice in our favors. My son you will get what you desire without shedding a single drop of blood. He will be a helpless toddler in front of me in the dice game, and I will win you his kingdom, his palace, his wealth, and whatever else you desire. Tell me Son, what more you want?"

Duryodhana accepted the proposal wantonly and stared dreaming of owning the throne of Indraprastha. The only hurdle was how to send the official invitation to Yudhishthira. It was impossible till Dhritarashtra accept the proposal and would agree to send the invites.

It was not difficult for Shakuni and Duryodhana to convince Dhritarashtra. On the pretext of friendly games and honor the prosperity of Pandavas, Dhritarashtra agreed to call the sons of his brother Pandu to Hastinapur. The invite was sent, and as expected Yudhishthira didn't deny. The importunate Duryodhana got what he longed for, "An invitation to Pandavas for dice game!" He laughed at his petite win over his weak-witted father. The blind father couldn't show the path of righteousness to his son. The orders were passed to erect separate halls for games similar to that of Indraprastha. Dhritarashtra sent Vidura with the invitation of dice game.

Yudhishthira was addicted to the dice game. He liked the idea of friendly game among brothers. But the most important part was he didn't want to dishonor his uncle by refusing the invitation.

~~

The day arrived. Yudhishthira and other Pandavas with Draupadi reached Hastinapur. Yudhishthira met Dhritarashtra,

Gandhari, grandsire Bhishma, guru Drona, guru Kripa, Vidura and other retinues of Hastinapur. All elite arrangements with best fruits nectar, wines, music, and never-tasted-before viands were made to welcome the king of Indraprastha. Yudhishthira was happy witnessing the arrangements and so were his other brothers.

The center stage for dice game was set. All the courtiers were sitting surrounding the center podium. Duryodhana, then asked, "O Brother Yudhishthira! I hope you are enjoying the hospitality of Hastinapur. You are emperor, a *Chakravartin Samrat.* We have taken utmost care in placing everything for your order and comfort. This special hall for games is designed to welcome the king of kings. You, my brother, have reached the epitome of success. It is indeed my pleasure to host you. If you permit, shall we start the game?"

Yudhishthira said, "I am here on the invitation of uncle Dhritarashtra. I like the game of dice, but I am in no favor of playing as this is game of chances and luck. Conquest in battle and not in the game of chance is the path of Kshatriyas."

To which Shakuni replied, "Are you afraid, O King! The game is to show your skills and use your intellect to convert the chances in your favor. It is not about right or wrong. It is mere entertainment and family union."

Yudhishthira's love for the game couldn't keep him away for long and he said, "Well! With whom I have to play?" In his mind he thought it would be Duryodhana but to his utter dismay he got shocked when Duryodhana said, "My uncle Shakuni will roll the dice for me and I will take account of the stakes."

Yudhishthira wasn't ready as he knew how expert Shakuni was in the dice game. The dice used to roll on his commands. All his life, Shakuni had practiced the game. Reluctantly, Yudhishthira said, "It is not customary that one man plays on other's behalf."

Shakuni knew it was about to come and he was ready with his taunts, "O king! I see you are forging excuses. The rulers and your acolytes are watching you. Are you afraid of future? If yes, you can walk away. Nobody will say nothing to you." Yudhishthira couldn't say no as it would be very embarrassing. He accepted the challenge and the game started.

~~

Dice rolled. Shakuni started getting the desired numbers. From jewels to ornaments, from silver to gold, from pearls to metals, chariots, horses, elephants, servants, maids, cavalry and the palace, Yudhishthira continued to lose. Cows, sheep, goats, cities, villages, and personal possessions of Yudhishthira, he lost everything.

He started losing the jewels of his brothers, possessions of his brothers and then finding no way out he put Nakul on stake. Traumatized assembly witnessed a human on stake for the first time in life. But it was not Yudhishthira's day. The dice rolled and he lost Nakul. Nakul became the slave of Duryodhana.

Dice rolled again and this time on wager was Sahadeva. Shakuni's command on the game was way beyond Yudhishthira's imagination. He lost Sahadeva too. Yudhishthira got aghast sensing the direction the game was heading too. It was no more the friendly game. He looked at Shakuni. He wanted to stop the wager. Shakuni sensed it and said, "O King! I know your love for Bhima and Arjuna is more than that for sons of Madri. Certainly, you will not put them on stake."

The words of Shakuni stung to now thoroughly reckless Yudhishthira. It was quick imputation from Shakuni which struck the king deep. He replied, "You think I differ between the sons of mother Madri and mother Kunti. You wretch, you will never understand the love among Pandavas." And then he did which put everyone in shock and dismay. He put Arjuna on stake and lost followed by putting Bhima as wager and losing him too. All his four brothers were now slaves of Duryodhana. Duryodhana laughed in the courtroom. He got what he desired but the game was not over yet.

Shakuni rolled the dice again and asked, "Is there anything else you can offer?"

Yudhishthira, shocked and bemused, "I put myself on stake. If you win, I will be your slave."

The dice rolled and Shakuni won again. Yudhishthira was no more the king. He became the slave of Duryodhana. The assembly was silenced, the courtiers were stunned but the Kauravas were laughing like demons. There was distress among the elders, but everyone was mute spectator. Nobody stood to stop the gambling. The friendly game was turning cruel. All five brothers were sitting like slaves without jewels, without crowns, and without their favorite weapons. The intelligence was being decayed and the wit was destructed. All the wisdom was silenced and then Shakuni turned to Yudhishthira and said, "O slave of Duryodhana! You lost everything in the stake, but I give you a last chance. There is one jewel in your possession. You put that on stake and if you win, you will be free."

Yudhishthira was left with no choice, "What is that jewel? I have lost everything including me. All my brothers and I are slaves of Duryodhana. All my wealth, my possession, my weapons, my palace, and my throne are lost. I'm left with nothing."

Shakuni smirked and mocked, "Slave Yudhishthira! You have your wife Draupadi with you. Put her on stake. It is her against everything you lost. If you win take back everything and enjoy your kingdom."

Yudhishthira agreed, "I pledge her."

Duryodhana and Karna shouted with exultation. Yudhishthira's unwitting pledge was not accepted by the courtiers. Putting woman on stake. Nobody did that before. The human race stooped at the fathom of humility.

Dice rolled again and Shakuni laughed excitedly, "O Yudhishthira! You lost her too."

Duryodhana laughed and entire courtroom got filled with his vilified laughter. He was the supreme power. He won everything he desired and all five Pandavas including Draupadi were his slaves. He mocked at Bhima, he teased Arjuna, and then ragefully he shouted, "Bring that maid of mine, Draupadi to this courtroom. That lady doesn't belong to the palace. She should be here standing with other servants and serving the princes." The entire assembly trembled with his rage. Vidura tried to pacify him but in vain. Under the influence of his lust, Duryodhana ordered a charioteer named Prathikami to bring Draupadi to the courtroom.

Prathikami went as per orders of Duryodhana, told Draupadi the entire episode but Draupadi stood strong, "O charioteer! Go and ask your master. Whom my husband Yudhishthira lost first? Me or himself? If he lost himself first, he has no rights to put me on stake and hence I am no slave. I will not follow the commands of that guile Duryodhana." Prathikami returned with Draupadi's message which made Duryodhana more furious. He turned towards his brother Dushasana and said, "Brother! Bring that arrogant Draupadi in this courtroom and make her sit on my thighs. Fetch her forcefully and fear not even if you have to drag her."

Pandavas were stunned but sat helpless. Nobody could stand against the lascivious desires and unlawful acts. Dushasana followed the orders of his elder brother and joyfully sped on his errand. He reached to the inner apartments of Draupadi and shouted, "Draupadi! Why do you delay? You are our slave now. Come brother Duryodhana is calling you in the hall of games. O beautiful lady! delay not. Now you have been won by us, make yourself affable to us."

It was time of her cycles and hence she was in single piece loincloth. She said, "Dushasana! I can't come to the main hall amidst all men. I am in single piece loincloth. A woman can't come in front of any man in this condition." But Dushasana was in no mood of listening. He broke open the door and entered the room. Trembled and grief-stricken Draupadi ran towards Gandhari's room but Dushasana darted after her, caught her by hair and dragged to the assembly hall.

~~

Draupadi was dragged in mid of all intellectuals, visionaries and masters of wisdom, but nobody raises their voices against the gory act of immorality. This was the inception of injustice! She shouted for help. She cried. But nothing happened. The leonine laughter of Duryodhana and Dushasana was overpowering the pleadings of Draupadi. And then the unexpected happened when Karna came forward, "These all brothers and their wife are now slaves of Duryodhana. What you call a woman who is married to five men? A harlot? O Draupadi! Your husbands are now slaves but don't worry, you will get hundred more husbands if you follow Duryodhana."

"O Duryodhana! You are the master of these mendicants. All their wealth, their jewels and even their garments belong to you. What are you waiting Dushasana, seize all which belong to brother Duryodhana?" continued Karna.

Dushasana with lustful eyes glanced at Draupadi and tried to pull the single piece of garment covering Draupadi. Finding no help, Draupadi implored divine mercy and succor, "O Krishna! Save me from this plight. You are my only refuge." She shouted and fainted. Krishna saved the helpless woman in his own way. People thought it was divine miracle, but it was Draupadi's trust for Krishna which saved her modesty by becoming the garments to clothe her body. Exhausted Dushasana sat down in sheer fatigue accepting his defeat before the ultimate power.

There was chaos in the hall. Whoever witnessed the barbarism couldn't control cursing Duryodhana and Dushasana. Bhima, who was controlling his wrath so far, stood up and vowed, "May I never enter the blessed abode of my ancestors if I don't drink the heart's blood of this sinner Dushasana. May I not live peacefully if I don't break the thighs of this wicked Duryodhana."

Dhritarashtra then realized that these could be the cause of his sons' destruction. He called Draupadi and tried to soothe her with his affectionate words. He said, "Draupadi! My sons have stooped too low and overpowered the humility. You are wielder of wisdom. O Daughter! Forgive my sons for their unforgettable follies. Ask what you desire from me."

Draupadi said, "In front of you, this all destruction happened. The princess of Kuru dynasty was dragged in front of all the courtiers. I am standing here in a single piece of cloth soaked in blood. My modesty is snatched. Even then you want me to forgive your sons. How could I? Nevertheless, I understand your love for your sons. But if you want to do something for me, free my husbands from the bondage of slavery and install Yudhishthira as the king of Indraprastha again."

"So be it", said Dhritarashtra. He then said, "Dear daughter, don't you want to ask anything for yourself?"

"As per the scriptures, a Kshatriya lady can ask for only two boons. I am pleased that you accepted my two requests. I don't want anything else.", said Draupadi.

Bewildered and bemused Pandavas with their wife Draupadi left that hall and departed for Indraprastha. This led to other serious and angry discussion between Duryodhana and his father, "O Father! Why you reverted the success of ours? I gained everything I desired. Once again Pandavas are favored over me. I won their wealth through my skills and you returned everything to them. Then how you expect me to be the emperor of emperors when my skills are underrated? What I won is lawfully mine. If you favor these Pandavas, I don't want to live in this palace. I will either retire to woods or enter the fire. What will I do when my own father doesn't favor me?"

"What do you desire O son?", asked Dhritarashtra.

"One more game of dice. But this time I promise I won't ask them to put any of their belongings and possessions as wager. The one game which will decide the fate. The game which will decide whose destiny is stronger. If they win, I will go to woods for twelve years followed by one year of incognito and if I win, Yudhishthira and his brothers with Draupadi will have to walk to woods and live life of ascetics for twelve years. And if in thirteenth year, they are recognized, it will be followed by another twelve years of exile.", Duryodhana put the condition.

The helpless and blind father couldn't do anything against the wile of his son. Pandavas were called again for the dice game. This time again Yudhishthira followed the summon, and this time again the dice rolled against him. Pandavas lost. Following the condition, they left all their possessions behind and walked towards the woods for thirteen years.

CHAPTER 0

THE YOUNG WARRIOR

The strength of a warrior is not defined by the wars he wins; but the times he seeks for peace.

"Twelve years have passed and it's time to go incognito!" said the eldest of all Pandava brothers. The five brothers and their wife had lived in exile for twelve years. Time flew, but the wounds had not healed.

The thirteenth year would be the toughest. All six of them would have to live in concealment, hiding their identities. That what the contract was. Even if by any remote chance, they were found or discovered by the Kauravas, they have to serve another twelve years in the forest! They must pick odd jobs to survive the last year in concealment.

"But where should we go?" asked the youngest brother Sahadeva.

"The spies of Duryodhana will be on our hunt for the entire year and if they find us, another twelve years of exile!", exclaimed brother Nakul.

There were many smaller kingdoms surrounding Hastinapur, the capital of Kuru dynasty. Arjuna, the third son of Pandu, expressed "How about the *Matsya* kingdom which was across the Yamuna?"

Matsya was ruled by the just king Virat and was both rich in heritage and resources. They had a strong army, immense wealth, cultivated a wide range of crops and reared various animals. King Virat was fond of a variety of games like wrestling, horse riding, dice games, and was very attentive of the welfare of the cows and steeds of his kingdom. It was the perfect hideout place for one year. All the brothers readily agreed to Arjuna. Yudhishthira then asked about the new identities of all the brothers and their wife.

Yudhishthira proposed that he would disguise as a Brahmana, with the name Kanka, learnt in scriptures and skilled in the dice game. He would request for the employment in the court of king Virat as the advisor and with his skills in the game, he would entertain the courtiers. The mighty Bhima suggested that he would seek the employment as a cook, expert in culinary arts, and would also entertain the king with his wrestling skills. He mentioned that his new name will be Vallabh.

Whereas Arjuna, a skilled archer and learnt warrior, declared that he would enter the kingdom as one of the neuter sexes and seek employment as the music trainer for the ladies of the royal family. He would wear the conch-bangles to cover the sturdy arms, a braid to hang from the head and deck ears with the earrings. Dressing in the women's clothes, and in the name of Brihannala, he would recite the poems and stories of valor of the warriors of various kingdoms. Likewise, the other two brothers, Nakul and Sahadeva expressed that they would disguise themselves as a horse trainer and a cowherd respectively. Nakul's name would be Granthika and Sahadeva would call himself Tantripala.

Yudhishthira then turned to Draupadi and asked about her plans. He was also worried about her safety. The beauty of Draupadi would attract the unwanted attention and would create ripples in the evil hearts. Draupadi replied that she would disguise as the waiting-maid of the royal lady of king Virat, Sudeshna. She would present herself as the hairdresser of the queen and assume the name, Sairindhri. The decisions were taken, all of them with the new identities proceeded towards the kingdom. Before entering the palace, the biggest hurdle was to hide the weapons they carried. If they enter the palace with the weapons, anybody would identify them as the five Pandava brothers. They decided to wrap the weapons in a big white cloth and hang them within the dense branches of a big *Sami* tree outside the entrance of the kingdom. They tied a corpse with the branch as well. The odor of the rotting corpse would not allow people to come near to the tree. This way all their weapons would be saved. The brothers then decided to enter the kingdom individually but Draupadi would be followed by Arjuna until she reaches the palace of the queen. Being in the guise of a transgender, Arjuna would not be stopped to enter the queen's palace and that way her safety would be ensured.

Everything went as planned and the five Pandavas commenced their stay with their new identities in the great kingdom of Matsya. The king offered the remuneration for each one and they were also given fitting places to stay. Arjuna disguised as Brihannala was tested for impotency and when the king was assured that Brihannala was transgender, he was sent to the inner apartments of the queen. The queen examined Brihannala as the music trainer for her daughter. The other brothers were asked to clear the assessments given to them and then befitting tasks were assigned to them. At last, Draupadi as Sairindhri entered the queen's chamber. As she walked into the palace, the other servants and courtiers were mesmerized with her beauty.

The queen was amazed to see a damsel with long hair, sharp toes, round bosoms, prominent heels, large lotus-shaped eyes, bent eyelids, pointed nose, rose petal lips, and slender waist standing in front of her, seeking employment as the maid of hers. Sudeshna, the wife of Virat became envious with the beauty and at first, refused to accept her as the maid. More than with the charm and beauty of Sairindhri, she feared that the damsel would attract the attention of the king. She was more than envious of Draupadi and considered her as a threat. The velvet beauty had the power to melt the hearts of the beasts. The queen, the first lady of the kingdom was afraid of seeing the divine beauty in front of her. Beholding the evident reluctance of the queen, Sairindhri explained that she was already married to five Gandharva brothers and they always watch her progress and protect her secretly. There was nobody who could overpower her and if anyone wished to do so, the Gandharvas won't spare the life of that evil-heart. Convinced, the queen appointed her as the hairdresser. They started living a normal life and there was nobody who could mark their real identities. As months passed, Kanka became dearest to the emperor. Vallabh entertained the king and his relatives with his wrestling skills and fed them with the best viands. Granthika trained many wild horses and helped the kingdom in increasing their cavalry. With the skills of Tantripala, the cattle in the kingdom populated in thousands and Brihannala became favorite of the young princess.

Life couldn't have been better, and the thirteenth year was about to end, when one day Kichak, commander of Virat's army and brother of Sudeshna, spotted Sairindhri in the queen's apartment. Immediately, he got carried away with her beauty and as *Kama* took over him, he desired to possess her. He reached out to her and tried to allure her. He expressed his desire to unite with her. The embellished Sairindhri and her spotless beauty drenched Kichak in the lust of having her in his abode. The maddened Kichak approached her and proposed to become his wife. He was ready to make his other wives as the maids of Sairindhri and promised to ornate her with pearls, shining metals, stones and anything which would be liked by the lady. His mind and body were completely carried away by Sairindhri's beauty and he started dreaming of her in his life. But Draupadi, in the guise of Sairindhri was not an ordinary lady. She was the princess and had chosen her husband as per her wish. Nobody else could mislead her. The firm Draupadi politely refused Kichak's offer. She didn't want anyone to know the truth about her marriage with the Pandavas, and as she departed, Kichak became furious.

Kichak, soaked in the evil emotions couldn't accept the refusal and he immediately rushed to his sister to seek the possession on Sairindhri. The sister couldn't resist the demands of a stubborn brother and agreed to send her to his chambers in the pretext of picking up wine for the queen. Kichak went back and asked his servants to prepare the best drinks and food. Next day, when Sairindhri went to the queen's palace, Sudeshna asked her to visit Kichak and collect the special drinks from his room. Sairindhri understood it was not the wine but the desire of a sister's brother which was forcing the queen to speak like that. The helpless Sairindhri couldn't call any of her husbands. There were still fifteen days left in the completion of the thirteenth year and she didn't want the real identities to get revealed before the completion of incognito period. She prayed to God begging his mercy and left the queen's chamber to visit Kichak. Kichak had already surrendered himself to *Kama* and was maddened by the thoughts of the damsel. Sairindhri entered the room, the room was filled with fragrance, beautiful flowers, ornate garlands and unguents. The room was filled with divine fragrance, apart from beautifully crafted furniture and gold threaded drapes. The man soaked in the lust, in the desire of winning the lady, pounced on her as she entered. She tried to resist but Kichak didn't understand. She warned him that if he didn't leave her, the five Gandharva husbands would not spare him. Maddened with hate and jealousy, Kichak couldn't bear the insult and tried to pull the upper garment of the lady. She managed to escape from his chamber and rushed towards the courtroom of king Virat. Kanka and Vallabh were seated among the other courtiers. As she reached the hall, Kichak grabbed her by her hair and turned her down on the floor. The hurt Sairindhri cried for help. Bhima saw it and the courtroom drama which had happened thirteen years ago flashed in front of his eyes.

It was the similar courtroom of king Dhritarashtra where the dice game was arranged between the two brothers Duryodhana and Yudhishthira. Duryodhana cunningly asked Shakuni to represent him in the game and Shakuni an expert in manipulating the speech convinced Yudhishthira to play against him. Shakuni was an expert dice game player and nobody could stand before him. He managed to defeat Yudhishthira consistently and with each set of rolling dice, Yudhishthira slowly lost his wealth, his ornaments, his servants, his army, his kingdom, his brothers, himself and in the end, to everyone's utter dismay, his wife Draupadi. Duryodhana was blinded with envy. His hatred knew no bounds against his cousins. The seed of jealousy which was sown in his childhood had transformed into a tree bearing poisonous fruits of vengeance. At the spur of the moment, righteousness decimated and amidst all those provocations, Duryodhana found the right opportunity to insult the Pandavas amidst everyone. In front of all the courtiers, he abused the innocence of the wife of Pandu sons; Draupadi. The lascivious desires tried to disrobe the modesty of the princess in front of intelligent courtiers, her husbands and the king; but alas, nobody stopped, rather stooped to the injustice; because as per the rules of the game, Duryodhana was right. His intentions were cruel, and his act was immoral. Everyone was a mute spectator and when all doors were seemed shut, Draupadi prayed to Krishna for help, who rescued the princess in his own way.

The actions happened thirteen years ago, the insult, the injustice, the vows, and the exile, all flashed in front of Bhima's eyes. He ground his teeth in anger and stood up to kill Kichak. Yudhishthira, the calm man, held Bhima's thumb and tried to pacify him. In loud voice, he then asked Vallabh to go out and cut the woods and collect the fuel for evening cooking. Kanka then ordered Sairindhri to retire to the queen's chambers. He assured that her Gandharva husbands would do the rightful deeds to prevent her modesty. Retiring to her room, Sairindhri tried to pacify the fire of hatred and self-pity inside her by sprinkling cool water over her head. She wanted to kill Kichak so that the remaining days in Matsya, would be peaceful for her, but couldn't as it would create unnecessary ruckus and will expose everyone. She reflected, "My life is becoming worse from bad! What am I doing? A princess once, slave today; I'm living on the mercy of the kings. A woman surrounded by maids once, today serving as a maid of a queen. How should I justify my birth? I am not afraid of anyone or anything! I must do something." But alas neither she, nor her husbands could do anything for the fear of being exposed.

The day passed without further incidents. The sun touched the horizon, slowly cooling the burning earth; but alas the fire inside Sairindhri couldn't be doused. Still in her anger, she remembered Bhima. Afflicted with sorrow and with grief in her heart, she wiped her tears and moved towards the kitchen where Bhima was sleeping. She entered the room and sat beside the man of strong built. Her sobs woke him up and he asked about the reasons for her visit to his place. She wept, wept inconsolably hiding her tears behind her palms. She put her head on the chest of Bhima and embraced him. She wanted someone to hear her miseries and help her find the answers. Bhima wrapped her in his arms and putting his hand on her chin, he asked her to tell everything she was hiding in her heart.

Draupadi told how angry she was with Yudhishthira because of his addiction to the dice game. Once a king, now he was serving another king for sustenance. He had reached to the present condition because of his addiction. He lost everything and was thrown to the forest just because he couldn't judge the mischief of his brothers. She continued telling how grievous she becomes seeing the mighty Bhima entertaining the ruler, the courtiers, and the royal ladies by fighting with animals. The burly built had become a piece of entertainment and that distressed her. She told how difficult it was to see her warrior husband in the attire of a woman singing and dancing in mid of all the ladies and maids. The warrior who destroyed the foes armies in hundreds and thousands, the warrior who was undefeated, was hiding his valor behind the instruments. The archer whose arms were meant to hold the bows were hidden behind the bangles. "The misery of a woman can't be known till she reveals", she added. Looking at the unprecedented conditions of Nakul and Sahadeva her heart used to melt each day. She was becoming pale each passing day and when there was the hope of getting over all this, Kichak came and he reminded her of everything happened with her years ago. She had never forgotten the miserable treatment meted out to her and on that day when Kichak pulled her hair, the act of Dushasana flashed in front of her. She told she wanted to avenge for the act of Kichak and if Bhima couldn't kill him, she would end her life.

Bhima tried to console her and promised her to slay Kichak the next evening. "O Dear! Worry not. Your agonies will end tomorrow.", remarked Bhima.

Draupadi's eyes sparkled. "How will it happen?", asked she.

"Invite Kichak to the dancing hall of the palace. That place becomes desolated in evening and is perfect to kill that wretch", Bhima shared his plan.

Draupadi understood that she should speak to Kichak in a sweet tone without alarming him of any danger. She knew what needed to be done. She went back to her room. Next morning, the warrior engulfed in lust, Kichak, again went to Sairindhri in the desire of convincing her. "I'm mightier than King Virat; I'm young, powerful, resourceful and more handsome than any man you will ever get. You should be grateful that a true King is proposing to a servant like you. Though you are just a servant now, if you marry me, I can change your fate! I'll make you the queen of Matsya and all other wives of mine will be your slave".

Not only was Kichak boastful and lustful, he sounded incredibly arrogant too. Draupadi, as told by Bhima, spoke kind words and invited him to the dancing hall in the late evening avoiding the notice of any servant or queen. She told her that this meeting of her should be in private and shouldn't come in notice of either his brothers or her husbands. Kichak, blinded with the beauty of Sairindhri couldn't sense the danger and agreed to come in the evening. The day passed and as soon as twilight fell, Kichak reached the desolated hall usually reserved for conducting the dance classes for the princess. Vallabh was hiding under the bed-covers and thinking him as Sairindhri, Kichak jumped over the bed. As he put his hand over the covers, Vallabh held him with his strong hands. He roared and told that he was the Gandharva husband of Sairindhri and came to kill him. Kichak unclenched himself and then the two men stood before each other like two elephants fighting. The duel happened and Kichak couldn't stand in front of Bhima's attacks. Bhima, the slayer of demons, who could uproot the trees like grasses, who could demolish the mountain with his bare hands, and who could crush the pebbles with his arms, lifted Kichak and threw him in the ground. Kichak couldn't survive the attacks and succumbed to the injuries caused by Bhima. To make the death look paranormal, Bhima inserted Kichak's head, hands and shoulders inside his body. The full-grown man became the ball of flesh with all the bones wrecked and the limbs shattered. Killing Kichak, Bhima quickly retired to the kitchen and then Draupadi called all the servants to show them what happened to Kichak. What her husband, a Gandharva had done to him. Seeing the condition of the dead meat, the servants believed that it was not the act of any normal man.

Kichak was dead but it was not the end of Draupadi's miseries. The next day when the relatives of Kichak gathered for the last rites, they exclaimed to burn Sairindhri with Kichak blaming her for the cause of the death. All the brothers and other relatives of Kichak then forcefully seized her and took to the cremation ground. They were not blaming Kichak for his acts but believed Sairindhri for the reason of Kichak's death. The miserable Sairindhri finding no way to rescue shouted for help. She was in dilemma, if she would call Pandu sons with real names, their identities would be revealed. If she would call them with their names for the Matsya kingdom, everybody would come to know about the truth of the Pandavas. Hence, thinking of other names of Pandavas, she called out, "*O Jaya, and Jayanta, and Vijaya, and Jayatsena, and Jayadvala* listen to me. These relatives of Kichak are taking me away. The Gandharvas, endued with illustrious energy, the rattling of whose chariots are loud, and the twang of whose bowstrings can be heard across welkin, listen to me, these men are taking me away." Even in the adversity, her presence of mind helped hiding the real identities of the Pandavas. Bhima listened to cries of Draupadi and jumped off his bed. He quickly dressed as a Gandharva, ran towards the cremation ground. The strong bull in the disguise of Gandharva killed many relatives of Kichak. Few ran away from the site and in midst of that chaos, Bhima ran back to the palace concealing as Vallabh. Draupadi also returned from the other route to the queen's apartment. The terrified relatives of Kichak reached out to the king and informed whatever happened in the cremation ground. They were afraid and confused. And all their anger worked against Draupadi and the king released the orders for her to vacate the palace. There were only thirteen days left in the completion of the thirteenth year and Draupadi wanted those remaining days to stay in the Matsya kingdom. With the hope of getting the permission, Sairindhri requested the queen and the royal lady accepted the plea of Sairindhri. She got permission to stay in the palace for few more days.

On the other side of the river Yamuna, in Hastinapur, the spies of Duryodhana returned with the lost hope of not finding Pandava brothers for the entire year. They searched the kingdoms, the villages, the palaces, and jungles but couldn't locate the five brothers. The spies informed Duryodhana how they searched the remotest possible locations but couldn't locate the brothers.

Grandfather Bhishma was confident that the virtuous Pandu sons would definitely survive the thirteenth year in hiding. He said, "Wherever the Pandavas would be living, the place would be full of wealth, free of enemies, the humans and animals should be living peacefully, and the king would practice justice for all." The courtiers listened to him carefully. "Yudhishthira, the just would ensure the justice has prevailed, Bhima would protect the place from enemies, the twin brothers would make sure the wealth of the kingdom increases and the warrior would ensure there was no place for fear. The country where the brothers were present would definitely be rich with culture and heritage and their treasury would grow exponentially from the effect of their devotion and hard work.", he concluded.

The spies were tired after months and days of hunting for the Pandava brothers and were exhausted, irritated and extremely unhappy with the empty results. They were awfully scared to tell Duryodhana that they were unsuccessful in their job! Most of them were very impressed with the clever deception of the Pandavas but couldn't express it to their master! But upon being questioned by Bhishma about a fully potent and happy kingdom, they zeroed it on the Matsya kingdom. The graceful and mighty kingdom was indeed near to perfect!

They shared the story of Kichak's death with Duryodhana. The spies explained how the commander of Matsya kingdom was dead and also elaborated on the brutal condition of his dead body. Duryodhana's close ally Trigartas were extremely happy to hear about the death of Kichak as they had personal enmity with Kichak. While Kichak was alive, he had defeated and humiliated

Trigartas on multiple instances and this news of Kichak's death came as a boon to Susarman, leader of Trigartas. Susarman wanted to capitalize the opportunity and expressed the desire of attacking the Matsya kingdom with the help of Kaurava army.

The Matsyas were famous for its rich heritage and they had thousands of high breed cows and other cattle which enhanced their wealth years over years. Susarman was confident that in absence of Kichak he would be able to seize the empire and capture the wealth. Duryodhana heard the words of Bhishma and then the description of Kichak's death. Duryodhana's experiences of life and high intellectual capabilities were trying to join the pieces of the puzzle. He believed Pandavas would be in Matsya but wasn't too sure and hence agreed to the plan of Susarman without opening up his thoughts and ideas to him.

The plan was set and on the decided day of the month, Trigartas together with the Kaurava army marched towards Matsya dominion. The army led by Susarman consisted of chariot warriors, elephant riders, foot soldiers and horsemen. The king Virat came to know about the attack. He was not prepared for the war, but the ruler had no choice. He commanded his brother Satanika; and sons Shweta and Sankha to prepare for the war. The Trigartas came with the large troop and the king Virat needed more warriors to support him. He proposed if Kanka, Vallabh, Granthika and Tantripala also prepare for the battle and help him and his brothers for the combat with Trigartas. The king asked his brothers to provide them the best weapons from his armory, the chariots with the best breed of horses, strongest metal armors, leather covers, and headgears.

The decked Pandu sons in the disguise of ordinary men then ascended the chariots and followed Virat for the battle. Yudhishthira told all his brothers to fight mindfully so that the identities remain incognito. This was going to be tough for the Pandu sons. They had to fight like any other but not fight like Pandavas. They had to show the skills of ordinary men, but not the skills of Pandavas. They had to handle the weapons skillfully, but not like the ultra-skilled true Pandavas. They all reached the battlefield following the king Virat and his acolytes. The Pandu sons were staying behind and letting Virat's sons and brothers fight with the army. Soon the battlefield turned red with the blood of the martyrs. The soldiers were being slaughtered mercilessly. Susarman entered the array of Matsyas and summoned king Virat for the duel. The Kshatriya warrior accepted the invite but Susarman in very short time succeeded to overpower Virat. Susarman broke the chariot of Virat and killed his charioteer and horses. He then pulled him on his chariot and ran away from the battlefield.

There was nobody to support Virat and then Bhima asked Yudhishthira that they must rescue the king at any cost. They had lived in his palace for one year and this was the time to repay. Yudhishthira agreed but asked Bhima to fight with bow and arrows. He knew that if Bhima picked the mace, it would be evident to identify the mace fighter as Bhima. With the permission of elder brother, Bhima took charge against the Trigartas and roaring loudly he entered the array of the foe's army. He destroyed the array formed by opponents and with the shower of his arrows, he killed thousands of soldiers. There was nobody in the Trigartas army to counter him and soon he reached near Susarman's chariot. Bhima defeated Susarman with his lethal attacks. Susarman couldn't stand longer and surrendered before Bhima. Virat was released. The happy king praised the valor of the Pandu sons without knowing their actual identities. He then sends his messengers towards the palace to disclose the news of their victory.

While the Matsya warriors and the Pandu sons were away from the palace and the city, the Kaurava army led by Bhishma, Drona, Karna, Duryodhana and other Kaurava princes seized the wealth of the kingdom. They captured sixty thousand cows, hundreds of horses from stables and destroyed the paddy fields. The frightened animal keeper rushed towards the palace in hope of getting some help. The army was already deployed to fight against the Trigartas hence the palace was left with the royal ladies, few gatekeepers, servants and the youngest son of King Virat, Uttar.

The cowherd told what happened to the animals and how the Kaurava army had captured them and taking them away from the city. He requested Uttar to help. He tried to encourage the young prince by telling him about the clan and valor of his brothers and father. The teenaged boy, who had never faced any battle and who didn't know the strength of Kauravas, got excited and exclaimed that he would defeat the Kauravas and rescue the cows. Little did he know about the strength of Kauravas and lesser was he aware of the valiant stories of Bhishma and Drona. The young lad enjoying his teenage in the inner apartments of the palace, mostly with his mother and maids, heard the news of that cow-herd, and climbed onto his high horse. He wasn't sure of what to do, how to plan, but just to boast his half-baked skills in front of young royal ladies, he said, "All the charioteers are gone away with my father on the battlefield, if I get a qualified charioteer, I will alone defeat the entire Kaurava troop and bring back the wealth of Matsya province."

Brihannala heard this and the warrior inside him woke up. He wanted to face the Kaurava army and mark his return in front of Duryodhana. And this was the best recipe he could have ever gotten. He asked Sairindhri to convince the young prince and make him as Uttar's charioteer. Sairindhri understood what Brihannala was up to, so she did as he desired. She convinced the young prince and then the servants were ordered to decorate the chariot for the young prince. The mother was overwhelmed, seeing her young boy going to fight for the pride of the nation. The younger sister was even happier and innocently asked his brother to bring silk clothes for her dolls while returning. Excited maids helped Uttar dress-up like a warrior and then Brihannala was also dressed up in the attire of a charioteer. The actions were set in motion! The prince mounted the chariot and with authority commanded his new charioteer to take him to the place where the Kaurava army was positioned. Brihannala smiled and commanded the steeds to rush towards the field. As they approached, an ocean of soldiers was waiting for them. The soldiers decked with swords, maces, javelins and many other weapons were ready to captivate the young prince of Matsya. Seeing the large troop surrounded all over, Uttar's overconfidence sublimated, all his hopes evaporated, and the boy started sweating. He had never seen such a large troop in all the seasons he lived.

"This will be my end", he reflected.

Thinking of his life, he asked Brihannala to stop the chariot and return to the palace. The terrified prince was more worried about his life than the prestige of Matsya kingdom. Brihannala reminded him about the oath he took in the palace, but Uttar wanted to go back to his mother's abode. And when Brihannala didn't stop the chariot, he jumped off and started running towards the palace. Brihannala didn't want this to happen, as after all, he was a warrior. As a Kshatriya, it was his duty to fight! But of course, one can't explain this to a kid!

He stopped Uttar and told him that if he didn't want to fight, Brihannala would fight alone and let Uttar be the charioteer. Uttar laughed. Brihannala asked Uttar to climb the *Sami* tree where they hide the weapons. Uttar refused. The ego of a young prince was stronger. No option left, Brihannala took out the bangles from his arms, tied his hair and head with a piece of cloth and revealed his actual identity. He told he was Arjuna, the third son of Pandu. Uttar was still not convinced. Then Arjuna told him the history of Kuru dynasty, he told about the incidents happened in past years and how the Pandavas ended in the Matsya kingdom. He showed his strong arms, the arms of a warrior. He showed the marks on his fingers, the impressions of bowstrings. He revealed the true names of Kanka, Vallabh, Granthika and Tantripala and told him how they all were living in concealment for the entire year.

Uttar was awestruck. He couldn't believe his eyes or ears! That Arjuna, whose stories his parents have told from childhood? That Arjuna who learned from Drona and who was friends with Krishna? That Arjuna who can defeat a thousand men in a war field! He was so shocked that he folded his hands and bowed down to the warrior with tears rolling down his pink cheeks. The young lad, seeing the real hero in front of him couldn't believe his luck.

Tears started rolling from his eyes, the tears of repent. He touched the feet of Arjuna and asked for his forgiveness. Arjuna embraced him and they both ascended the chariot. "We have a war to fight! Let's fight together!" he said smiling to the prince. The roles were reversed and the positions too. Uttar led the chariot near the tree, climbed the tree and brought down the weapons of the Pandavas wrapped in the cloth. After one year, Arjuna touched his *Gandiva*, and as he stretched and tied its string, a great twang filled the welkin. He put the arrows in the quivers, hanged the sword at his waist, put on the armor, wore the leather bands on his wrists and mounted the headgear. The warrior was ready. Uttar was mesmerized seeing the fully dressed Arjuna, the warrior. Arjuna blew the conch marking his presence on the field.

The conch and the twang were not unknown to the Guru Drona. He declared Arjuna was back. Listening to the words of Guru, Karna in envy uttered that no matter if he was Arjuna or any other warrior, he was prepared for any combat. Guru exclaimed, "Alone who saved the Kauravas from Gandharvas, alone who destroyed the *Khandava* forest, alone who led the life of Brahmacharya for five years and learnt the science of war forms, alone who took Subhadra in his chariot and defeated the Vrishni army, alone who fought Rudra, and alone who spread the fame of Kuru dynasty all across, the wielder of *Gandiva*, the third son of Pandu, Arjuna is back from the exile." And while the master was praising his favorite disciple, he was greeted by two arrows penetrating the soil near his feet. This was Arjuna's greetings to his master. The two other arrows then passed hitting the earrings of the master, as if the disciple was sharing the glory he achieved in these years. The Guru was overwhelmed, the grandsire's chest filled with pride listening to the praise of Arjuna. The rattles of the chariot wheels were nearing, the noise of the conch was increasing and the emotions of the Kauravas changing. Duryodhana was joyfully terrified. He knew the prowess of Arjuna, but he was cheerful knowing that the years of exile was not over. As per him, there were still few days left in the completion of thirteen years and if they found him, the Pandavas would be thrown to another exile of twelve years. And the grandsire would never want it to happen to his favorites. The guru ordered the soldiers to form the array and give protection to Duryodhana.

"I will today set a fire in the Kuru forest and will slay everyone coming in the way", shouted Arjuna. Uttar was surprisingly handling the chariot brilliantly and the four steeds tied with the leather ropes were following every command of the young boy. Arjuna asked Uttar to first take the chariot to the place where cattle were kept. Uttar followed the command. Arjuna released multiple arrows towards the soldiers covering the cattle and blew his conch to give direction to animals. The cows, calves, bulls and steeds started running towards the city, breaking the ropes tied to them. The mooing of the cows and the bleat of calves filled the field. The cattle were rescued but the work was not completed. Arjuna wanted Kauravas to know that he was back and thus he rushed towards the army commanded by Bhishma. After rescuing the cattle, Arjuna rushed towards the Kaurava army.

Meanwhile, Duryodhana believing that he found Arjuna during the incognito period, rushed towards Bhishma and asked to pass the ordeal of another period of exile for the Pandavas. He was confident and overjoyed that another twelve years he would enjoy the wealth of Pandavas. Bhishma listened to him patiently and then he did his calculation based on the calendars and the scriptures. They were the descendants of the Lunar dynasty and they followed the lunar calendars. Based on the changes in the celestial cycles and planet positions, Bhishma declared that every five years there was the increase of two lunar months and with that calculation, Pandavas had already spent five months and twelve nights more in the exile. They were entitled to come back to Hastinapur as they followed all the conditions put before them. Duryodhana didn't agree to it and he approached Karna and Drona to counter Arjuna and if possible, slay him on that day itself. Least did he know that Arjuna had spent all these years of exile not randomly escaping life! In fact, he had put in harder work and effort into refining his already amazing skills of war. He had made all efforts in learning the science of war forms and received and invented many powerful celestial weapons.

Arjuna came nearer to the Kaurava army. Karna, Drona and brothers of Duryodhana were all ready for the combat. Bhishma tried to pacify the anger but there was nobody to listen to the words of old man. Arjuna came into the target range blowing his conch. He was ready like an angry tiger to pounce on the prey. Arjuna released the shower of arrows on the Kaurava army, killing hundreds of soldiers. The angry opponents tried to seize the lone warrior but Arjuna cut off each arrow targeted on him. Uttar couldn't believe the massacre; it was gory for the young eyes. The blood, the crushed arms, and the motionless mortals, all were the first experience for the teenager. Arjuna then called the missile capable of making people unconscious.

Arjuna mounted the arrow on his bow, closed his eyes, recited few mantras, and then released one of the powerful weapons from his quiver. The universal missile launched from his bow blasted few meters above the ground where the guru and grandsire positioned. The powerful missile with blast released smoke making it difficult to breathe. The people standing in its range lost their senses. In minutes, the entire field got filled with the numb bodies. The warriors on chariots, the elephant riders, the foot soldiers, the entire cavalry became motionless. Arjuna's one attack and everyone surrendered. Arjuna asked Uttar to take off upper clothes of all the chariot warriors as clothes for his younger sister's dolls. He should be fulfilling the young girl's wish. Uttar did so. Arjuna told Uttar not to reveal anything that happened on the field and there would be an appropriate time for people to know the truth. The roles once again reversed and Brihannala drove back the chariot to the palace.

The entire Matsya empire and its citizens were amazed believing Uttar alone defeated the large army of Kauravas and praised him for his powers. The father's emotions were flying high and with the great sense of pride, he boasted his son's valor before Kanka. Kanka smiled and said the victory was sure as Brihannala was riding the chariot. King Virat took that as the insult of his son. In the heat of anger the king snatched dice from the hands of Kanka and hit him. The blood oozed out from wound. The angry father insulted Kanka. Meanwhile, Uttar and Brihannala arrived at the palace. Beholding the anger of his father, the prince wanted to tell the entire events happened in the field. He wanted to share the excitement of witnessing Arjuna as warrior and wanted to reveal the true identity of five sons of Pandu but was stopped by Brihannala. He pacified his father and asked for Kanka's forgiveness. Kanka left the court and told Virat that he would return after three days.

Three days later, as promised, the five brothers decked with their mighty weapons and dressed in silk robes entered the courtroom of Virat's palace with Draupadi. The king was amazed to see the five warriors with their celestial weapons. He asked for their real identities. Uttar, who was sitting in the hall, stood up and bowed down to Arjuna. The father was surprised to see this. Uttar then told the courtiers and his father, the true identities of those five brothers. He told how Arjuna alone defeated the entire Kaurava army and helped in bringing back the cattle. The emperor was speechless and regretted for his behavior the other day. Recovering from his state of mind and remembering how the four brothers helped him in conquering the Trigartas, he offered Yudhishthira half of his kingdom and wealth. He also proposed that the valiant Arjuna should get married to his daughter Uttara, youngest of all his children.

Arjuna with all due respect to the king's proposal mentioned that he would not be able to accept the offer. He had spent the entire year in the inner apartments of the ladies while in the guise of Brihannala. He told that he had always treated Uttara as his daughter, and he didn't want the world to think otherwise. The warrior was concerned about the prestige of the young princess. But a direct refusal could also be deciphered as an insult and Arjuna didn't want that to happen. He really did love Uttara as his own daughter. Hence, he proposed an alternative. He said, "With all respect to the desire of king, I, son of Pandu, accept Uttara as my daughter-in-law and request to get her married to my dear son, Abhimanyu."

Virat asked about Abhimanyu as he had never heard about him before.

"In righteousness, in deeds, in intelligence, in fame, in prosperity, there was and there will be nobody better than Yudhishthira. In strength, in destroying the foes, there is nobody equal to Bhima. In humility, in counselling the monarchs, in bravery and in prowess, there is nobody else than Nakul. In the knowledge of scriptures, in the sweetness of speech, in the beauty of person, there is nobody equal to Sahadeva. And people say that there is no better wielder of bow and arrows than me. All these qualities possessed by the Pandavas, in unison is in Abhimanyu. Abhimanyu, born in the abode of Krishna, lived in all luxury but learnt the roughness of life from Balarama. He is learnt in all the scriptures and in young age has achieved the great feat of fighting with the skilled warriors. He is the wielder of all known weapons and has learnt different war forms. He is the ideal son, a boy who is a boon to his father. A boy who is the future of Kuru dynasty is perfect for your young daughter as the husband, Dear king Virat.", said proud father Arjuna.

Virat was impressed by what he heard from Arjuna. He had heard about the skills of the Pandavas and had witnessed their prowess during the war with Trigartas and Kaurava army. He accepted the proposal of Arjuna and requested to invite Abhimanyu, his mother Subhadra, Krishna and other relatives for the ceremony.

THE YOUNG WARRIOR

Thirteen years have passed. When the young boy was just three, he was forcefully separated from his father. He always remembered the days when he was in Indraprastha with his father and other family members, living the life full of luxury. There was no sign of pain, no tears, no separation, and no fear till the *Rajsuya* yagna happened in Indraprastha. It was when Duryodhana first saw the treasury and possessions of Yudhishthira, it was the first time when he saw the palace of illusions, it was the first time when his ego was hurt, and his desires grew multi-fold. That was the day when filled with greed, envy, and desire, Duryodhana planned to snatch all that wealth from Yudhishthira. And then cunningness reached its epitome when greedy Duryodhana and wily Shakuni developed a plan. They invited Pandavas for a friendly game of dice and summoned Yudhishthira to play with Shakuni. Yudhishthira trusted his cousin, but then, destiny had some other plans. The dice rolled and the king of Indraprastha lost his wealth, his possessions, his honor, and landed into exile of twelve years with an additional one year in incognito.

"Am I permitted to enter the room, dear sir", asks a servant.

My train of thoughts break, and I open my eyes at the knock of the door. I ask him to enter my room. He hands over a letter that he brought with him. I open the roll, my eyes glitter. It's the letter from my elder uncle Yudhishthira. A drop of tear rolls down my cheeks from the moist eyes. It is the moment of joy; the time has come to meet the elders. It is the invitation to go to the Matsya kingdom with mother and uncle Krishna. I feel elated with the thought of meeting my own blood. I run towards the chambers of my mother. She already knows it. She embraces me and the tears of joy fill the room. We will soon meet my family, my uncles, and my father.

Subhadra was a young girl when her marriage proposals were being discussed. Arjuna, at that time, was on his self- imposed exile and was roaming across different countries. He reached Dwarka to meet Krishna and he saw Subhadra for the first time. It was what one calls "love at first sight". When the two pairs of eyes met, Subhadra had already made up her mind that she wanted to spend the rest of her life with this Man! But there was a problem, permission of big brother Balarama. Balarama, the elder brother of Krishna wanted Subhadra to get married to Duryodhana, but the illusive Krishna had some other plans. Krishna, the best friend of Arjuna, wanted his sister to be married to the best warrior of world. Krishna hatched a plan. He advised Subhadra to elope with Arjuna. He arranged the chariot with special features. Subhadra and Arjuna were all on-board with the plan and were excited to start the new journey of their lives. Balarama when came to know about this, sent troops in hundreds and thousands to rescue the princess. However, it was not possible for any troop to stop Arjuna. And moreover, Subhadra was a very strong woman who was unshaken in her decisions. Hence, in presence of Krishna, Subhadra and Arjuna got married. Abhimanyu was the love child between these two young lovebirds.

My joyful mother and I prepare to leave for the Matsya kingdom. Krishna, Balarama and other relatives also join the caravan. The chariots loaded with pearls, jewels, gold and other precious goods also follow the family. Gifts to a king should be after all befitting from a king! The gifts will be presented to the *Matsya Maharajah*, as the token of gratitude for allowing the Pandavas in his realm, albeit unknowingly. After days of travel, the caravan reaches Matsya region. The fertile fields, the flocks of livestock and the smiles on people's faces sing the glory of Matsya Kingdom and its prosperity. The sign of happiness remarks that this prosperous kingdom must be led by a just king!

Moving towards the capital city we saw a lot of suburban towns and villages reflecting the wealth of the nation. Behold the grand palace! The entire place is decorated in opulence to welcome us. The floral garlands, the unguents, the scented water everything fills the air with divine fragrance. The chirping of birds, the ringing bells and chuckles all around, reflect the happiness in the kingdom. The unmistakable charm and humility of people greet us at every step. I reach the main hall with my mother and uncles. King Virat is seated on his throne, and upon seeing us, the ministers present in the room rise from their seats to welcome us with folded palms.

I am decked with shining armor, garlands made of pearls and precious stones. The quiver with bows at my back and the mighty bow, *Raudra*, on my right shoulder are the sign that I am Arjuna's son. I walk towards the majesty; while rose petals and many more flowers are being showered on me. The ruler comes down from his throne, walks towards me and embraces me and I reciprocate. The queen, Sudeshna, pecks my forehead and welcomes me into the palace, "Dear son, your charm is more than what your father told. You majestic truly reflects the regime of Kuru dynasty. Welcome Son! Welcome to Matsya."

Everyone is happy seeing us in the palace but my eyes search for my father. I'm restless. I don't want to hear praises; I don't want to see or meet anyone! I have waited so long to meet him! The thirteen years of separation was less grievous than these moments. My anxiousness is probably visible on my face and I look around the hall and finally I see him.

My heart melts, time stops, the buzz and hum of people around cease to exist, the eyes get moist, the tough boy becomes a three-year child and I run like a toddler towards my father. I bow down to my father and the tears are unstoppable. My father lifts me up in his strong arms and embraces me. The affection melts through the eyes. I'm ecstatic, elated, overjoyed. My love and happiness know no bounds. The entire palace is filled with the emotion of love. My mother and many others shed tears of joy seeing our reunion. The thirteen years of separation, the pain of not living with my father and not seeing my uncles has filled the emotions to the brim. He puts his hands on my shoulders and lifts me up. I can sense the charm in his eyes. "The broad shoulders decked in armors, strong arms, wide chest, tough built, it all resembles, you, my son, are the true lineage of Pandavas," my father exclaims joyfully.

I bow down to my uncles and seek their blessings. The embrace of uncle Bhima almost flattened my lungs and my shriek makes every soul in the hall laugh their hearts out. Uncle Yudhishthira calmly blesses me. I embrace uncles Nakul and Sahadeva. And when I reach near mother Draupadi, her eyes couldn't control her admiration for me. She gets overwhelmed seeing me after so long. For her, I am still a three-year-old. She pecks my forehead and blesses me.

Amidst my meetings with uncles and mother Draupadi, my father sees my mother. The memories of fleeing away together at a young age brings smile on his face. He embraces her. She shies like a young bride. The family meets and then father walks towards his best friend, uncle Krishna. The two friends meet after years. The infinite smile on uncle Krishna is hard to decipher but at this moment my heart is exploding with love and joy. This is indeed the happiest day of my life.

THE PRINCE MEETS THE PRINCESS

The conversation between my father and I seemed eternal. King Virat and queen Sudeshna are happy to see us all gathered in their palace. "It's a privilege to host you all" she says with a pleasant smile and the kind nod in assent. The King asks his queen to accompany Uttara from the inner chambers to the hall and make arrangements for the first meeting of Uttara with the family. Queen Sudeshna nods her head and heads towards the inner chambers with a few maids. "A young girl who was playing with dolls till yesterday will become a woman and soon be part of your family" King Virat said in excitement while a drop of tear trickled down his cheeks.

"Uttara…" I heard the name but absolutely paid no attention to the words of the king.

I'm absolutely unconcerned, unaware and uninterested in the proceedings of the hall, as I'm gripped with never ending exciting tales narrated by my father and like a toddler, I'm mesmerized with his tales of valor, courage, war and I obviously don't want to leave my father. I'm continuously probing him about the exile and their experiences of the past thirteen years, when suddenly, I see a young girl draped in silk robes entering the main courtroom. The young girl coming with the queen and other maids steals my vision away from my father. I'm mesmerized at her charm. My father's voice slowly faints in the background. All of a sudden, his voice, his tales become irrelevant in comparison to the jaw dropping beautiful damsel who was walking right in front of me. I'm star-struck! Is this a dream; is this a reality? For a few moments, I can't feel myself. The black long hair, the lotus petaled eyes, the curved eyelashes, the pointed nose, the rosy lips, the grown bosoms, the slender waist, and the round bottoms. "The young girl is no less than a divine", I mutter. My eyes can't move away from the demoiselle. My mother looks at me, the mother knows what her son is thinking.

Uttara looks at Arjuna. Her eyes can't believe that he is the same Brihannala who was her dance teacher for the entire year. She looks at other Pandava brothers and gets charmed to see the world leaders in her father's courtroom. She walks towards her father and passes through the place where I am seated. The four eyes meet. And in one glance the young hearts decide that they are made for each other. The proud father and valiant Matsya ruler Virat in a loud voice then announces, "The marriage of valiant Abhimanyu with the beautiful Uttara is fixed and I request sire Yudhishthira to invite all his relatives and guests." The ceremony date gets fixed and the messengers are sent with the invitation. My heart couldn't ask for anything more, the young fairy of millions of hearts will stand beside me in couple of days.

The day arrives. The entire palace and the city are decorated with the fragrant flowers. The conch, the cymbals, the drums fill the entire city with the sound of happiness. A princess' wedding is supposed to be extravagant and so is it! For past few days, King Virat didn't leave any stone unturned to make it a grandest event of the country. "Let the gold flow like ocean", the organizers are instructed. Guests from far and wide have reached Matsya in chariots, palanquins and elephants. They have brought the finest produce from their empires as gifts for the newly weds. For more than a week, different quality viands, wines, juices are being served in the entire city which my eyes witnessed for the first time. The grandeur is mesmerizing, the arrangements are impeccable and so is Uttara. I have never seen such rosy cheeks, big eyes and heart melting smile. I am head over heels in love.

The Brahmans perform the celestial yagnas, the priests perform ceremonies in the temples and the gurus chant the mantras for the future of the new couple. The joy kills the pain, the happiness engulfs the sorrow and the bliss removes the grief. The pain of thirteen years ended with this joyous moment of union. The union of two souls, the alliance of two empires and the unification of two families.

The queen and her maids doll up the young girl soon to be a bride. As she enters the mandapa set for the nuptials, the priests chant the mantras and the maids shower the flowers. Uttara decked in every possible ornament and draped in the silk robe looks no less than a fairy.

The entire hall blossoms with the fragrance of unguents and a variety of floral garlands. My eyes meet the eyes of my mother and I blush. My father and mother look at each other and they seem to be very content. I'm elated to see everyone around me smiling. I feel that the sadness of separation of thirteen years has finally come to a halt. And I'm the reason. That makes me feel so proud!

My father accepts the daughter of King Virat as his daughter-in-law in front of all elders and the nuptial knot ties us. The king Virat, today as bride's father, offers the seven thousand steeds, two hundred elephants, pearls, jewels, expensive stones and much more to the newlyweds and in front of the Brahmans accepts me as his son-in-law. The ceremony gets over and then both the families gift the Brahmanas, the sacred priests, and the servants, a plethora of clothes and jewels. All the guests at the royal wedding receive gifts as per their order.

FORMATION OF THE ARMY

As the ceremony gets over, the guests retire to their beds but the euphoria and the sparkle in everyone's eyes remain. The course of the royal evening comes to the end. I am directed to my room with my newlywed wife. This is the start of my new journey. It all happened at a pace I couldn't imagine. The room is decorated with the floral beads, the smell of scented water and fragrant wax fills the entire room. The bed is decorated with red rose petals and the finest silk sheets. The lights are dimmed and the entire palace cams down to the soft music and tries to grab some sleep. It's been a busy day!

Next morning, uncle Krishna calls everyone in the discussion hall. King Virat and his sons, king Drupada and his sons, the Pandavas, uncle Balarama, uncle Satyaki, my father's ardent follower and disciple, and other close aides are gathered in the room. Uncle Yudhishthira, who was supposed to be the King of the greatest empire on earth but lost it all to a dice game, is as calm as ever. I have always been intrigued by his composure and had a curiosity of knowing the secrets of his self-control. I sit behind my father. I look around and observe that the hall is filled with innumerable valiant warriors.

Uncle Krishna rises from his seat and speaks, "The Pandavas have successfully completed their exile of twelve years and the one year of incognito without coming into the knowledge of anyone. Duryodhana promised that he would give the wealth and kingdom back once the five brothers complete their exile, but it could be devil's promise. All present in this room know that the wealth snatched from Yudhishthira was the cunning affair of Shakuni and Duryodhana. It was injustice done and the time has come to seek justice. We are here today to decide which side we are. In case, Duryodhana doesn't agree to return what belongs to Yudhishthira, the result could be war. Not to punish the unjust, is the injustice in itself."

Everyone listens to his words silently. Uncle Balarama breaking the silence in the room rises up and opposes his younger brother's views, "Yudhishthira had lost everything without being forced. He was requested to play the game and he could very well refuse. Moreover, he could at any point end the game, but he didn't do it. He took decisions following his wit and in all his senses. Putting the wealth, his kingdom, and sadly his wife too on stake was purely his decision and hence Duryodhana can't be blamed for the injustice. It was arrogance, ego and the lack of judgement of Yudhishthira, and not the cheating of Duryodhana."

Uncle Balarama makes his point clear and says, "In case the war is called, I'll not participate from either side."

For him, both the groups are equal and Duryodhana is not guilty. Satyaki rises from his seat bows down before Balarama and says, "O sire! The dice game could be justified, but the immorality with Draupadi can never be. No matter what the situation was, no matter in what circumstances Yudhishthira lost the stake, the Kauravas had no right to dishonor the princess. The dishonor to a woman is the dishonor to the entire family and Draupadi is the princess of Kuru dynasty. So, stealing her modesty was equal to denting the Kuru kingdom. I'll favor punishing the people responsible for immorality."

The debate went on for hours with multiple people presenting their views and opinions. Finally, King Virat advises uncle Yudhishthira to send the invitation to all the allies, friends, rulers, and warriors of different regions. In case of war, Yudhishthira will need the support and he speculated that Duryodhana, the clever one, must have started forming allies.

Uncle Krishna adds his point, "I feel, as the kingdoms surrounding Hastinapur have equal relations with both the groups, it should be on the wit of the rulers and the warriors to decide which side they want to represent. Let's not force anyone."

He suggests that king Drupada is a respected ruler and hence he should send a message to the Kaurava prince that if the peace treaty can be signed with equitable terms, the brotherly sentiments will not be hurt. But in case, Duryodhana refuses the peace agreement, then the fate of the Kauravas will be decided by the wrath of *Gandiva.*

I am sitting quietly in the corner listening to all the commotion of my elders. I know that the wrong has happened with my sires and my godmother, but my heart sinks for my wife, who's a new bride. She is a born Kshatriya, but still a very young girl. My heart melts thinking of the plight of my new wife. I haven't spent even a day with her. Not gotten a chance to know her, not seen the seasons of blossoms with her, and the elders are talking about the war. The young girl whom I met a couple of days before, got married yesterday, what is her fault that her husband will be thrown to war in a couple of days. And in a war, no one knows who'll survive to see the light of the day and who'll perish! "Life's not fair" I tell myself!

The misfortunes of a father are gifts to his son. I met my father after thirteen long and painful years and before I could share the feelings of separation, I was arranged to marry the young daughter of king Virat. "Was it the decision for my future, or the political arrangement to prepare for the war?", my mind reflects. But I don't have any answer.

"The young man whose eyes have seen only sixteen summers, who have just started to learn the beauty of life, is going to be dropped in the middle of a war against the mighty warriors of Kuru dynasty.", reflects my mind. I don't know if I would survive the war or not, I don't know if I will get the time to spend with my wife or not, but I will be one of the faces in the war, that I know surely. Silently sitting in the corner, multitude of thoughts crisscrossed my mind and my face is decorated with a tense smile. I smile at my fate, I smile at the time, I smile at the events happened in the past and I smile at myself. I only have questions to ask, only answers to seek from my dearest uncle Krishna, but he's too busy. Is he intentionally avoiding me? I don't know!

The invitation for alliance reaches to the remotest kingdoms. Some accepted, some rejected depending on who's dearer to which kingdom and some simply don't want to participate.

And in few days, the contingents start arriving at the base of Pandavas, *Upaplavya*, a small territory in the Matsya kingdom. The Pandavas manage to arrange seven *Akshauhini* of the army, with one *Akshauhini* consists of twenty-one thousand eight hundred and seventy chariots and an equal number of elephants, thrice as many horses and five times the foot soldiers. The weapons and ammunition are being arranged for the soldiers and cooks are being called to serve food to this large cavalry.

PEACE TREATY

"War is certain.", every soldier has this thought in mind. The seven *Akshauhini* allied with us start practicing for the battle day and night. Uncle Balarama already left for the pilgrimage and uncle Krishna on request of my father accept to favor Pandavas. Albeit he already expressed that he would not pick the weapon but there are certain relations which are beyond desires. The friendship of my father and uncle Krishna is one such.

"Krishna asked Duryodhana and me to choose between his entire regiment and himself. He also put the condition that he would not pick weapon during the battle. I was given choice to choose first. How can I select anything on top of Krishna!", told my father when I asked him how allies were formed. "I requested

Krishna to be my advisor and then he chose to be my charioteer in the war.", my father concluded.

I am speechless beholding the trust between two friends. On the other hand, Kauravas managed to arrange eleven divisions, with the warriors like Bhishma, Drona, Ashwatthama and Karna on their side. The fierceness of the battle can be imagined with the strength of cavalries, the preparation of the armies and the types of weapons being procured. All the soldiers are being trained in smaller groups to ensure they understand the code words, array formation and commands during the war. I am also getting training on the new weapons and the knowledge of different array formation. The gurus tell about the strategies to protect the king and the group leaders help the soldiers learn to handle new additions to the weaponries.

The Brahmana sent by king Drupada as the messenger for the peace treaty to Kauravas has returned with no positive news. He tried to explain to the Hastinapur ruler, Dhritarashtra about the law and righteousness. He explained that the kingdom should belong to the descendants of the Kuru dynasty and by law, it should be divided among Kauravas and Pandavas. He told that the Pandavas would go for the peace if the Kauravas return their wealth and give equal honor in the kingdom. But greed overpowers wisdom and distorts the wit. Duryodhana declined the proposal of giving the wealth which belongs to his cousins. The king Dhritarashtra conveyed that he would send Sanjaya, his close aide and intelligent courtier of Hastinapur, as his messenger of peace.

Sanjaya is sitting in the middle of the room with the letter sent from Dhritarashtra. We are gathered in the meeting hall and on the advice of Yudhishthira, Sanjaya starts reading the letter, "Dear son, you are the son of dharma and patience is your biggest weapon. You have learnt the scriptures and followed the righteousness all your life. My sons are perverse and don't listen to the advice of even grandsire Bhishma. But you should not lose your patience. The possessions gained through the war can never bring happiness, the killings of own brothers can never bring bliss. I, as your elder, in the capacity of your father, advise you to refrain from hatred and keep on following the path of dharma. You can retire to the woods, perform yagnas, read the scriptures and make your sires proud with the intellect you gain with years of devotion and learning. I always want the welfare of all you brothers and bless you for the blissful life."

Everyone is silent, listening to Sanjaya. The intention behind the sugar-coated words is inevitable. Sanjaya extends the salutations to all present in the room and leaves for Hastinapur. Uncle Yudhishthira, the one true king turns towards uncle Sahadeva and asks him to write a message for grandfather Dhritarashtra.

He dictates, "Dear Uncle, the wealth, Duryodhana, cunningly snatched from us was earned by us. It was not your generosity. You have given me the throne of the emperor once, and we brothers with our intelligence and strength have earned the wealth and made treaties with numerous kingdoms. The wealth which belongs to us was stolen by your sons and now when we have successfully completed the condition imposed on us, you are denying giving back which rightfully belongs to us. The world is rich with wealth and heritage and everyone can live here peacefully. There is room for everyone, big or small, rich or poor. There is no necessity of hatred and I, the eldest of all the Pandavas, extend my hands towards the peaceful world. I urge you to give us five villages viz. Avisthala, Vrikasthala, Makandi, Varanvata, and one of Duryodhana's desire; if not half of the kingdom. We, the five brothers will be content and follow the path of peace."

Uncle Yudhishthira continues, "Krishna will go to Hastinapur with this new peace proposal between the brothers." Beholding king's desire, uncle Krishna turns towards us and asks for the wishes of each Pandava brother. The eldest has already shared his opinion by offering the peace agreement in lieu of five villages. He turns to his friend Arjuna. Albeit my father is capable of defeating the entire Kaurava army, he still advocates for peace. Uncle Bhima, the strongest of all, the one whose anger can disrupt the volcano, the one who has the strength of hundred elephants, also suggests for the peace, if Duryodhana agrees to the demands. The twin brothers also join the forces of the peace treaty. I listen to each one of them. The strength of a warrior is not defined by the wars he wins, but the times he seeks for peace. The true warrior doesn't believe in taking the lives but rather saving them. I feel proud to be part of the lineage which has valor, strength, anger and calmness at the same time.

Krishna prepares to leave for Hastinapur. The king is concerned about his safety as the Kauravas can't be trusted. He asks Satyaki to join Krishna and be in his close proximity while Krishna speaks with Kauravas. The two emissaries leave for Hastinapur. It will be sleepless nights for us till they return. The days pass, the sun and the moon change their positions and after few days, uncle Krishna returns.

Nobody can tell, seeing the face of Krishna, what's in his mind. Not even his close friend Arjuna can demystify the mystic, and I am too young to judge him. Even though I have lived with him for years and my education was under his supervision but knowing him is a mystery. Krishna enters the palace and the eager Yudhishthira asks all family members to gather quickly. Krishna greets the elders; the youngsters seek his blessings and we all get seated to our places. For the moment, the room is silent, the whiz of the air can be heard with naked ears. Everyone waits for Krishna to speak and the desperate eyes look at him.

Krishna speaks, "Dear all, present in this courtroom. I met grandsire Bhishma, Dhritarashtra, mother Kunti, Duryodhana and other Kaurava brothers, Vidura, Guru Drona and Karna in the palace of Hastinapur. They welcomed me with the fullest of their capacity. I was allowed to present the views and the peace message of Yudhishthira and as he desired, I spoke about giving Pandavas the five villages, if not the half kingdom which they actually deserve. I urged for peace. The grandsire was happy with the peace message of Yudhishthira. Duryodhana mentioned that when Yudhishthira had lost the wealth in the game, there is no point in asking it back. As per him, he is being framed as the offender. And, when I tried to convince him to settle with the five villages, he roared in anger and said he would not give the piece of land, equal to needle's point and left the courtroom. The

Kauravas are not ready for any peace agreement, even after the advice of the grandsire and Vidura. My dear, all who are present in this room, the time has come to punish the guilty. This is the time to teach lessons to the offenders and the time to rise above the attachments of blood. This is the time to look back at the injustice and to look for Kshatriya dharma. My dear warriors, stand, rise and walk together. WAR is certain."

DAY 1

Chapter 1

THE BATTLEFIELD

Individually we are brave; united we are fearless

Both the sides couldn't reach any conclusion. No peace treaties helped. The pearls, jewels, ornaments, chariots, steeds, elephants, cows, weapons, arms, soldiers, servants, and other untold wealth with the capital city lost in the dice game thirteen years ago is still in the control of Duryodhana. He is not ready to give even the land equal to needle's point back to the Pandavas. The dice game which was organized for entertainment resulted in the biggest mistake of our lives. The humility, the reasoning, the justice, the laws, and the respect, everything was on stake and the Pandu sons lost it all. The elders were mute spectators, the evil laughter of the Kaurava brothers engulfed the pride of Pandu sons. They did not even spare the princess and the clan's daughter-in-law. Nobody reacted to mother Draupadi's dishonor, and everything was in the control of Duryodhana. It was the epitome of injustice and the lowest point of intelligence. Draupadi cried for justice, argued for the immorality, and fought her heart out before calling her last hope, Krishna.

When worldly desires of Duryodhana overpowered humanity and when war was the only option left to get justice, we gathered together. Today, in the hope of winning pride again through killing own brothers, and in the hope of cultivating the righteousness through the unethical means known to humankind, we are gathered in numbers of hundreds of thousands.

Today, we are gathered on this field of Kurukshetra. The land in the dominion of Kuru dynasty, pride of the trailblazers of Kuru empire will witness the dreadful mutilation of humans. The open land spanned across till the eyes could see is today flooded with the soldiers, steeds, elephants, and chariots. All gathered in one hope to win over other. The warriors, the Gurus, the disciples, the virtuous, the seekers, the soldiers, and the warriors, all are gathered to witness the cruelty knocking at our front door.

RULES OF THE WAR

Later in the day, the elders gather to define the rules of the war. From side of the Kauravas, mighty grandsire, guru Drona, Duryodhana, Dushasana, Karna, Shakuni, and Salya came to the center of the field. From our camp, king Yudhishthira with all Pandava brothers, Dhrishtadyumna and uncle Krishna proceed towards the same place. The grandsire Bhishma in presence of all the great warriors takes the center place and speaks, "Today we are gathered here in the virtue of our Kshatriya dharma. All the kings, greatest of the warriors, soldiers and heroes from different Kshatriya clans, I don't know what the result of this combat will be, but we all in our defined capacities will perform our duties. One who follows the dharma, sticks to the rules, don't overpower the weak, follows the ethics of the war, will be remembered always. The men with great skills, supreme powers, who know how to defeat the foes and save the friends, will be welcomed in the heaven. I, in the authority of commander of the Kaurava army, invite Yudhishthira to set the rules of the war."

Listening to this, uncle Yudhishthira goes forward, bows down before the greatest hero of Hastinapur and says, "With the knowledge, I gathered reading the scriptures, and with the lessons, I learnt during the training under Guru Drona, I will tell the rules of the war with the permission of the grandsire." He continues, "It is mentioned in the scriptures that people with equal skills must encounter each other. The weak should not feel that he is being molested and there will be no contest of words. Those who will be wounded, and will ask for the retirement from the war, will not be slain. Those who surrender, will not be killed. The warriors sitting on elephants will combat with similar opponents and it will be true for the warriors sitting on horses, and chariots. The foot soldiers should get other foot soldiers as their opponents." Listening to this, the other warriors give their consent.

The grandsire then steps in and says, "The battle should be fought within the rules defined, per the Kshatriya dharma. The great warriors present here are skilled in different weapons and arms handling, and hence the two warriors should give notice to each other, in case of any duels. Nobody should strike the other who is not prepared or unarmed. The one whose weapon is unfit or the one who loses the shield should not be attacked." He adds, "The ones who are driving the chariots, ones who are ferrying the weapons, the animals, the drummers, and the conch blowers will never be attacked."

Once the rules are defined, the warriors acknowledge and return to their respective camps. The Kaurava group is standing in the western part of Kurukshetra and the Pandu sons face the west. I am the chosen one by the Pandu brothers, to always be in the close vicinity of our king Yudhishthira. I am instructed to protect the king in all situations and in the close combat take decisions as taught during the practice sessions. Along with me the other brothers, sons of mother Draupadi, my brother-in-law Uttar with his other brothers and father form the large army.

As per advice of King Drupada, uncle Yudhishthira had sent messengers around the world seeking the support of various kingdoms. During the glorious days of Pandavas, they had made several treaties, and because of the excellent relations with great warriors, many turned up to support the war. We managed to make the large army of seven *Akshauhini*. Although it is almost one and half times lesser than that of Kauravas army; but all of us are enthusiastic and energetic and ready to fight for one cause.

The Kaurava army floods the western part of the land. Hundreds of thousands of soldiers, horsemen, charioteers, elephant riders and other skilled warriors are standing in front of us. The grandsire Bhishma committed to Hastinapur kingdom is leading the foe's army. He, the mighty warrior, who learnt the war skills from *Parashuram*, capable of handling untoward war incident, ready to save his motherland is standing firm like a wall. Because of his numbers of conquests across the world, many kingdoms formed the ally with Kaurava army. Some came with fear, some due to past commitments, and some in the greed of wealth; came to participate in the battle. They together form a big army of eleven contingents with a large troop of soldiers.

THE BATTLE

We are positioned in the battlefield. From the point, where I am standing, I can see the ocean of men standing firm with swords, javelins, bows and arrows, and shields and innocent animals carrying them. All these men are ready to lay their lives in one command. With the command, I see the different regiments have started taking their respective positions, each regiment being led by different warriors have only one goal, to protect the prince Duryodhana. I see Duryodhana and his other brothers, who are my uncles too, are being surrounded by the array of thousands of foot soldiers, hundreds of horsemen and an equal number of elephant riders. The charioteers array themselves to protect the inner army and then a large group of soldiers are placed in front for the combat. I could hear the uproar of soldiers, neighs of steeds, trumpets of elephants, the loud noise of hooves of running horses, and can feel the turbulence being caused because of the movement of the armies. This is certainly not going to be an easy combat because each and every soldier present in this land today is skilled in multiple war forms. They have proved their worth in various past combats and have shown the intelligence in many difficult situations. This is not the war of power only, it is about the skills, energy, intelligence, pace, and decision making as well. I see the firm wall being formed in front of us to protect the Kaurava brothers and each of their chariots are being protected by many other skilled soldiers.

Life is so strange! When I was born, all the Pandava and Kaurava brothers were living in harmony, together in one kingdom under the blessing of the grandsire. But today the same brothers, albeit cousins are on opposite sides of what would be a bloody, inhuman and sorrowful battle! Greed, ego and worldly desires have overpowered dharma and logical thinking. Duryodhana is out there to prove to the entire world that he deserves everything, and he is the most powerful amongst us all. What dark shadow is overpowering his humanity I don't know, but I feel terrible knowing that once a good man has dropped his morality for a contest of blood bathed game of life!

Or was I completely wrong from the beginning? What if uncle Duryodhana was always greedy, what if he was always evil and faked his generosity till the dice game? Well, I'll never know now!

Arjuna, my father, a man with dark complexion, large eyes like lotus leaves, warrior of the warriors, a man with broad shoulders, with the strength of a lion, and intelligent like a sage, is standing in his chariot, with Krishna as his charioteer. But he looks restless today. His chariot is full of quivers and hundreds of arrows and venomous missiles. His *Gandiva* hangs on his right shoulder, the sharpest sword hangs by his waist, and a heavy metal shield covers his chariot. He is wearing a thick metal coat covering his body to protect himself from the enemy's shafts. He resembles a complete warrior on this field of Kurukshetra. The man, world bows down before whose caliber.

A man who single-handedly destroyed the *Khandava* forest, who gave tough fight to Rudra (in the disguise of forester), who studied the science of weapons from Indra, and studied the art of handling the weapons and array formations from Guru Drona, who is the dearest disciple of all his mentors, who alone made Bhishma, Karna, Drona, Ashwatthama, and Duryodhana run away from the combat while rescuing the wealth of Virat kingdom, greatest of men, stands in the middle of the field with his dearest friend Krishna. I look at my father and bow down to him seeking his blessings. He nods his head and signals me to take my position. I follow what he signals but he doesn't look positive.

His eyes don't sparkle. His face looks bemused and seems his heart is not in synergy with his mind. He looks at the array of the soldiers in front of him, who are ready to die for him and asks Krishna to drift the chariot across the field.

I see him going to the field observing minute details of the positions of friends, brothers, relatives, and other soldiers. He stops in the middle of the battlefield from where he could see everyone. It looks like he is standing on an island surrounded by an ocean of men and animals. I see Krishna and Arjuna talking. What could be the discussion about? The battle can start any moment, the signal to attack can come anytime. We should be arranged in the array for today's attack. I arrange my quivers, my arrows, and other shafts and lances. The four powerful steeds are yoked to my chariot. I look at them, put my hands on their faces and they gently nudge as if they are reassuring their commitment for me. These quadrupeds without even knowing about the jealousy cruising on this field commit themselves for the greed of humans. They haven't committed any crime, they haven't done any wrong deeds, then why punish them? But alas, questions are all I have. Answers I seek in vain!

I look at my charioteer Sumitra. He is busy feeding the animals. I tap his shoulder and smile. He smiles back. For my life in this war, he is going to be my closest friend. The reins in his hands will decide my destiny on the field.

Amidst all these unspoken emotions and unexpressed feelings, I see the two friends coming back and my father appears more confident now.

Uncle Yudhishthira approaches Arjuna and asks him to decorate the counter array. My father is given the responsibility to form an array in such a way that it should not look lesser than Kauravas army. Albeit we have one and a half times lesser regiments than our enemies, the array should be firm and difficult to penetrate. My father reaches out to all of us and commands to form the array in the form of Vajra, with each end should be governed by a strong warrior in our cavalry. King Yudhishthira should be placed at the center and surrounded by sons of Pandava brothers. This means the sons of mother Draupadi and I have to be in close vicinity of the king. The next layer will be surrounded by the soldiers and the outer layer will be led by the four Pandava brothers. Uncle Bhima will be in front, uncles Nakul and Sahadeva will cover east and west part of the array and my father, Arjuna will govern the tail of the array.

Happy to see the formation, Yudhishthira, in the hope of seeking blessings from the elders, asks his charioteer to move towards the Kaurava army. Looking at him pacing towards the foe's army, uncle Krishna, asks few of us to follow the king in order to counter any unjust acts from Duryodhana. As per the command, I start following the king and with me comes a few more warriors. Uncle Yudhishthira, on reaching near the Kaurava army, asks the foes to clear the path for him as he wants to meet the grandsire. I'm amazed at the number of soldiers that Duryodhana has managed to bring to his side. Kings from far flung kingdoms have agreed to join his side. But why? Greed, jealousy or merely friendship? He seems to be a master manipulator! While these thoughts weave in my mind, I see the wave of soldiers moving away from our path on the permission of the grandsire.

Reaching near to grandfather Bhishma, we all bow down. Yudhishthira touches his feet and asks about his health. Grandsire Bhishma, always firm and confident is looking feeble today. I see the dampness in his eyes when with the great affection he hugs uncle Yudhishthira. The eldest Pandava asks for his blessings and his permission to be part of the war. Bhishma blesses him saying, "Victory must be yours". To which a visibly surprised Yudhishthira asks, "How can someone win the situation against the grandsire? Until the great wall is standing protecting the lands of Hastinapur, not even a bird can enter the area without your permission."

Grandfather Bhishma understanding the eagerness replies, "A man is the slave of the wealth, but wealth is slave of nobody. For my entire life, until today, I am bound to serve my motherland. Even though I know that justice will prevail only when the Pandu sons will win the combat, but I will make sure till my last breath the country which I built with great affection will be saved." with a smile.

Hearing this, everyone in the Kaurava army gets confused, but starts applauding and jumping with super confidence. I know it is not easy to cross the lines drawn by the grandsire and it will be most difficult to penetrate any of the arrays arranged by him. But somewhere I know the grandsire's blessings are not just hollow words. He really meant every word he just said. There is a power in his wishes and blessings which we cannot see or can never explain with logic but must be known to Krishna and my father Arjuna. When the lighter clouds cover the sun hiding its glory, they forget that a wave of wind will drive them away. The hollow ambitions of Kauravas resemble these clouds which are overjoyed thinking the glory of Pandavas is dead.

Everyone has their own flaws. The trick is to find your opponent's flaws and to exploit it to win. Any group, any country, and any army have their inherent weaknesses. The winner overcomes them but the loser surrenders. We just have to work out the perfect plan and be firm and confident in any of the unforeseen circumstances.

After taking grandsire's blessings and permission, uncle Yudhishthira moves towards Guru Drona. The mentor, the Guru, the trainer, and the well-wisher, who has devoted all his life to the service of Kuru dynasty, today also, is standing with the Kauravas.

When the Pandava brothers were sent to exile thirteen years ago, and all their wealth and belongings were kept in the captivity of Duryodhana, the Kaurava brothers needed someone to take care of the kingdom of Pandavas. And then, it was decided that Guru Drona would manage the kingdom. Guru Drona, who always wanted to have powers like the king accepted the offer and seems today he is repaying by helping Kaurava brothers. Truly, a man can become the slave of wealth, no matter how skilled he is.

We reach near Guru and bow down before him. Uncle asks for his blessings. The Guru with great affection blesses the king. And when asked by the king, how can we be victorious when we have to fight against him, Guru replies, "There is nobody present on this land who can defeat me in the war. Nobody, except Arjuna, can penetrate the array formed by me and nobody has the answers to my weapons. Until I am standing with the arms, I am invincible. But if the battle steals all emotions from my heart, if a situation on this war field turns my eyes moist, if my mind seeks for peace, if my soul desires to set free, if I am forced to leave the arms and if I sit in meditation, I can be killed."

I see the smiling face of uncle after listening to the words of the Guru. I am bemused but seems he knows the secret message Guru shared. We depart from the place and move towards Guru Kripa to seek his blessings. Kripa blesses us and asks the king to remain just in the war.

"No matter what the situation could be, you should be unmoved from the path of truth and you must be the followers of rules.", says Guru Kripa.

Uncle Yudhishthira replies, "I have followed the truth my entire life and I would never be moved away from the path of justice."

Kripa blesses him for victory and both of them part their ways. We then reach the place where Salya, the king of Madra, brother of grandmother Madri, and uncle of Nakul and Sahadeva is standing. The king bows down to him and asks for his blessings too. Salya with great affection and tearful eyes hugs him. I can see the repentance in his attitude because he unknowingly has committed a mistake.

While he was coming to meet us, post invitation sent out through the messengers, he was greeted by the servants of Duryodhana on his way. He was fed well, treated with utmost care, and thus he got allured with so much care being showered on him. In this mood, he gave the boon to Duryodhana to ask for any support and the cunning Duryodhana, asked for his support during the war. Devastated Salya visited uncle Yudhishthira in our training camp and apologized for his folly. Uncle listened to his story and then advised him to become charioteer of Karna in case duel between Karna and Arjuna happens in battle. Which is certainly inevitable!

Salya is a skilled warrior with extreme acumen. He is as good as Krishna in the role of a charioteer. But the agreement of riding Karna's chariot happened on the cost that Salya would not miss any opportunity to demean Karna's ability. His main target will be to belittle Karna's effort before Arjuna. This is about placing the foe in the form of a friend, sometimes to get insights, sometimes to demoralize, and sometimes to distract. In a tough situation, the motivation of the closest person plays a pivotal role. Motivation can make an ant climb the mountain and discouragement can make people forgetting their skills. And, certainly, this was the agreement between Salya and uncle Yudhishthira.

While meeting Salya, uncle reminds him of his promise and asks for his blessings as well. Salya blesses the king and we depart from Kaurava regiment. The king after getting the desired blessings looks confident and asks in a loud voice, "Who here present in the battlefield wants to support the Pandavas, anyone who wants to join our side is most welcome." Acknowledging the invitation, one of the Kaurava brothers, Yuyutsu, who is the son of Dhritarashtra and his maid, accepts the invitation to change the side and willingly wants to support us. Happy to hear this, the king welcomes him and asks his charioteer to drive towards Pandavas army camp. We follow the king and reach the camp.

With the blessings and permissions of the elders, Yudhishthira asks his brothers to take the positions in the array formed. All following the instructions reach to the respective positions. Uncle Krishna asks us to blow the conch and signal the readiness for the war. All the Pandu brothers and Krishna take out their conches. It is a loud roar in the battlefield, like a thunderbolt strike. Arjuna blows his conch *Devadatta*; Yudhishthira blows *Anantvijaya*; Bhima, Nakul and Sahadeva also put full pressure to create the loudest noise with their conches, *Paundra*, *Sughosha* and *Manipushpaka* respectively.

Listening to the noise from our camp, grandsire Bhishma takes out his conch and responds to the invitation from us. Drona, Duryodhana, Dushasana, and other Kaurava brothers follow the suite and the entire battlefield gets filled with the deafening noises. The animals are getting threatened and because of fear the horses' neighs, the elephants' grunts and the birds fly away. The foot- soldiers start thumping their feet and javelins, the animals jump and the entire field fills with the dust storm. The sun cannot be seen from the earth because of the thick blanket of dust being formed and nobody can open their eyes properly. It continues for several minutes and then the noise lowers. The warriors put down the conches and put on their weapons.

Arjuna ties strings of *Gandiva* and the string twangs with thunder striking noise. He arranges his quivers with hundreds of arrows surrounding his chariot. Krishna with a smile on his face is seated at the charioteer's seat. The calmness in his gesture hides many mysteries of his life. Bhima, a ruthless slayer and powerful mace fighter, lifts his heaviest mace equal to the weight of thousands of clubs and waves it is giving the sign of crushing the foes. The anger in his eyes is evident. He grinds his teeth and gives a loud roar like a lion, which can be heard from a great distance. Yudhishthira, a skilled javelin fighter and learnt scholar of scriptures arrange his weapons too. Nakul and Sahadeva also tie the strings of their respective bows and manage the swords, arrows, javelins, and maces in their respective chariots.

The sons of the Pandava brothers including me stand at the positions told to us. We bow down to elders seeking their blessings. I fill my quivers with hundreds of arrows, deadly missiles and other venomous shafts. I take out my sword, check the sharpness and keep it back in the leather sheath. I check the positions of each of my other weapons and then ask my charioteer, Sumitra, to take me near my father. He takes me to the place where my father and uncle Krishna are positioned. I bow down to them, touch their feet and seek their blessings. My father advises me to stay strong and follow the path of wisdom in any unfavorable condition. And take decisions not based on the scriptures, but on the real situations. I take their permission and come back to my place near king Yudhishthira. We are standing at our respective positions and we see Kaurava army approaching towards us. Uncle Bhima, who is leading our array alarms us and roars loudly.

His roar is no less than an angry elephant's grunt, listening to which the horses of his chariot start neighing. The charioteer controls them, and, on his order, those emphatic steeds start running towards the western part of the battlefield.

All of our soldiers following the command rush towards the foes with the deadliest weapons in their hands. The chariot warriors have taken the positions with the arrows pulling the bows' strings and their chariots are cruising on the field, the elephant warriors with long javelins and shafts are running towards their counterparts. The foot soldiers with their thirst for the blood of their enemies are running like tigers with swords and shields in their hands. In no time, the whole field is filled with the thundering noise of striking swords. The splendid bows on the command of their masters release venomous arrows in hundreds and thousands. The entire field is covered by the thick cloud of the arrows and the fleeting dust makes it difficult to target the enemy. I see the Kaurava brothers, Duryodhana, Durmukha, Dushasana, and Vikarana have started killing the soldiers mercilessly. The arrows being released from their bows look like snakes and when strike the soldiers, in no time take their lives away. The chariot warriors from our army counter the released arrows from enemies and try to nullify the impact.

The brutal Bhima, ferocious Nakul and speeding Sahadeva penetrate the enemy's army and give the fitting reply in the combat. I, as told, am very close to the king and making sure no enemy's arrow should reach near him. Suddenly I see that a giant creature is approaching towards us, he is Alamvusha, a warrior from a *Rakshasa* clan. I sense the danger and ask brother Ghatotkacha, son of Bhima, half Rakshasa and half human, to counter Alamvusha. Ghatotkacha with the lightning speed strikes him and the fight shakes the earth, creating turbulence.

Meantime, the king of Kosala, Vrihadvala, attacks me. I, like an alert tiger, duck the attack. His arrows hit my charioteer, Sumitra, and he loses the control and the horses too. I lose my grip and jump off the chariot with my sword. I run towards him with the sword in my hand. The blink of eye and I pierce him. My sword tastes the first human blood and it is the start of the battle for me. Vrihadvala, in anger, strikes a couple of more arrows at me and I, in return give him equal fight. I manage to bring him down and release his soul to Yama's abode. This is the first strike, the first kill, and the first victory for me. I am elated. I am excited. The battle will see my prowess. The teachings of years will not go for waste and my father will be proud. I wave my sword in air marking my victory over Vrihadvala.

The cheerful heart boosts the confidence in my veins. I can hear Uttar, my brother-in-law, cheering for me from behind. But it is just the beginning. We have entered into the ocean of fearless and merciless combatants, who are ready to slash each other to satisfy their thirst. As the crocodile clenches its prey, as the tiger pounces on deer, as the bull strikes with its horns, these endless soldiers in hundreds of thousands are killing their antagonists.

As the combat continues, the killings increase. The grandsire Bhishma in his desire to captivate the king Yudhishthira rushes towards him with five warriors including Kripa and Salya. Bhishma's intention is clear. He is fighting for his motherland; the land which he nurtured for years, generation after generation with care and affection. Though he loves both the groups equally, he knows that the war is a result of injustice done by the Kaurava brothers but his obligations and duties towards his country don't allow him to shower affection towards anyone who raises eyes against his kingdom. His mind is certainly a bigger battlefield than the one on which we are standing. Everyone knows he wants to support us, but his responsibilities are not allowing him to do so. He with great energy rushes towards the king, and I, being in the closest vicinity of the king, am expected to save the unprecedent situation. I ask Sumitra to rush towards the great grandsire. I pick the arrows from the quivers while he directs the chariot towards the grandsire. To fight with the son of Ganga, who did not let even Parashuram overthrow him in a duel, is going to be tough for me. My chariot rushes towards the five warriors approaching with grandsire Bhishma, and in no loss of time, I start showering the arrows. My hands are working with agility, and my arrows are striking the targets. I shower multiple arrows at each of the warriors including the grandsire. The grandsire smiles as if he acknowledges my learnings and weapons handling skills. I bow down to him but even in that very second of gesture exchange, both of us don't stop shooting arrows at each other.

The grandsire then impetuously showers thousands of arrows at me and in no time, I am surrounded by the cloud of arrows without a single one hitting my body.

"How clever and skillful" I mutter under my breath.

Meantime, the other chariot warriors also start releasing their deadly arrows. Seeing the situation getting adverse, Uttar raises alarm and the ten warriors from my side rushes towards me. The sons of King Virat, Uttar and Shweta, take the charge, and uncle Bhima quickly rescues me. I am now in the safer place on the battlefield and the head surgeon of our camp starts treating my wounds. The celestial weapons, venomous arrows and deadly missiles have caused damage to my body. I have been asked by the king to retire for the day and get the wounds nursed. I am in the nursing camp but not far from the battlefield.

Uttar and Shweta, after taking the charge, continues to fight against Kaurava warriors. Uttar, from his chariot full of shafts and arrows and other weapons, attacks Salya. In response, Salya, also pierces multiple shafts at him. Salya, a skilled warrior, releases arrows at Uttar, in return, Uttar tries to give fitting reply. But as they say, "the experience counts." Uttar being a young warrior, participating in the first combat of his life is facing trouble in handling Salya's strikes. Salya continues his attack and releases the sharpest shaft at him. Uttar is not able to handle the attack, and the shaft penetrates his shield. He loses control and falls off his chariot. The mighty young warrior couldn't survive the attack and succumbs to his injuries. My wife's brother, who's like a younger brother to me, dearest to all in Virat's kingdom, is now lying with no soul in his body. The soldiers lift his body and take to the safer place. It's the personal loss to me as well. Uttar was not only my wife's brother but also a good friend. My heart sinks. Uttar laid his life for the family, and for the cause, he was born for, in the Kshatriya clan. He made all of us proud but this feeling of being proud always comes with hefty price. Sometimes, the cost is effort, and sometimes, the cost is life. My heart is mixed with the thought of killing the foes and the guilt of throwing young Uttar in the field. He had not seen even fifteen springs of his life. Yama will never be happy seeing the young soul in his palace.

Shweta, the elder brother of Uttar, is continuously fighting with other warriors and rulers. He kills many soldiers in the Kaurava army and continues slaughtering anyone coming in his way. The death of Uttar has made him more dangerous and merciless. His wrathful killing is continuously increasing. He rushes towards Salya, with great rage. The red eyes are filled with anger. He showers a hundred of arrows and other deadly shafts on Salya. The revenge of his brother's death is evitable in the speed with which he is targeting Salya. Salya is surrounded by the deadly strikes of Shweta, and to rescue Salya, Duryodhana immediately orders the king of Kalinga and other princes to rush towards Shweta and distract him. Salya was rescued by the forces and Shweta is now surrounded by the hundreds of soldiers and other skilled warriors. But the intensity of Shweta's attack is not lessened, and he is continuously attacking the princes and warriors from different races all around. He has killed many warriors and many others are wounded by his attack. The situation is getting tense and the kings from remote locations who came to support Duryodhana are getting terrified by the attack. No single warrior coming in front of Shweta lasts longer. He either is killed or surrenders before the mighty chariot warrior. Nobody knows if the blood in his eyes shows the anger or the grief of his brother's death.

Sensing the agility and swiftness of that incredible warrior, grandfather Bhishma takes the charge. Seems, he is only one left in Kauravas army today who can counter Shweta's attack. Bhishma in his counter-attack showers hundreds of arrows at Shweta, some pierces him, some he manages to duck. It is now a duel between the two callous combatants. They are fighting like the two angry tigers fighting for their respective territories. The grandsire, as ever, is firm and stable. There is no sign of apprehension in his face and neither his aims are distracted. He, on one side, is commanding the army to continue attacking on our other troops and on the other has taken the front of managing Shweta's attacks.

Shweta is dexterous today and seeing the attack coming from Bhishma, he releases a range of shafts and other supporting missiles and covers Bhishma with them. Shweta's attacks have killed soldiers in great numbers. The damage in the opponents is evitable. His continuous rage is working like the fuel in Duryodhana's fire of worries. Looking at the frantic prince, sire Bhishma furiously attacks with hundreds of venomous arrows on Shweta. Some of those arrows hit the charioteer, and some hit the steeds. Losing the control, Shweta jumps out of the chariot. Bhishma, the just warrior stops the attack with arrows. Shweta takes out the mace from his artillery and in loud voice invites Bhishma for the duel on the ground. The mace fight between the two happens but Bhishma, the skilled handler of mace takes away the rays of life from Shweta's body.

Shweta is dead now. I was struggling to find the ways to disclose the death of Uttar, and now it becomes tougher for me. In a single day, I lost two of my wife's brothers. The entire Matsya kingdom is present in the battlefield just because I'm married to Uttara. The brothers were fighting for the dynasty to which they have given their sister. They are not committed with any pledge, but they are compelled by the responsibilities. The responsibility of protecting the family of their sister's husband, the responsibility of keeping the promise which they made to themselves. I see the corpses, then I look at the battlefield, it's not only me whose heart must be sinking at this moment. The intensity, the rage with which this war is going, in coming days, certainly this turbulence of emotions will overpower many. The voids can be filled but not the emptiness, the battles can be won but not the lives.

Seeing the death of the second son of Matsya kingdom, the third son Sankha, rushes towards Bhishma. This is serious for me, third son of the same family, encountering with grandsire now. I know, the mighty grandsire will defeat Sankha anytime. My father understands the situation and asks uncle Krishna to take his chariot towards Sankha. Krishna in no time reaches the spot where Bhishma and Sankha are combating. My father covers Sankha and takes the charge. If there is anyone who can stand against the tornado created by the grandsire, that would be Arjuna. The warrior who at numerous instances has proved his strength and skills is now standing in front of Bhishma. And Bhishma also knows, he is the only one in the world who can give the equal fight to him. The grandsire seeing Arjuna approaching him takes out his deadliest arrows from the quiver surrounding him in the chariot and showered hundreds of them towards the Pandava army. His arrows are slaughtering anyone coming in the way. The high-end missiles, the venomous arrows, and the deadly shafts being released by him are causing damage all around. His chariot rushes in great speed and penetrates any array formation. The sound of all these impacts is so high that nobody could hear anything. But the blood flowing in all directions is easily seen. Arjuna is trying to counter with every possible measure, but the fierce strikes from the circular bow of mighty Bhishma are unstoppable. The soldiers are losing control, the animals are fearful. The sun is slowly losing its strength and with the painful noises all around, it sets. And with this the first day of the war is called off. The day was controlled by the grandsire and there was nobody who could stand against him.

DAY 2

Chapter 2

THE VALIANT ARJUNA

The fear of losing can make a calm mind restless

The first day of the war ends. Grandsire Bhishma, wrathful as the God of death fought fiercely and was dominating throughout the day. Whoever came in his way was mercilessly slayed. The commander, when silent is like the moon but when furious can become impetuous like burning sun. He has proved that he is the wall of Kuru dynasty and to protect his motherland, he can go to any extent and slay anyone. In our camp, we gathered to perform the last rites of the Matsya brothers, Uttar and Shweta. Every soldier in our army is praising the valor of the heroes of the day. If Shweta wouldn't have distracted the sire, he would have caused much more damage to the Pandava army. Our king, Yudhishthira praise the bravery of both the brothers and with the moist eyes we give farewell to the brothers. For me, it is not only a loss of two brave and skilled warriors but also the loss of two friends. There is no end to the pain of my wife, Uttara. She is inconsolable. At an age suited for being in gurukul, the valiant but young warriors laid down they lives for us. Uttara can't stop crying and no one including her father and I can't console her.

King Virat, the father of the glorious sons is trying to hide his moist eyes behind the eulogies being sung by the panegyrists but alas it's too evident. Can you really console a grieving father who has to bid farewell to his children forever? Never! The vacuum cannot be filled with words or any other form of consolation. I feel very guilty because it's not their war. The reason of war is not clear to me as well. Moreover, King Virat has nothing to do with our family feud and why does he have to participate? While these thought play havoc with my conscience, I see my uncle Yudhishthira walk towards the podium.

He calls for a meeting. He wants to discuss the strategy and plan for the next day. My uncles and my brothers, the noble princes and warriors, and uncle Krishna, all congregated. The King asks us to sit as he takes the center stage. Looking at Krishna with his dampened eyes and in very low energy, he speaks, "O Krishna, with the energy the grandsire is fighting, if he continues in the same way, it will not be easy for us to protect our army. If I am not able to save our friends and well-wishers who have gathered here on my request, there is no point in continuing the war. These noble princes and skillful warriors have gathered on my request. The safety of their lives is my responsibility, but it seems I am forcefully throwing these souls in the well of death. Instead of heading towards the annihilation, I would rather retire in the woods with my brothers and live life like a mendicant."

The fear of losing can make any calm mind restless. The king whose mind is as calm as the rays of the moon, who is as patient as the earth, and who is always in the control of his emotions, today, on seeing the dance of death in the battlefield loses the control of his mind. His mind and his heart are not in synergy. The king who has unfathomable knowledge, and who has learnt the war strategies from the greatest mentors, is not able to cope with the fear of losing. He surrenders as a frightful young boy.

While king Yudhishthira is worried, uncle Krishna on the other hand is calm. The smile on his face never fades away and this makes me worried. What does he know, which we don't? Why and how is he so calm and quiet when the calmest man on earth is as scared as a toddler? While I'm deep in thought, Krishna starts speaking. "O Dear Elder! This is no time to allow fear to overpower your wisdom. We are in the battlefield and we always knew facing grandsire would not be easier. I advise to make Dhrishtadyumna, the skilled warrior and brother of Draupadi, as the commander of the army for the next day. O king! think of an array formation which is suitable for both the new commander and the army. The array which is failsafe as per the scriptures and which the warriors in our camp can control."

Listening to Krishna's suggestions the king says, "With the rays of sun diminishing in power, we stopped today's battle and I noticed that the current strategy and the today's array formation was not enough to control the grandsire and his commandants. With today's formation of our army, we tried to counter the foes but Bhishma had answers to all our strategies. Bhima, on one hand, fought like an angry elephant leading the array, my two other brothers supported the array as desired, the Matsya brave-hearts kept the grandsire and Salya distracted. And at last, Arjuna managed to save the soldiers from the tornado of the grandsire. But all this was dwarfed before the priggish grandsire."

"I, the eldest of Pandavas, in front of the great warriors and the biggest strategist Krishna, with all my knowledge from our ancient scriptures and warfare, suggest forming a *Krauncharuma* for tomorrow's battle", continues, the king. Hearing his words, all the warriors give their affirmation.

I know, the formation of this array is not easy. It requires multiple layers of armies gathered in the form of a crane. Someone will have to be the head, two have to become the eyes, and many other warriors will have to be part of the wings of the crane. We have practiced forming these kinds of various arrays during the training sessions, but tomorrow is going to be the real test!

We will be fighting not only against the foes, but also to help Yudhishthira overcoming his fear of losing it all. Fear of losing hope is the greatest fear of all. Winning a war against your foes seems nothing compared winning against your own fear. If you can conquer the fear in you, you can become invincible!

The new commander Dhrishtadyumna then takes over from uncle Yudhishthira and starts explaining the positions of soldiers and animals in details. Everyone listens attentively, but my eyes are trying to read the mind of my uncle. I observe the king and conclude that his emotions are ruling his thoughts and hence he too like some of us are divided on the outcome of the war.

Yudhishthira, the son of Lord Yama, was born with the power of mantras mother Kunti had. As per the name, he is stable in any untoward situation. He is a learnt scholar, who has read the scriptures and has been following the path of dharma as explained in books. He had established equality in his kingdom and thus, people from different domains had migrated to his empire with immense faith in him. The farmers, the merchants, the cowherds, the horsemen, the soldiers, the mentors, the scholars, the teachers, the charioteers, everyone, irrespective of domiciles happily founded shelter in Indraprastha, the capital of his kingdom. He always believed in endowing the winners, giving shelters to needy, and helping the poor. During his leadership, Indraprastha was as glorious as the sun, as great as the Himalayas, and flourished as the ocean. Along with his brothers, Yudhishthira has acquired lands, immense wealth, jewels, pearls, gold, ornaments, chariots, immeasurable cows, fastest steeds, strongest elephants, deadly weapons, venomous missiles, and other ammunition from all over the world. The flora and fauna were blooming in his kingdom without any fear. Justice was meted out to everyone, the guilty was convicted and the innocent was acquitted. He performed many rituals during his tenure as king and all the brahmans, teachers and mentors were happily finding homes, respect and wealth in his abode. He encouraged the spirituality in his kingdom and strived for knowledge and learning. He believed in giving equal opportunities and chances to the people from all classes and always surrounded himself with learned people. Even his foes couldn't find any fault in him. The man who has followed righteousness all his life, who is always fearless, who is a firm follower of rules, who always oblige the elders, and who has never gone against dharma in his life, today, is affrighted of the fierceness of the grandsire.

Next day, as the sunrays hit the battlefield, we gather in the field. A large group of soldiers, horses, chariots, and elephants face the western hills. As decided last evening, Dhrishtadyumna commands the army to get arranged in the crane shaped array. King Drupada with thousands of soldiers and multi-thousands of chariots in his troop become the head, Kuntibhoja, father of grandmother Kunti, and the ruler Saivya are the two eyes. Hundreds of warriors and more than twenty thousand chariots become the neck of the crane. The twin brothers Nakul and Sahadeva with Yudhishthira and other warriors become the wings. They are supported by more than ten thousand chariot warriors. The back of the crane is formed by millions of soldiers. At the end of the wings, a large group of the strongest elephants is placed to give the protection to the soldiers. The back of the crane is protected by King Virat and ruler of Kasi with more than thirty thousand chariots. The array in the battlefield is a juxtaposition of both beauty and the notoriety. What looks beautiful now will definitely be a bloody pile of meat and bones at sunset. I am positioned near the King Yudhishthira, with other brothers. The crane shaped army now waits for the signal to attack. The neighs, the grunts, the roars tremble the welkin, and with the thumps of animals, dust engulfs the air around us. The energetic soldiers are ready to kill and die for their motherland. On one command, they are ready to fill the ground with a river of blood and flesh. The vultures and the hawks are flying high above in the sky in the hope of feasting on the flesh of dead animals and humans. What a concoction of life and death!

The foes' army also starts gathering in the western side of the ground. Being led by the grandsire and under the supervision of Guru Drona, mighty Kripa and skilled Salya, Duryodhana's army looks more confident today. Their army in the defined array led by distinguished warriors is divided into different groups. The thousands of soldiers, the multi-thousand chariots and horses surrounded by strong elephants in the same numbers together look like an ocean ready to engulf the enemies. The arrows, the shafts, the spears, the maces, the swords and many other different weapons in large numbers are ready to paint the ground red. All are assembled in the ground waiting for the signal and then Arjuna takes out his conch and blows it. In the resonance uncle Krishna, King Yudhishthira and other Pandava brothers also blow their conches. This is the signal to start the day. Answering the signal from us, grandfather Bhishma and other sires blow their respective conches and both the armies rush towards each other resembling the start of the fierce day.

The soldiers on chariots take on the soldiers with the similar capacity. And as per the rules defined on the first day, the other combatants select their antagonists. The sword fighters, the mace fighters and the javelin fighters take on the respective counterparts. We advance towards the foes in the form of a crane with our new commander, Dhrishtadyumna instructing the commandments. The entire group as supposed is running in synergy so that the formation shouldn't break. King Drupada being the head of the crane is attacked first by the opposite army and he responds to each attack flawlessly. The pace of the soldiers increases as the two groups come closer. The battle is in full swing. The number of arrows being shot cover the sky and make it hard to decipher whether it's morning or evening!

The arrows cruise all over, the maces pound hundreds of skulls and break thousands of bones, the spears pierce thousands of hearts and swords cut other thousands of heads. The fury is all around, and the hatred is at its peak. The neighs, grunts and roars penetrate the eardrums. The dust looks orange as the sun rises higher. Our array is ruthlessly removing the souls away from the bodies of our enemies hundreds at a time.

Suddenly Dhrishtadyumna is attacked by Guru Drona's son, Ashwatthama. The two skilled warriors in their individual capacities, able to combat with thousands of soldiers single-handedly. They now face each other releasing arrows in hundreds, a few of those manage to pierce each other. Every arrow released from one is receiving a befitting reply from the other. While I'm amazed at the sight of two merciless warriors engaged in the deadliest combat, I suddenly notice an arrow flying towards me, followed by the rattle of chariot wheels approaching. While dodging the arrow, I look up and see Lakshmana, Duryodhana's son rushing towards us. He is inviting me to a duel as he intends to reach the king Yudhishthira. I, standing closest to the king, am the wall for him.

Anyone trying to reach the king should pass through me. Lakshmana releases multiple arrows in series, not targeting me but targeting the king, but I am prepared for the counterattack to bring his arrows down. I reply to him with multiple shafts. The arrows from my quivers cruise through the air and pierce him. The strikes are limitless from both sides but each time my arrow breaks his arrow I see the pain and anger in his eyes. I smirk at his amateur attitude.

To each of his attack, I have the counter and the bigger counter. Seeing the fierce combat between us, Duryodhana comes to the rescue of his son. He releases many shafts at me, and I am now surrounded by hundreds of arrows. My father sees me. He knows I might not be able to counter Duryodhana's fury braced by the grandsire and I need backup. I see him coming to support me. In no time, my father on his chariot, being driven by Krishna is now standing at the place where I was attacked. With his counter strike, he frees me from the coming danger. His skills are way above anyone's imagination. He can break any arrays and can defeat any number of warriors. Duryodhana knows well that he can never defeat his, at least in the bow-arrow duel. Father attacks at Duryodhana and his arrows make Duryodhana immovable. He is unable to counter the attacks and asks the grandsire for his rescue. The grandsire with the pace of light advances towards us and in fraction of a second, he breaks the array. His agility and dexterity make the counterattack difficult.

The duel which started between Lakshmana and me is now turned to the battle between grandfather and my father. Grandfather Bhishma cannot be conquered easily. No intelligence, no war skills, no strength could overpower him. And so is my father. He is not being vanquished by the attacks of the wall of Hastinapur. Looks like the two warriors would continue fighting till the end of the era. Duryodhana knows that the victory can't be his, until the two warriors fight with equal strengths. He commands the other warriors with thousands of foot soldiers and hundreds of horse warriors and chariot warriors to cover Bhishma and suppress the attacks of valiant Arjuna.

The other warriors in hundreds each carrying deadliest weapons advance towards the two tigers fighting. Due to the movement in high numbers, the entire ground looks like the high tides in the ocean. The roars, the rush, the charge, everything is causing the huge tornado of dust making things invisible around. There is a series of release of the arrows, shafts and other venomous weapons. When they reach within the range of Arjuna's arrows, he releases the arrows in hundreds and thousands. His *Gandiva*, with the tension of stretching the string, turns circular, each time he releases the arrows. Krishna, the perfect charioteer for the pioneer warrior, makes the steeds run at top speed. The fastest running horses are making it impossible for the foes to target him. His chariot is running in a circle and makes the illusion of Arjuna targeting the enemies from different directions. In no time, the army of a hundred thousand starts reducing. No place in the field is left where the enemies could hide, and many of them are finding place in the lap of death. The fierce combat results in a pool of blood on the field and the piles of flesh can be seen as far as the eyes can see. The Kaurava army seeing the furious Arjuna, trembles and run back to their camps. Guru Drona tries to stop the running soldiers but in vain. The loud cries, roars and the sound of shrieking, reaches the welkin, and makes people around terrified. This dance of death is being continued since the noon and Arjuna hasn't spared anyone. Those who could find a way out of Arjuna's fury became the victim of Dhrishtadyumna's anger. And the remaining soldiers who came in numbers from remotest regions are being sent to Yama's place by mighty uncle Bhima. Once brave men; praised, loved, and often envied, are now lying motionless.

The sun's shine is gradually diminishing, the rays are not strong. It is the evening – evening of our lives, evening of the day. The soldiers, and the warriors are killed and the ones alive, ran out of the sight. This is the clear victory for us on the second day of the war. The victorious Arjuna and Krishna blow their conches to announce the victory and we all resonated. All the soldiers are retired to the camps. It was tiring, but the horrendous day. The day two ends, and my father was present everywhere on the field. His attacks, his skills and his intelligence have proved that he is "the warrior" on the field. He saved many lives but at the cost of many other lives. Ironical! But this is the war.

DAY 3

CHAPTER 3

THE ANGRY KRISHNA

You are always in truth; and the truth is always in you

The second day of the war ends and Pandava warriors gather at their camp as customary to the daily routine to reflect on their actions of the day.

I am amazed to see the enthusiasm in our camp despite the bloodbath and the huge number of losses of men and animals. Some lost their brothers, some their best friends, some probably their fathers or sons. As customary, every dead body is set on pyre and burned with utmost respect. But everyone is so devoted to the cause of "Upliftment of Dharma", that they brush aside their sorrows and join the party to cheer up each other.

The rest of the evening is devoted to praising the valor of Arjuna, my father. Every warrior present in the camp applauds Arjuna and appreciates how he vanquished the opposition's army. Everyone is happy with the way he fought. Not only he but the way uncle Bhima and our commander kept the foes on their toes is being appreciated by the panegyrists. It is the victory for Pandavas. But it is not the end, as the journey has just begun. Uncle Yudhishthira then takes the center stage and initiates discussion about the strategy of tomorrow. Seeing the valor of my father on the second day, the king makes him the strategist for third day and asks him to share his views.

Bowing down before the king, my father says, "I am obliged to be the decision maker for tomorrow's combat. I appreciate the efforts of all the skilled warriors and soldiers who helped me in achieving the feat. It was truly a team effort. We followed the instructions of our commander but also used our intelligence whenever needed. It was valor mixed with ingenuity."

He continues, "In my opinion, I felt that today's array formation was perfect, and all the soldiers were perfect for the positions given to them. My sons and nephews, along with my brothers and friends fought with great skills, but we have to continue with the same strength in the days ahead. One victory begets the burden of carrying it day after day. We shouldn't forget that they have the grandsire with them. The grandsire will definitely come back with a master plan for tomorrow."

All of us were listening to father's words when Satyaki rises up and asks about the array formation for next day.

Satyaki, a valiant warrior, is friend of Krishna and the disciple of my father. When Krishna gave his entire army to Duryodhana on his request, Satyaki stayed back to fight in favor of us along with Krishna. I have seen him fighting relentlessly for the past two days. He is as energetic as my father, and as tactical as Krishna. All his moves are so calculative that the foe's army can't predict "what's next". His agility, dexterity, energy and valor are of enormous lessons for us.

Satyaki asks, "O mighty Arjuna, your skills are known to everyone, the grandsire always appreciates your intelligence and today's array formation was so flawless that their army was not able to penetrate the formation, till Bhishma and Drona took the charge. We should understand that to counter our strategy for today, they will definitely return with a much difficult array formation. We should be prepared for any unknown danger and clever strategy which might be presented against us by the great grandsire."

Listening to Satyaki's concerns, my father smiles and says, "You, my friend, speak the truth. In a war, we should never undermine the strength of the foes. It may be our victory today but certainly; they will plan their array more carefully now. And we should be prepared for the coming days."

Addressing to all the warriors he continues, "With the strength we fought today, we will maintain the same without the fear of death. The fear of death comes to the cowards, the valiant lives without fear. Individually we are brave, united we are fearless. Thus, with the knowledge and experience I have gathers over the years, I advise that tomorrow we should create an array in the shape of the *crescent moon*. Thousands of soldiers will be packed in multiple rows. The front row will be headed by the key commanders and the entire array will be commanded by Dhrishtadyumna."

Hailing his idea as the best so far, our entire camp roared with assent. On this note uncle Yudhishthira requested everyone to take rest as tomorrow is another big day!

I reach my tent, exhausted but enthusiastic. The energy is drained but the commitment is not. I place my bow on its place and take out quiver and leather sheaths from my body. Uttara is glancing at me. She is still struggling with her inner turmoil. The pink face has become pale, but she is keeping smile on her face. I know this is for me to remain stable and confident in war. This is our battle, on field and off field too. I walk towards her and place my hands on her shoulders. She shrinks. The petals on her face move as she wants to speak but she chooses to remain silent. My heart melts at the condition of this young *Kshatriya* girl. Just few months before she used to ponder around the *Matsya* palace with her colorful dolls. But today, the colors of her life are being stolen by this brutal war. I embrace her and she places her head on my chest while we close our eyes on our bed.

Next morning, as the sky turns orange, we start moving towards the battlefield. As per the commands of father last evening, we position ourselves at our distinct places to form the array. From the right side, my uncle, the mighty Bhima takes charge, next to him, king Virat, my father-in-law, and king Drupada, my father's father-in-law, are seated in their chariots. Behind them are the troops assigned to them in large numbers. The chariots, the foot soldiers and the elephants are gathered in large number. Next to king Drupada, warriors from Kasi are positioned. Dhrishtadyumna and Shikhandin take the middle position of the array. Both of them are again followed by a group of troops in large numbers. As decided, next to Shikhandin, King Yudhishthira with five sons of mother Draupadi, namely, *Pratinvindhya, Sutasoma, Shrutakarma, Satanika, and Srutasena* place their chariots.

These five are lookalike of each Pandu son. Born with the powers and strengths of each Pandava, these brothers possess the qualities of their fathers.

The king Yudhishthira is today protected by Satyaki and me. All of us have formed the *crescent* moon shaped formation and when brother Ghatotkacha and the superior Arjuna place themselves next to us, the array completes. This array is capable of engulfing any formation from the opponents. The formation is governed by the two mighty brothers, Arjuna and Bhima. The formation looks strong. Satisfied with the placements our commander Dhrishtadyumna then asks us to move in synergy. He commands that the attacks should happen in parallel to counter any formation by the opponents.

As we have assembled in the field, the opponent army also reached with their own array. From this side of the field, when I stand on my chariot, it looks like they are positioned in the shape of *Garuda*. The grandsire is experienced in forming impenetrable arrays and *Garuda* is one of them. Sire Bhishma himself has taken the lead and stands at the beak of the bird. Guru Drona and Kritavarman are the two eyes. Kritavarman has joined Kauravas with the army of Gopas given to Kauravas by uncle Krishna. He is a committed commander of Dwarka, the city of Krishna and Balarama. The three most skilled warriors are leading from the front.

When the leaders get on the grounds, the acolytes get pumped with confidence by themselves. Bhishma, Drona and Kritavarman are such amazing leaders. They are not scared to get hurt, hit, and never fallback in protecting their fellow men. This attitude injects copious portions of confidence among the soldiers and they become ruthless, knowing there's always someone to protect them.

The head of the bird is formed by Ashwatthama and Guru Kripa with hundreds of warriors from the Trigartas clan. The formation looks deadlier as I see the warriors of enormous strengths being positioned layer by layer. At the neck of the *Garuda*, Bhurisravas, Salya and Jayadratha, brother-in-law of Duryodhana, are present with another hundred warriors. The back of the array is formed by Duryodhana, Vikarana, Chitrasena, and other Kaurava brothers. And finally, the wings and tail are formed by the rulers of many other kingdoms, including Magadha and Kalinga warriors. Grandsire Bhishma, then signals all the warriors to advance towards the eastern side of the land where we are positioned. The conches from both the groups are blown signifying the start of the third day of the war.

With the signal, the battle starts, and we rush towards the opponent in the crescent moon formation. The array protected by Arjuna and guarded by Bhima is too strong to break. And in the same way, the *Garuda* formation, being governed by Guru Drona and Bhishma is difficult to penetrate too. The bloody combat is underway, the greatly skilled bowmen are releasing arrows in hundreds and the opponent warriors too release powerful arrows countering the attack. The elephants, while running, shake the field and affright the soldiers coming in the way. And in few minutes, the mutilated bodies and blood falling on the earth make it a treacherous sight. Blood flows like a river. The unrecognizable bodies of soldiers form a pile of flesh, and the cries of the injured shiver the heart.

As the troops advance towards each other, uncle Bhima and his son Ghatotkacha create havoc in the foe's army. They agitate the soldiers like a grinding machine. Uncle Bhima, with his heaviest mace crushes the skulls of anyone coming in his way. And his son with his skills of creating illusions, befool the opponents. The soldiers in the opponent camp can't find a way out. I clear all hurdles coming in the way of king. My strikes pierce the flesh of mortals ensuring they should not live in dichotomy of immortality. Both the sides are furious and ready to gulp the opponents. The father-son duo continues to go deeper into the opposite camp and get engaged in combat with the key warriors.

Shakuni from the other side of the array attacks us without signaling. In the hurry of reaching the king, Shakuni's troop attack Satyaki and me. They first attack Satyaki's chariot and break that into pieces. Satyaki fell off his chariot and gets surrounded by multiple warriors. He is at Shakuni's target, but his life shouldn't be at the mercy of the rolling dices. Shakuni can kill him barring the rules defined. There is no time to wait for the next move. I see the danger and I rush my chariot towards Satyaki. With the speed of light, Satyaki mounts on my chariot before any harm befalls him. We both share the same chariot and Sumitra, my charioteer, an expert rider, takes us to right position from where we both can aim at the opponents. The arrows and shafts in thousands are being released from our bows giving fitting reply to Shakuni's group of skilled, yet helpless soldiers. The troop is now scattered and tremble in fear of death. They start running towards their camps and Satyaki and I, both stationed in the same chariot, make sure that they reach out of the range of our arrows.

Satyaki has learnt the war skills from my father. He is an intelligent archer and is skilled in movements. I see him taking control as soon as he positioned himself in my chariot. I never had an opportunity to see my father fighting, but I guess watching and observing Satyaki, fulfilled a part of my desires. His aims are flawless, he can release hundreds of arrows in a series, and can handle different types of weapons. He gets tougher as we continue slaughtering the soldiers advancing towards us. I learn a lot from him. For me, it's like I am learning from my father in close proximity. I never had a chance to learn archery, the war skills, the array formation skills, the array penetration techniques from my father, as he, along with my uncles was illegally sent to the forest. I would never forgive Duryodhana for snatching away my childhood!

But, today, as I see Satyaki fighting, I get an enormous boost to my confidence. It feels that if my father would have taught me, it would be the similar experience. I am trying to follow his moves while fighting my own battle. Satyaki, also, with great pleasure explains techniques to me while I shoot at the foes. Releasing multiple arrows from multiple threads of the same bow is a skill. Satyaki is Master of It. He explains how to arrange fingers while releasing arrows from multi-threaded bows.

Meantime, sires Bhishma and Drona come near to Yudhishthira and starts slaughtering the group of soldiers trying to protect him. Nakul and Sahadeva, the twin brothers, cover the king and make sure that the king remains unhurt. All three of them give an equal response to the Guru and the grandsire swiftly. They have slain their army with shafts, swords, maces and other powerful weapons. At the same time, Duryodhana with his troop is engaged with uncle Bhima. Both the warriors are burdened with the hatred for each other since childhood. The childhood rivalry shaped into adulthood envy with time.

Replying to each-others strikes, the violence between the two reaches the zenith. Bhima is not only a skilled mace fighter but also a learnt bowman. Both standing on their chariots are today engaged in the fight with bow and arrow. Uncle Bhima then showers multiple shafts at Duryodhana, swooning him. He loses control and falls on his chariot. This turns to a dangerous situation for the Kauravas. Bhima, knowing that it is the luckiest chance for him to capture the prince alive, strikes again. But Duryodhana's charioteer cleverly takes him away from the target of uncle Bhima.

Satyaki, on the other hand, is continuously making life miserable for the Kauravas. I hear the cries of pain, heavy last breaths, and roars surrounding us. My father also strikes them, like the cloud showers rain. The helpless Kaurava soldiers run towards their camps trying to save their lives, trembling with fear.

We happily blow our conch now. This is the clear victory for us in the first half of the day. All our soldiers are elated and sing the victory song with joy. The grandsire sees this all. He smiles looking at the wielder of *Gandiva*, and my father bows down at him. Seems grandsire Bhishma knows that it's not easy to vanquish the army where Arjuna is the guard and Krishna is the protector. He moves back towards his camp with Guru Drona silently. This sight sends a chill down my spine, as it could be silence before the high tides, the lull before the storm! Drona is bound to the vow of saving his kingdom at any cost and certainly, he will come back with the fiercest strategy. I, then, move back to the camp with mixed emotions in the mind. The second half of the day is waiting for the coming tornedo in the form of Bhishma. And at his best the grandsire can't be touched by *Daitya*, *Danava*, *Gandharva* or even the *Narayana*. A needle becomes two-edged sword in the mighty arms, and grandsire has those arms.

When we reach our camp, Krishna advises us not to get carried away with the victory in the first half of the day. He also asks us to remain calm and focus on the targets, not to worry about the pain and the emotions, not to become sad with the cries on the battlefield.

Krishna addresses the soldiers and warriors, "For us, the only aim should be to protect our king and get back our kingdom. There shouldn't be any deviation from the path of our aim. The target should be aimed with firmness and confidence. The waves from the ocean can break the heavy stones at the shores, but the emotions on the ground should not break our confidence."

"Remember! Duryodhana will certainly not digest his defeat. And, the grandsire, stiff like a wall, is a tough combatant when it comes to the protection of Hastinapur. Strengths help in creating opportunities and weaknesses amplify threats. Always maintain the balance. Victory is assured when opportunities ride with strengths and weaknesses are addressed.", he concludes.

After the midday halt, the soldiers are arranged again. My mind tries to understand the counterattack. I was diving into the depths of my emotions when I hear the conch. This is the signal to start the battle again. The armies of both the camps are ready to attack. With the conches, I hear the steeds running towards us. Crossing the river of blood, heaps of scattered limbs and unattended dead animals, the chariot carrying the grandsire reaches close to the Pandavas army. With his furious eyes, the tense muscles, the fingers stretching the strings of the bow, the grandsire starts releasing the arrows in the numbers of hundreds of thousands mercilessly. The chariot is rushing with the speed of the wind and it seems it's flying on the field. The soldiers are frightened by the wrath of Yama in the avatar of Bhishma. All the warriors in the field cry for their life, but nobody is capable of controlling the flood of death. Like the high tides take away the solid rocks, like the thunderbolt cuts the mountains, like the fire engulfs the woods, and like the lava of the angry volcano, that disciple of Parshuram is unstoppable. He is punishing everyone coming on his way. He is striking with full strength and creating a lot of havoc in our camp. His anger can convert a calm pond into a ferocious ocean.

Looking at the disaster happening, Krishna turns to my father and says, "My friend, the mightiest warrior, the time has now come to strike Bhishma. The time has come to stop this nerve shivering wave. Behold this heart-wrenching scene where Bhishma is no less than a destroyer of mother earth and is ready to feast on the death of our army. Seeing the scattered army, the flesh and blood all around I'm agonized. My hands tremble, my vision burs with tears, my heart wrenches to stop, but alas, this is not a decision I can take." "This one man is capable of defeating any vast army in this world or any other. And the warrior, who can control this wrath is "you", my friend. Thus, I command you to lift your *Gandiva*, pull the string and let your arrows sing with the tune of grandsire's arrows.", Krishna shouts at my father.

I then hear, my father asking Krishna to rush towards the grandsire. He with great energy says that he will throw down the invincible and save his men. I am also following them in my chariot clearing the path for them to reach near the grandsire faster.

Seeing the two greatest of men approaching towards him, the grandsire first smiles, praises my father for his war skills and weapon handling techniques, and then he invites him for the battle. Grandsire says, "I am pleased with the way you have fought so far, O mighty Arjuna!" I feel proud listening to the praises of my father. Every single soldier on this field have heard the abilities of this ambidextrous throughout his life. I real proud moment when in the middle of battle the most ferocious opponent praises you. What more a warrior can ask for?

The two warriors from different generations of Kuru dynasty stand facing each other. I am guarding for wicked souls of Kauravas army, if they attack without signaling. My father takes the position with *Gandiva* in his shoulder and quivers full of hundreds of venomous arrows tied in his chariot and his back. Grandsire, in rage, starts showering arrows at his opponent. Krishna, the charioteer, commands the steeds to run in a circle. This motion helps Arjuna to duck many of the arrows coming on his way. But nothing is working in front of grandsire's wrath. The arrows hit the target stealing many lives on the field. Our army is soon getting decimated and the soldiers guarding king Yudhishthira also look terrified.

The situation is getting out of control and if this tornedo is not stopped it will lead to destruction of the entire army. I feel helpless in front of the mightiest grandsire. My father looks for the opportunity to counter the attacks but in vain. Krishna looks tense too. He raises his voice, "Arjuna! Take charge and find the way out to control Bhishma." But any attack from him gets a fitting reply from grandsire Bhishma. The furious Bhishma is consuming our army in hundreds and thousands. If this continues, Bhishma can slay the entire army in one day. I'm really tensed and scared!

The way grandfather is targeting and striking us using his weapons is not because of his anger but his commitment for the soil of Hastinapur. He is no less than lord of death today and his strikes command the mortal puppets to jump into the pyre of death.

The soldiers want to run away but Bhishma is so fast that they can't find a way out. This becomes an opportunity for Duryodhana to take the control over us and he doesn't want to let it go. I notice, then, Drona, Vikarana, Jayadratha, and Kripa and other powerful warriors run towards Arjuna to cover him from all sides. They know if my father is captivated, there will nothing be left in the war. Once Arjuna is trapped, the war is already won!

The soldiers on Duryodhana's command approach towards us, but Krishna senses the danger. He knows Bhishma is uncontrollable today and all these warriors will try to overpower Arjuna. Albeit, Arjuna is not easy to win, but Bhishma is in no mood for mercy today. Krishna knows that if Bhishma is not stopped, the tide of the war will be in the favor of the Kauravas. Enraged, his face turns red and the furious Krishna leaves the reins controlling the horses rises on the chariot.

Beholding unstoppable grandsire, he shouts, "I still remember the vow I took years ago. The moment when the piece of my cloth became the loincloth of Draupadi I vowed that the guilty would be punished. Today, if Arjuna, you are unable to control this angry old man, I will throw him down from his chariot. I will slay him to stop this anguish."

He jumps off the chariot leaving the steeds on their own. His discus is whirling on the first finger of his right hand. He runs impetuously towards the grandsire. His saffron clothes wave high in the ground and his eyes are red in anger. He was not this furious even when he slewed *Sisupala* years ago, but today the reasons are different, the context is changed, and today he is going for Bhishma.

Everybody looks aghast seeing him jumping into the quagmire of war. Everyone including me are petrified at the sight of an angry Krishna. No one has ever seen his angry avatar! We all thought this benevolent person is ever-calm, ever-composed. But alas! Today, Krishna seems to be denizen of some other world.

As he advances towards Bhishma with his discus, he is no less than the angry Shiva. His anger resembles the wrath of death, and his eyes are fiery red. With that fierce, Krishna reaches near Bhishma and shouts, "O sire! You are responsible for this slaughter. You, keeping mum towards the inhumanity happening around, have certainly given it fire to grow. Being the wisest minister in the Kuru dynasty, you should have led the kingdom to the righteousness and restrain the king from the enmity. You always have followed the rules set by you and not the ones instructed by sages. You under the influence of your oath have left the throne to be captivated by people with less intelligence and when the rightful heir was about to take care of the kingdom, you again abandoned the intelligence and let the misfortune happen. Today, for this destruction, this killing, this slaughter, you are the root."

Listening to angry Krishna, Bhishma, with the smiling face greets him and politely says, "O Krishna, the lord of the universe, I bow to you. I urge you to throw me out of this chariot and free me from this slavery. Slewed by you, O Krishna, my dignity will shine in the three worlds and I will rest in peace. I can no longer bear the burden of enmity on my shoulders. Both the groups are dear to me, but my oath doesn't allow me to celebrate the victory of my dear ones. O greatest of all men present on this field, I take refuge in you. Please free my soul from this body."

I couldn't believe my eyes. Because of the destruction caused by mighty Bhishma, Krishna who corresponds to serenity and peacefulness, has lost the tranquility of his mind. He is running like a young warrior forgetting his promise of not lifting any weapon in this battle. I am sure my father wouldn't want his friend to break his promise. He jumps off the chariot and runs behind his best friend. Everyone is stunned. The striking is paused. My father tries to stop uncle Krishna from breaking his vow.

With great difficulty, he manages to stop Krishna and says, "O *Madhava*, your mind is always concentrated on truth. O *Krishna*, you are the significance of the existence of eternal peace. O *Vrishabhakshana*, you are learnt in all Vedas. O *Damodara*, your effulgence is unmatchable. You are the creator, the preserver and the destroyer, O Lord, you are the one who is eternal and possess complete knowledge. You are always in truth and the truth is always in you. Then, why, my dear, have you forgotten your promise of not slaying anybody in this battle. Your prowess is equal to *Vishnu*, and your speech is equal to *Brahma*. I, third of the Pandavas, urge you to quell your wrath. Remember the promise you made of not picking any weapon in the war. You are my friend, my mentor, and my advisor. I can never let you break your promise."

Krishna stops looking at my father and says, "I know what I avowed."

"Then why you lifted your discus?", asks my father.

"O Partha! You are dear to me. My oath is significant for me. But the one I took before Draupadi has more relevance.", says Krishna. "The world already calls me coward, one who ran away from the battlefield years ago. But these accusations don't stop me from not following the righteousness. I do what I believe is right.", he continues.

I am listening to every word coming out of his mouth. I see the three greats in front of my eyes, the mighty grandsire who is ready to get slewed by Krishna, the invincible Arjuna who doesn't want Krishna to lift the arm, and Krishna himself. It is exquisite to see them together. The striking is still paused in this part of the field. No soldier dares to lift his weapon beholding the angry avatar of Krishna.

Krishna reminds my father the oath which he took years ago. He says that he has taken the oath to give the fitting reply to inhumanity which tormented Draupadi in the central court of Hastinapur and promised to amply avenge the heinous act. And today when he saw the furious Bhishma, he decided to pick the discus in his arm and protect the oath made in front of Draupadi. I believe Krishna judged the situation and weighed his two promises, the one made with his friend of not lifting the weapon and the other with mother Draupadi to avenge the cruelty. He picked the latter one today.

I am in no capacity to judge anyone. But in but in my opinion, I have seen too many people taking too many oaths and for what joy I cannot fathom! It seems to me that it's just an egoistic way of expression. We shouldn't promise anything at the spur of a moment. I feel that whatever is right and just must be done, no matter we announce it to the world or quietly achieve our goal. Otherwise we would be overburdened with only oaths and ultimately not achieve our prime target. I firmly follow that we should be pragmatic and take decisions based on the situations in which we live.

My father listened to his friend patiently and realizing the truth behind Krishna's anger bows down to him and says, "O Krishna! I follow all your words. I will not get digress from the ultimate goal. This war is called to punish the guilty and the purpose of the battle will be served. I will slay the foes. My friend! You refrain from attacking the grandsire and return to the chariot."

Gratified Krishna returns to the chariot and my father follows him. Rising on the chariot, he blows *Devadatta* signaling the resumption of the battle. I too get ready at my position.

With eternal energy the wielder of Gandiva pulls the string, the twang of which reverberates in the welkin and resembles the thunderbolt. Confident, my father once again starts striking blazing arrows in all directions frightening the enemies and killing anyone in his way. Then he invokes with the mantras, the highly powerful and terrible weapon called *Mahendra*. He releases it in the air and with the power of the weapon, thousands of arrows are released killing the soldiers in high numbers. The continuous release of the shafts from his bow penetrates the flesh and bones of anyone in the way. All the noises of pain and cries, all the shrieks, all the blares are being silenced with the twang of *Gandiva*.

Realization, I am sure it is my father's realization of importance of this battle. The mystic has done his magic once again. Before my father deviates from his goal, Krishna pulls him back.

The striking and killings are multi-folded. Nobody dares to advance towards the target area of Arjuna's arrows. Seeing the valor and energy of leader, the warriors in our troop get elated and with immense confidence counter their antagonists. The warriors on chariots, on elephants, and on foot, all look energetic and in synergy.

The sunshine gradually diminishes, and the third day is called off. Today, Arjuna alone has slain ten thousand chariot warriors and more than seven hundred elephant warriors. I'm not sure if it was the anger of Krishna or the valor of Arjuna which killed a greater number of warriors; but I'm certain that death danced on Krishna's flute.

DAY 4

Chapter 4

THE BURLY BHIMA

We needn't consume everything life throws at us

The third day got over with massive human losses on both the sides. The soldiers and animals have been merciless, and the brutality was on display in the field. Each evening when the sun sets, it brings the loud cries of sufferings in the form of crying, shouting and screaming to our ears. The dead soldiers in both the groups get cremated with all the rituals and leave us in pain with teary eyes. The wounded get treated by the physicians and attendants. While there's hope for some to recover, some cannot be saved and worse still, some become paralyzed for the rest of their lives!

It's anyhow extremely difficult to see so many people getting cremated every day and on top of it, to get ready for tomorrow to kill some more is just treacherous. No matter how many battles a warrior has fought but to cope with mental distress after seeing enormous killings is no easy. Each warrior, each soldier, each man representing the groups knows that its survival of the fittest. If you kill, you get to live, else you get killed. It's that simple. I think it's a cruel, ruthless game, which given a choice I would easily quit, but again, I don't call the shots here.

Today is the fourth day of the battle. The armies again gather on the field. Yesterday's array formation has caused much trouble to the Kaurava camp and hence, the commander Dhrishtadyumna suggested adopting the same form today also. We are again arranged in the form of a crescent moon with slight changes in the warriors' positions. Uncle Bhima is leading the array today and with him, his son Ghatotkacha stands like a wall for Pandava army. The sky is turning orange and the rays start falling on us as if sun God is wishing us to be virtuous. The warriors on chariots, on elephants, on horses, and on foot with their distinct weapons create a loud uproar signifying start of the day. The opposite camp too is on the field and once again mighty grandsire, like a solid wall is leading their army from the front. When both the army groups are positioned, the commanders of both the groups blow their respective conches to signal the armies to advance towards each other. The conches blare, the drums beat, the steeds run and the soldiers shout, the day four starts.

I see that a large group of armies led by grandsire Bhishma is advancing towards my father's chariot. Certainly, he doesn't want my father to create more damage today. He showers multiple arrows, but Krishna, the expert charioteer commands the steeds skillfully ensuring the safety of the warrior on board. Meantime, my father Arjuna seizes this opportunity and pulls the string of his *Gandiva* and showers hundreds of arrows towards the advancing Kaurava army. Every time, Arjuna releases arrows from his mighty bow, it triggers a thundering twang which can be heard from any corner of the field. The sound of his bow is a symbol of our dominance over the opponent army.

Grandsire Bhishma with Drona, Kripa, Salya and Duryodhana, attacks Arjuna sensing the impending disaster and all of them release multiple shafts at him simultaneously. Surrounded by powerful warriors, father releases multiple arrows to counter them. He's probably more skilled than all of them combined. I feel elated seeing his unfading glory.

The collision of the arrows creates a sound piercing the eardrums of all living beings. The five great warriors of the opponent army don't give breathing time to Arjuna. Gradually I observe, it's becoming a challenge for my father to counter multiple arrows from all the directions. The ambidextrous warrior releases arrows aggressively but as the strikes from the opponents' increase, I see him getting tired and probably losing focus too. The sweat from his forehead is flowing down to his cheeks and probably reaching to his foot. His face looks like a shining armor as the sun's rays fall on his face drenched in sweat.

The clever me thinks that this is the time to intervene and provide back-up to my father or these five warriors will overpower him. I ask my charioteer, Sumitra, to advance towards them. I blow the conch to signal the opponents and Sumitra commands the steeds to rush towards Arjuna's chariot. I strike with great impetuosity and agility at opponents. After all, they should know the son of Arjuna is approaching towards them. Some of the arrows strike the grandsire and some pierce the guru. I, without losing time keep continuing. Bhishma, Drona and Salya in return attack me and some of their arrows penetrate my armors and guards. The arrows pierce, the wounds bleed, but there is no time to think about my pain. I should strike and support my father no matter what.

Father, seeing me as his backup, is filled with pride and energy. And now we both counter the attacks of these five warriors. I see my father, attacking like an enraged lion. Due to circumstances, I never got an opportunity to learn the skills of fighting directly from my father. When I was three, they went into exile leaving me behind with my uncle Krishna. Uncle Krishna always tells me that I am a born warrior. The teachings of Krishna are helping me today to judge the situations and respond with intelligence. Though uncle Krishna has not left any stone unturned to upskill me with every possible knowledge of war form, I always wanted to be a disciple of my father. And today, I believe is the day when I have the chance to see my father combating from the closest vicinity. Both of us replying to the attacks mercilessly.

Duryodhana, seeing the attacks from us falls back and calls for more support from Ashwatthama, Bhurisravas, and his brother Chitrasena. All three of them, on his command attack at me. I, with my full energy and the knowledge of celestial weapons start countering them. My charioteer, Sumitra, commands the steeds to run and help me to get different angles and opportunities to shoot the arrows against each of them. Sumitra, I must admit is extremely skilled. His judgement of every situation and his reaction to them is just perfect. I have never had to tell him or request him. He seemed to read my mind too! This perfect synergy is always required on a battlefield. A battle is not fought by just soldiers. The supporting men, physicians, the supporting family and unfortunately the animals too play a very crucial role.

With all the strength, I strike the opponents with the best arrows I have in my quiver. My hands are moving with full agility and my bow turns semi-circular when I shoot the arrows for maximum speed and distance. My arms are moving briskly, my eyes rotating to cover the directions, my veins are ready to come out of the skin, my heart pumps blood faster than usual but my mind is calm like the moon. I am striking all of them with great prowess and seeing my immense energy on the ground and my war skills, my father roars like a lion with pride. This roar to me is like his wishes for me and it motivates me to fight emphatically. His eyes are full of love and the smile on his face is an assurance that I have been able to make him proud.

Both, my father and I, have overpowered the opponents and they now find it difficult to counter our attacks. Duryodhana then sends a troop of twenty-five thousand soldiers towards us. He with his other nine brothers, Vikarana, Dushasana, Vivinsati, Durmarshana, Dussalan, Chitrasena, Durmukha, Satyabrata and Purumitra, approach towards us. They are advancing faster and we will be surrounded by them soon. Sumitra signals Dhrishtadyumna about the attack and the commander, with uncles Bhima, Nakul and Sahadeva, and five sons of mother Draupadi, and soldiers in thousands rush towards us for the backup. Dhrishtadyumna, with mace in his hand crushes the skulls of soldiers coming on his way. He showers arrows in great numbers at the opponents when Salya cuts off his bow and surrounds him with his shafts. I attack Salya to rescue the commander and force him to fall back. Meantime, Duryodhana with his nine brothers reaches near to us and the warriors from our camp with Dhrishtadyumna then counters their attacks. The showering of celestial weapons, arrows and missiles from both the groups has covered the sky and refrain the sunrays from coming on the ground. This is getting more dangerous and awful. The anger and the hatred are getting exchanged with no fear. The humans today are no less than the devils. The animals in the field are tensed and terrified. The affrighted souls are not finding the place to hide. The blood-soaked mud, the heaps of flesh lying on the ground makes it difficult for the armies to move.

The fearsome battle is getting more intense. The strikes seem never ending and then suddenly we hear the uproar. The roar is like hundreds of elephants are shrieked together. A roar which trembled the welkin, a roar which can create cracks in a mountain, a roar which has already filled the animals on this field with fear. There is a great thud on the ground and the earth shakes a little. I turn back; this is uncle Bhima with his mace who has just jumped off his chariot. A tall man with broad shoulders, a man with the power of hundred elephants, a man with mighty arms and thighs like trunks of ancient banyan trees stands like a mountain in the mid of the field.

Bhima is the second son of mother Kunti who was born with the blessings of Lord Vayu. He has the strength of a hundred elephants put together since birth. He is the slayer of Jarasandha who had captivated hundreds of rulers, and destroyer of Bakasura, a demon who had terrified many empires. Bhima is so strong that when he walks in anger, the earth shakes and when he roars, even the heavens quiver. Duryodhana and he share a unique enmity since childhood and Duryodhana had tried many ways to kill him when they were young. His food was poisoned, he was thrown into the river full of snakes, and he was tied to get drowned. But every time, he came back stronger. He eats like a hungry wolf and he has the strength to slaughter an elephant with his bare hands. His love for his brothers and mother Draupadi is beyond explanation. He is so strong that he can shake a mountain, can divide the ocean but his emotions are so soft that at times, he can't even hurt a butterfly. He is like a thoughtful sage with full of fire.

Uncle Bhima is standing in middle of the field with his heavy mace. The anger is in his eyes and death of enemies is in his mind. He advances towards the Kuru brothers. Duryodhana knows that trying to stop angry Bhima is like trying to control the high tides of the ocean with bare hands. He gathers an army of ten thousand elephants with the ruler of Magadha to counter Bhima. They all advance towards Bhima, but Bhima is in no mood of mercy today. He rushes towards the army of elephants like the God of destroyer. He starts slaying elephants and warriors sitting on top of elephants. His single mace-strike is enough to kill a huge elephant. I behold the power of Bhima for the first time and I'm awestruck. All around, there are motionless strong elephants and their controllers. Bhima is doing Tandav in anger and his mace is no less than Yama himself.

With my brothers from mother Draupadi, I follow uncle Bhima to cover the counter attacks from the Kaurava camp. The ruler of Magadha, sitting on the mightiest elephant like that of Indra approaches Bhima from behind, which I felt is a cowardly strategy. He also showers the arrows on us. I immediately strike back with a multitude of shafts and my arrows pierce the Magadha king. His soul lefts his body before we could realize or react. Uncle Bhima continues the killing of other elephant warriors. Our immediate surrounding is filled with broken tusks, bones, crushed human skulls, butchered bodies, and a stream of blood. There is no escaping for the foes, as each one of them is getting the fitting reply for their deeds. Bhima has crushed the troop of ten thousand elephants mercilessly, not caring about the men riding on top of those jumbos. In a battlefield, all that matters, is the victory. No one cares about the devastated families that the soldiers have left behind.

The army is now decimated, and the remaining affrighted soldiers are fleeing away. Duryodhana asks fourteen of his brothers to attack Bhima simultaneously, hoping to finally kill him. The fourteen Kaurava brothers, Senapati, Sushena, Jarasandha, Sulochana, Ugra, Bhimaratha, Bhimavega, Viravahu, Alolupa, Durmukha, Dushpradarsha, Vivitsu, Vikata, and Sama are asked to form the array and surround Bhima. They all in their excellent chariots with quivers full of venom-soaked arrows start advancing towards uncle Bhima. Seeing the army coming towards Bhima, his charioteer Visoka, commands the steeds to take his chariot near him. With the speed of light, the powerful steeds take the chariot to Bhima and he quickly jumps onto it. Bhima uproars and shouts "I will slay all of you in presence of everyone in the ground without any doubt." He then blows his conch signaling his readiness for the fight.

He lifts his bow. He pulls the string, mounts multiple arrows on the string, and releases them at the blink of the eye. The arrows being released from the strong hands pierce deep into the bodies of Kaurava brothers, and deeper into the soul of Duryodhana. His powerful shaft removes the head of Senapati, multiple arrows pierce deep into Jarasandha's heart and both of them are dispatched to the other world. He then targets Sushena and Ugra. Both of them are killed with a single strike of Bhima. The Kaurava brothers are terrified with the blow of the furious lion. Bhima attacks Viravahu, Bhimaratha and Bhimavega, and he slaughters them all. We are mere spectators of this slaughtering and fierce combat of mountain-strong Bhima. Till now he has killed eight of the fourteen brothers who were approaching him. The affrighted remaining six ask their charioteers to move away from the reach of Bhima and they all flee away. Bhima licks his lips as the wolf does after killing deer. He uproars and invites the other Kaurava brothers for a combat but the death of eight of them was enough to prove the anger of burly man. The strong arms crushed the opponents and the powerful blows break the bones. He roars and shows his anger by thumping his foot on the ground.

None of the Kaurava brothers is willing to have the duel with Bhima today. The furious Bhima is unstoppable, and nobody can think of a tactful counterattack. He continues releasing the arrows ragefully and thousands of other soldiers on chariots and elephants are being killed. Bhishma sees the angry Bhima and orders the army of another thousands of soldiers led by Bhagdatta to captivate or kill uncle Bhima. Bhagdatta is a skilled warrior and ardent follower of grandsire. He carries numerous deadly weapons in his cart and with the mace in his hand he asks his charioteer to run towards uncle Bhima. Thousands of soldiers with Bhagdatta then rush towards Bhima with the intention of annihilating him. We all take our positions to secure Bhima from any untoward situation. Ghatotkacha, son of Bhima, other brothers, the commander and I are standing in an array to keep a check on the attack from Bhagdatta and his army. Bhagdatta attacks uncle Bhima and one of his supreme darts strikes his body. His body goes cold and he fells unconscious. Ghatotkacha immediately runs towards Bhima's chariot and attacks at Bhagdatta. Visoka then gets time to rush away from the sight. The horses at his command take the chariot towards the camp where the physicians are ready to take care of him.

Here, Ghatotkacha fights with Bhagdatta and frees his soul from the body. Bhishma commands the other troops to attack Ghatotkacha, but he is a different warrior. He has the skills of fighting like both human and demon. He terrifies the army with his illusions. He creates the illusion of several warriors attacking the army from all directions, the terrified army cries for help and run helter-skelter. They don't get the right direction to attack as they can't differentiate reality from illusion. Ghatotkacha, at one time, increases his size like a giant mountain and other time becomes like an ant. The army couldn't find the way to counter his illusions. He crushes the soldiers, he throws away the chariots, and he terrifies animals too. Everyone in the ground is tired, they are running in all direction and Ghatotkacha laughs wildly as if he enjoys killing.

Ghatotkacha is the son of Bhima and Hidimbaa, from the Rakshasa clan. It was the time when the Pandava brothers escaped the trap of Duryodhana during the pilgrimage in Kasi. They were trapped in a palace made of wax which was burnt during their stay in the palace. The five brothers and mother Kunti, managed to escape through tunnel. They went incognito hiding from the Kaurava spies as they didn't want to reveal that Duryodhana's trick was unsuccessful. They travelled for miles and miles, from forest to forest, from days to nights. The tired family then reached the forest which was in the control of devil Hidimba. He lived there with his sister Hidimbaa. When the Pandava brothers reached there, the devil asked them to either leave or have a duel with him. Bhima the strongest of all them had a fight with the demon and killed him. Hidimbaa, impressed with the valor of Bhima, surrendered herself before him and asked him to take her under his protection. They both with the blessings of mother Kunti got married. And then the half human, half Rakshasa boy, Ghatotkacha was born with the head like a giant pot. He has power of Rakshasas and intelligence of humans. He has skills of warriors and strength of a demon. He is skilled in creating illusions and can change his body to any size. His roar is like hundreds of lions roaring together. When he walks, the welkin shakes. And when he fights, no human warrior dares to oppose him.

The second half of the day was controlled by Bhima and Ghatotkacha. They both fought brilliantly, and when the sun was about to settle in the west, grandsire Bhishma called off the tired and terrified army back to their camp. The signal was given to call the fourth day of the war and we all returned to the camps. We are sitting near uncle Bhima. The effect of the venomous arrow is now gone. The physicians have helped in his faster recovery. He opens his eyes and smiles while looking at us. As if the eyes want to say that they have witnessed many such venoms in past.

Uncle Bhima has killed eight Kaurava brothers today. The Pandava camp is joyous and everyone admires the valor of Bhima and Ghatotkacha. They are the heroes of the day. I, sitting in the corner of my tent, am thinking about Duryodhana. His condition today is similar to mine when we lost Uttar and Shweta on day one of the war. No difference, we both have lost our dearest ones. I can feel the pain of Duryodhana. I can feel the tears in his eyes, and I can empathize with his plight. But all this is the result of his own ego, his own greed, his own stubbornness. The brothers of both the groups are fighting with each other because of the greed of one person, and because of mistakes of many other. But at last who is suffering? "Everyone!" my inner self roars.

The war is still on, how many more lives It'll take, nobody knows. The situation created by Duryodhana because of his greed has today pushed him into the deep pain. The pain is all ours, we are of pain. Do we need to consume everything life throws at us? Thinking about all of this I doze off!

DAY 5

CHAPTER 5

THE CONFUSION

Confusion incepts conflict; Conflict begets lawlessness; and lawlessness results in chaos

The fifth day begins, the tears and sorrows of the previous day are vaporized, and the soldiers are ready to face each other again. The Kaurava camp, especially Duryodhana looks furious today. Like the high tides of an ocean brushes the shores and washes away anything in its vicinity, Duryodhana and his brothers want to eradicate the opponents from the field. Bhishma, the mightiest, is leading from the front. He is an untiring warrior who always remains firm, no matter what the situation is. No emotions can break him, and mercy is not his favorite word. They are today positioned in the form of a *Makara*, a sea creature who has a long snout, a long tail and four strong legs. Bhishma is standing at the head of the snout, Salya and Drona form the two eyes, Duryodhana with his other brothers form the back of the creature. Bhurisravas, Kripa, Dushasana, and Chitrasena are positioned at the four legs. Shakuni and Jayadratha with a large troop of soldiers form the tail of the *Makara*. Together it looks a beautiful creation of grandsire Bhishma. The array is an impenetrable formation with the outer layers covered by a large elephant cavalry.

At our side of the camp, the soldiers are getting positioned as per the instructions of the commander Dhrishtadyumna. Today, we are commanded to form the *hawk* array. The hawk is a bird with sharp eyes, strong wings and pointed beak. Uncle Bhima of immense strength who sent eight of Kaurava brothers to Yama's abode yesterday is standing at the beak. He is filled with unquantifiable energy and looking at him nobody could imagine that he was knocked by a powerful venomous arrow yesterday. Following him, standing tall on their respective chariots are Shikhandin and Dhrishtadyumna, as the two eyes of the hawk. Satyaki, the man with undoubted prowess is the head of the array. Before him stands father with his *Gandiva.* Each warrior is surrounded by a number of skilled soldiers with their unique weapons. The shafts, the spears, the swords and the shields are the ornaments of these soldiers with unmatchable energy. The wings of the hawk are formed by two groups of large regiments with elephants, steeds, chariots, and foot soldiers. The wings are governed by King Drupada and his trusted bowmen. My brothers and I are positioned at the back of the hawk with the elephant troops. The tail of the hawk is formed by King Yudhishthira, the excellent Javelin warrior and the twin brothers, Nakul and Sahadeva.

Both sides are ready with the array formation for the day. Ready to combat once again and ready to mark their presence in the sand of history. The soldiers, the warriors, the gladiators, the swordsmen, the bowmen, the knights, and the guards, everyone on the field seems to have unbeatable energy and enthusiasm. The pain of yesterday has been brushed aside and the will of today is unmatched. The tears have dried up leaving no trace on the face, but I'm sure the scratches on the heart and soul can't be mended.

No terror, no fear, no anxiety, just the will to fight and win at all costs is all that remains. The soldiers unite on the ground and share the same excitement. The warriors roar to massacre the foes and the animals' shrieks to match the emotions of their masters. The whole field is filled with one wish, VICTORY.

The conches are blown signaling the combatants to prove their authority. The soldiers again rush against each other and the dust on the ground rises in the air to blur our vision and the noise of hooves and wheels deafen the ears. Uncle Bhima, the leader at the beak of the *Hawk* enters the *Makara* with the shower of arrows. Father protects his brother Bhima from the counterattack of foes and allows him to enter deep into the opponents' array. Shikhandin approaches towards grandsire Bhishma, but as

Shikhandin origins from feminine gender, the former following the Kshatriya rules avoids fighting.

Shikhandin was born as a girl in King Drupada's family but her desires were to fight like a warrior and king Drupada raised her as a male warrior. She learnt the skills equal to her brothers and hence she is part of Pandava camp as a male warrior.

Grandsire, true to his principles, avoids attacking Shikhandin. Uncle Bhima is quick to spot this loophole and enters deeper into the opponent's array. Drona knows if Bhima gets near the Kaurava brothers, he will again cause havoc like yesterday. And then the unthinkable happens, Drona attacks Shikhandin with over a thousand soldiers giving time to grandsire to control Bhima from causing excess turmoil. Bhishma attacks Bhima with the series of pointed arrows which pierce Bhima's body at several places. Bhishma with a group of hundred warriors comes closer to the Pandava army and the titans of both groups clash with full energy. The thunder of maces, the twang of strings, the clangs of swords, fills the entire ground with extreme negative emotions and only thoughts of looming death. Bhima's troops fight with equal strength and make the foes' progress difficult.

Suddenly out of nowhere Shakuni, with the support of thousands of *Trigartas* and *Gopas*, army of Krishna fighting from Kaurava side, and King Jayadratha with his supporters of hundreds of thousands of soldiers penetrate our array formation to our utter dismay. Keeping in tandem, Dushasana and Lakshmana, with groups of more than ten thousand soldiers also attack from other directions. We are surrounded from multiple sides.

Sensing the impending disaster, Dhrishtadyumna commands me to take control of one side and requests father to control the other side. The twang of *Gandiva* is enough to fill the warriors with energy and terrify the enemies. Father, like a raging bull controls the attacks of Shakuni and Jayadratha. At the same time, I, with my brothers, take charge to outwit the attacks of Dushasana and his nephew Lakshmana.

Dushasana strikes at our army with multiple pointed arrows. The venomous arrows are so deadly that even if it touches your body, you will most certainly die a very painful death. The attack is so fierce that our soldiers find it difficult to move ahead. Fear seeps into their mind and they start rushing back to save their lives.

I'm appalled because this can cause damage to our camp as the soldiers are losing their confidence. At the same time, Dushasana is getting out of control and my army and I are gradually being surrounded by him and his troop. Soon, the other brothers of Duryodhana join the force, and this steps-up their attack.

I can't lose patience at this moment. It is crucial for me to take care of my army, my younger brothers and of course myself. I look around, my father, Arjuna and uncle Bhima are quite far, and they are engaged in a fierce combat with the grandsire and the guru. I can hear the distinct twang of the *Gandiva* clearly. I introspect, "This is the time for me to prove my worth of being Kshatriya. This is a live or die situation"

I gather all my courage and ask Sumitra to command the steeds in the direction of Kaurava brothers. I strike Chitrasena and Purumitra with many pointed shafts. In return, Purumitra hits me with seven-pointed darts which penetrates my shield and touches the body. The nerves and veins tremor. I shriek in pain and my blood starts oozing out. I strike back both of them strongly and cut off the bow of Chitrasena.

Once the troops following me see me striking from the front, they gain enormous confidence and immense energy and all of them uproar to shake the confidence of foes. The foot soldiers with their swords and spears and darts attack aggressively. The bowmen shower innumerable pointed arrows and leave the opponents terrified. The rush of emotions and actions all around fills me with greater confidence. I feel the troop is ever ready to strike, ever ready to take control of the situation, and hence with this incident I learn that sometimes the right leader can be the only difference between winning and losing! As I come to the forefront, the once terrified men of my camp conquer their fear and come out stronger. This shows their trust in me and I have to ensure to return the favor by ensuring that their confidence is not broken.

Chitrasena, Purumitra, Dushasana and Lakshmana along with their large troop keep on coming towards us and the propensity of arrows and darts being targeted at us from every possible direction escalates. Sumitra knows that if I remain at the center, I would not be able to counter the attacks from all directions. Hence, he commands the horses and takes my chariot to a spot from where I can strike the enemies and can cover my troop as well. The horses change directions as per the master's wish. Sumitra indeed is a clever charioteer. Once my chariot is positioned at the right place, I am able to target my antagonists easily. I take the strongest bow from my arsenal, tie the string and pull it to release the thunderous twang. The loud noise of the string of my bow attracts the attention of the warriors of my camp and each one of them nods their heads in affirmation with a smile on each of their faces. I pull the string with a bunch of arrows clenched with my fist and release them in the air. This continues multiple times and hundreds of arrows cover the sky. The arrows strike the soldiers mercilessly. Cutting through the armors, the arrows pierce the breasts, shoulders, thighs, skulls and hands of foes. My wrathful army is now united, and they too strike at enemies with their greatest strengths. The whole scene is awfully bloody for me, but for the warriors, it's a sight of splendid beauty. The paradox of earth!

Our anger erupts like lava from a dormant volcano and consumes anyone in the vicinity. Nobody is being spared. The wrath of soldiers creates havoc in the Kaurava army and the continuous strike from the mightiest weapons is enough to terrify them. The darts soaked in venom, the darts with fire, the sharpest arrows, the spears, all these pointed weapons are piercing the enemies and I can see the corpses are all around. The darts and arrows and pointed shafts flying above the ground resemble the fierceness of the warriors. I continue my strikes with the indomitable energy just like the enthusiasm of my regiment. The fight is getting indignant and the opponents get fitting reply to their strikes.

The danger of the foes' army increases and then Lakshmana, son of Duryodhana, takes to the front and smites my troop. The igniting arrows from his bow start piercing the chests of the warriors. The shield is not enough to stop the soul from going out of the body. The intense strike doesn't give enough time for my soldiers to guard themselves and many of the courageous men are consumed by the nonstop strikes from his side. He releases the couple of sharpest arrows towards me which strike my shoulder and my arms. Some of them I managed to duck but the storm of the arrows is not giving me enough time to take the position and counter his attack. His lightning strikes seem to be endless. I have to judge his movements and then strike back. He is a learnt scholar from the school of Guru Drona. He knows how to mount multiple arrows in one shot. He knows the use of fingers to give angle to the arrows while shooting. Each move is difficult to understand. He is a perfect antagonist for a duel. Duryodhana must be proud seeing his dexterity on the battlefield. I smile within.

Finally, I get an opportunity and I pick a bunch of arrows from the quiver, pull the string and release the arrows towards him. They strike all at once. Some of them pierce the horses of his chariot, some strikes his charioteer. His charioteer loses the control and his horses lose the consciousness. They run for some time and then fall on the ground separating themselves from the ropes tied to the chariot. Lakshmana's chariot is broken, and he is on my target. One strike and his soul will leave his body, but this will be against the rules decided. The chariot fighters shouldn't be attacked if their chariot breaks. I am unsure, should I follow the rules defined, or should I kill the enemy standing in front of me. What is most important? the winning or showing respect to the warrior when he is helpless? The war defines the winning or losing, but the moral defines a human. In war, it may be a crime to lose but in life wading away from humility is atrocity.

My thoughts struggle in my brain the same way the warriors combat on the field. I pull the string and decide to strike him but not to kill. I shoot with the mild arrow to make him unconscious so that he doesn't cause any harm to my troop. It's my decision to spare the life of a foe but it's my responsibility to safeguard my regiment. With the strike of my arrow, he falls to the ground totally unconscious. My fellow soldiers jump with joy and shout to kill him. But this is not what I decided. Kripa, seeing Lakshmana down, rush towards him showering arrows at my troop. He reaches the spot, picks Lakshmana and takes him away in his chariot. He looks at me thinking I would kill both of them. I look at them, smile and ask Sumitra to command steeds to take us to the other part of the battlefield. Baffled Kripa rushes towards Kauravas camp. Kripa stares at me with certainty that I desperately stroke Lakshmana to kill him, but I know it was my attempt to save my troops. I am sure this confusion will give birth to another rivalry. Confusion incepts conflict; the conflict begets lawlessness; and lawlessness results in chaos.

The sun is gradually setting, the soldiers are exhausted, the animals are tired. The battlefield is crimson, just like the sky. But the sky is beautiful, romantic, the battlefield is not. What an irony! The same color which is beautiful in God's sky is so terrifying on the earth! Corpses are everywhere. The clangs of swords, the strikes of maces, and the twang of bowstrings are gradually decreasing. The final conch blows, and we call it a day. The emotionally and physically drained soldiers with sweat and blood over the body make a move towards their respective camps. The poor animals cry for water and shelter. The whole day of ruckus is now silenced. The sun completely vanishes in the horizon, the twilight welcomes us, and we retire to our camps. Another great day comes to an end. Thousands of soldiers lost their lives, hundreds of animals were killed, and hundreds of thousands of weapons were fired. The field is burning, the wounds are paining, the deaths are increasing, but there is no mention to stop the carnage. Peace is the last word Kshatriyas want to talk about. The painful cries have filled the air. How can a man sleep and prepare for another day? But it's time…

DAY 6

Chapter 6

THE PROWESS OF ABHIMANYU

Commander commands; But Leader paves the way

The morning rays hit the earth bringing with it new possibilities. Perhaps in a distant village, far from this carnage the calm morning knocks, the flowers blossom, the birds chirp, the cattle moo, the steeds run as if they want to touch the horizon, all unaware of the destruction in the field of Kurukshetra! I open my eyes to experience the blue sky; the white clouds cover the crimson hue while a cool breeze passes through my ears. Uttara is fast asleep. The serenity of her beautiful face is a far cry of a normal married life which I haven't experienced yet.

The animals sound happier today. The soldiers are getting ready with their armors, and the keepers feed the animals and clean their wounds. The charioteers are checking the strength of the ropes tied to the chariots, and attached with the long pole, the flag of our army is waving strongly. All this view soothes the eyes and for minutes I have forgotten that I am in the war field. This is the sixth morning of the war. Both sides have faced unfathomable loss so far but still, the war is on. The valiant warriors of both the groups have shown their tremendous skills and nobody has lost their commitment for the battle.

Dhrishtadyumna with my father, Arjuna and uncle Yudhishthira comes out of the camp and commands the group leaders to gather around him for the morning brief. All the group leaders who head a unit of soldiers of different skills gather and wait for fresh instructions. Krishna has also joined the conversation.

The successors of Pandavas stand next to Krishna. My father and Dhrishtadyumna jointly announce the plans for the day, the array formation, and the strategy while everyone listens carefully. This is each morning's routine.

The commander-in-chief tells that King Drupada and my father Arjuna will lead today's combat followed by my twin uncles, Nakul and Sahadeva. He elaborates further and tells the positions of each warrior. After sharing all the intricate details, he asks if anyone has any issues in arranging the formation. When all the group leaders affirm their stand, he, in loud voice cheers the soldiers. All the soldiers resonate in a similar way and the rhythm sounds like music to ears.

The morning meeting concludes, and we advance to our camps to get ready with our body armors and weapons. I arrange my quivers and tie the string of my bows. I lift them and Sumitra helps me in putting the quivers on my chariot. All the four horses of my chariot are then tied with the strong ropes to pull the chariot. We are ready to approach the battlefield. Sumitra commands the steeds and the chariot wheels start rolling. I reach the place and other soldiers with the group leaders and the warriors also reach the place. With the command of the chief, all the soldiers start arranging themselves in the array. The array formation of the day is Capricorn, a sea creature. King Drupada and Arjuna becomes the head. The twin brothers Nakul and Sahadeva become the eyes. Bhima with his troop follows the twin brothers. I along with sons of mother Draupadi, brother Ghatotkacha, valiant Satyaki and uncle Yudhishthira are stationed in the neck. The king Virat with Dhrishtadyumna and another group of a large number of soldiers and strong chariot warriors form the back of the creature. A large set of skilled bowmen form the two wings of the creature and two legs are formed by king Kuntibhoja and Satanika. Shikhandin the courageous and learnt archer with other warriors form the tail of the Capricorn. The entire structure is then surrounded by a large group of elephant warriors and well-guarded foot soldiers. The complete formation is now arranged and then the conch is blown by Krishna, Arjuna and

King Drupada signaling us to advance towards the center of the field.

The opponents are also gathered. They have formed a *crane* like array led by guru Drona as crane's beak. His son Ashwatthama and brother-in-law Kripa form the two eyes. The warriors came from the southern part of the country with Duryodhana and Surasena are positioned at neck of the *crane*. The other warriors with unmatched skills and expertise in many different forms of warfare are positioned at the different parts of the crane's body. The other Kaurava brothers with mighty Bhurisravas are positioned at the tail of the array, completing the formation of the crane.

Bhurisravas, an old but energetic and skillful warrior is cousin of grand-sire Bhishma. He is son of great grandfather Shantanu's elder brother. He is a great fighter and his skills are no less than Bhishma. His energy and skills in the war can make any young soldier feel dwarfed. His unmatchable swordsmanship, the lighting fast hand movements, and rage like an angry bull can petrify the enemies. Since the inception of the war, he has been incredible and invincible.

The conches blow signaling the start of the day. The formation of the arrays by both the groups is so meticulous that even the strategists and planners find it difficult to penetrate into each other's territory. The arrays as written in the scriptures, the moves as explained by the experts and the use of weapons as told by the masters are followed by both the groups. The commanders of both the armies make sure that even the youngest soldier of the army is well aware of the tactics and as the day begins, nobody has to explain to the other about the movements. The entire army moves in a predefined pace. The charioteers command the steeds to maintain consistent speed, so that even the last foot soldier is not left out. This is the accumulated experience of decades and the practice of many more. The positioning of the warriors and the king is done in such a way that the opponents of similar caliber get to face each other. As far as I understand, a lot of art and science is involved in the formation of the arrays.

Guru Drona's chariot runs towards my father. The mentor and the mentee, the guru and the disciple, both full of energy are in front of each other. Disciple releases his first arrow which lands near the foot of the guru. This is his way of greeting the teacher and seeking his blessings! The guru replies with the smile on his face. Then the series of arrows are released by the Guru, but each gets countered by the disciple. The teachings of years and the hardship of months are getting paid today. Arjuna releases few celestial weapons with enormous powers, but the Guru strikes them down with more powerful arrows. The strikes are endless, the piercings are limitless. The arrows make the deep hole in the body but deeper in the mind. The shafts shake the body, but the anger shakes the heart. Each day the hatred reaches its zenith and creates enormous destruction.

The second Pandava brother Bhima has become uncontrollable since the day he has killed eight of the Kaurava brothers. At the same time, the Kaurava brothers look for every possible opportunity to kill Bhima. In the rage of killing him, Dushasana asks his other brothers to form a separate array inside the crane with the help of hundreds of foot soldiers and attack Bhima. Hearing the command of Dushasana, the other brothers, Durvisha, Dussaha, Durmada, Jayasena, Chitrasena, Vikarana form the array and with the loud roar invite their prime antagonist Bhima for the battle. The foes army gathers in front of Bhima, but he is unmoved. He picks his heaviest mace and asks Visoka, his charioteer, to move the chariot towards the Kaurava brothers. Visoka, as per the master's wish guides the horses but Bhima senses that the arrows are coming from different directions. Visoka finds it difficult to move the chariot so Bhima jumps off and with great pace penetrates the array formed by the Kaurava brothers. He continues striking everyone coming his way with his heavy mace. The skulls are crushed, and the shoulders are trashed as Bhima runs inside the array. He continues the merciless killing and his powerful blows keep Yama-dutas busy. He has now gone deep inside the array of Kauravas, some of them are crushed to death, some are deeply injured, and Bhima is also out of sight now.

Dhrishtadyumna sees the vacant chariot of Bhima. Terrified, he asks Visoka about Bhima and when he comes to know that

Bhima alone has gone inside the mini array formed by the Kaurava brothers, he gets cowed. Although he knows that an angry Bhima is no less than death but being commander of the army, it is his prime duty to safeguard the warriors. He decides to go behind Bhima and runs into the direction Bhima went. Hours later, when both Bhima and Dhrishtadyumna don't come back, the king Yudhishthira gets conscious. He asks me to take twelve chosen warriors, lead the team and get to the Kauravas camp to rescue Bhima and the commander. I immediately turn towards the standby team and select twelve heroes of great prowess and enormous strength to form the rescue team.

I, with the five sons of mother Draupadi, and other rulers form an array, *Suchimukha*, a bird with the pointed beak. This sub-array inside our *Capricorn* array is designed to get into the direction where Bhima and Dhrishtadyumna are combating and also to be with the other supporting troops. I am the leader of this small array and with the permission of our king, we start moving towards the foe's army.

Bhima and Dhrishtadyumna have already done enough damage in the Kaurava army and when we advance, as per the King's command, we start shooting endlessly. This creates much havoc in the army and the soldiers are struck with the fear. They start running towards their camps. The time it appears that *Suchimukha* array overpowered the array of the Kaurava brothers, the guru on his well-armored chariot rushes towards us shaking the land. In no time, he has released hundreds of arrows and this sudden strike breaks the chariot of our commander. The two horses of the chariot are also killed, and the charioteer is badly injured. Dhrishtadyumna was not ready for this unexpected attack and when his chariot broke, he was left with no choice to jump off it. He is now on the ground surrounded by other foot soldiers combating with his sword. Drona's chariot rolls on the ground as a shark in the ocean.

Sumitra understanding the situation commands the steeds to run towards the place where chariot-less Bhima and the commander are fighting. Within a moment, before Drona could reach the spot, I rescue both of them. They are now in my chariot and we rush towards the place where another chariot for the commander is ready. Visoka too advances with Bhima's chariot towards us and midway, uncle Bhima jumps off my chariot and ascends to his. Dhrishtadyumna gets his chariot and before leaving my chariot he pats my back. I have successfully rescued the warriors as per our king's wish. But this is not the end of the day. I have to rush back to the spot where the other twelve warriors are fighting. Drona's attack is endless, and it fills every soldier's heart with fear. All the terrified soldiers need support and I have to be their support today. I blow my conch signaling to them that they should not be fearful, and I am on the field.

Vikarana, Chitrasena and Durjaya, the Kaurava brothers then strike at me and my troop with many pointed arrows. The arrows soaked in venom when pierce the body, in no time release the soul to the other world. I continue striking the Kaurava brothers and nonstop release of the arrows and shafts from my bow doesn't give them time to strike. I can see the relieved faces of my soldiers. That smile in their faces injects tremendous energy in me to keep striking. There is nobody in the field who is ready to give up the fight. As the day advances, the energy increases. There is only one desire: to be victorious. There is only one dream: be glorious.

The sun reaches its maximum, it is the midday. Duryodhana who was smitten by uncle Bhima in the morning and lost his senses is back again in the battle. He attacks at Bhima.

Outrageously Bhima roars, "O Duryodhana! the hour has come to dispel the sorrows of mother Kunti and Draupadi. This is the time for which I was waiting for years. I will slay you today and avenge for the injustice Shakuni, Karna and you did many years ago. The betrayal, the humiliation, the dishonor, and the disgrace we faced because of you will get the fitting reply today. Each drop of your blood on the ground will tell the stories of treachery. You will be slain today as per my oath, and the justice will prevail."

A provoked Duryodhana, who was also waiting for this opportunity for years to kill Bhima, accepts the challenge and invites him to a duel. The two bulls are ready to combat, no limit on selecting the weapons, no limit of strikes, and no limit of argument. Like two angry lions fight for their territory, these two men are ready now to slay each other. The others are mere spectators in their combat. I tell Sumitra to keep an eye on the foe's army, there should be nobody attacking the raging Pandu son from behind. While I am dealing with other Kaurava brothers, my father is controlling Drona and Bhishma from more destruction and the twin brothers take their maternal uncle Salya as the antagonist.

The duel between the two strong, muscular and stubborn warriors starts. The endless strikes of shafts, the twangs of bowstring shake the heaven. Time seems to have come to a pause. The other soldiers want to experience this extravagance. I can hear nothing else other than the sound of metals striking together. The fire coming out of the powerful arrows is enough to engulf the soldiers in hundreds. The entire field is filled with the wrath of two adamant men facing each other like angry elephants. There is nobody who would want to intervene, we are mere spectators. The day enters the third set, the sun is getting milder, but nothing is changing between the two. Hundreds of arrows have been released, tens of bows are shattered but neither of them is willing to give up. Bhima then calls for the crescent-moon shaped arrow and targets towards Duryodhana. In the blink of an eye, the arrow strikes the chariot of Duryodhana crashing it completely. Duryodhana and his charioteer jumps off and are on the ground now. Duryodhana is on the target of Bhima and he is no mood of mercy today.

Duryodhana searches for a corner to safeguard himself. He picks his mace and one big shield to protect himself from Bhima's strike. He calls for his brothers to help in fear and a helpless state. Jayadratha and Vikarana hear him and turn their chariots in the direction of Bhima. Kripa at the same time rushes his chariot and reaches to the point. Duryodhana ascends to Kripa's chariot and Kripa with great pace rescues him. Jayadratha, followed by thousands of other soldiers, surrounds uncle with only one target, slay Bhima. Vikarana also adds his hatred with the sudden strikes towards Bhima. Seeing uncle Bhima surrounded by foes, I advance towards him, smiting the soldiers and Vikarana and Jayadratha. Jayadratha looks at me as a hungry wolf looks at its prey. He couldn't take that my arrows smote him. His ego is hurt with the piercing in his body. He picks his strongest bow and showers arrows in hundreds and thousands. It builds a cage around me and my chariot becomes immovable. Dhrishtadyumna then with his powerful strike clears the cage and I am freed. I rush towards Jayadratha striking him again with many arrows and shafts. He stares at me horrendously, as if he wants to slay me there only. I am backed by Dhrishtadyumna and other warriors who came with me in the sub-array, *Suchimukha*.

Vikarana strikes us with many shafts and pointed arrows. The other Kaurava brothers not letting any moment go to waste. We are in a tough combat today. Father is held by Drona. Twin uncles, Nakul and Sahadeva are fighting with King Salya and Shakuni. Uncle Bhima with Jayadratha. And the gang of twelve men lead by me are dealing with other Kaurava brothers. The sun is gradually moving towards the west, the mildness of sun is increasing, and it gives us the sign that soon we will have to call it the day. The energy is diminishing, the soldiers are tired, the charioteers' palms are bleeding, and the animals need rest.

Grandsire Bhishma signals the Kaurava troops to fall back and uncle Yudhishthira also calls his soldiers to retire to the camps. The day has been called off. The exhausted troops are coming back to their respective camps. Bhima was wrathful the entire day. He killed people in hundreds, injured animals and humans in thousands.

My arrows have also pierced hundreds and sword tasted the blood of other hundreds. The stains of blood are clearly visible on my chariot and on my body. The wheels of the chariot while rolling on the ground get soaked in soil mixed with blood. The pain has filled the air once again. The people are getting heartless day by day. The sixth day of the war comes to the end. When we reach the camps, our king embraces both uncle Bhima and commander Dhrishtadyumna for the unmatched valor they have shown the entire day. Everybody praises the strategy of Dhrishtadyumna. Then, Yudhishthira reaches near me and embraces me patting my back. I feel pleased, I feel spirited, and I feel elated. After all, I helped to save the strongest branch of Pandavas.

"You fought like a strong warrior; you not only rescued your uncle, but you have also shown vital leadership skills. You led the team of twelve valiant warriors and made sure nobody in the group gets hurt during the battle. A leader is not the one who commands, a leader is the one who protects, who encourages, who strengthens the power of the group and the one whose presence makes things possible. You have shown the ability to deal with the responsibilities given. You are a true warrior and a great young leader. You will become a glowing example for the generations to come." The words of uncle Yudhishthira are still echoing in my ears. With the feeling of pride and yet more responsibilities coming, I retire to my bed.

DAY 7

Chapter 7

THE END OF MATSYA LINEAGE

Future can be created; the truth can never be altered

Last evening there was no end to my exuberance with the sea of praises from the King. The kind words of the king are still making my eardrums buzz with happiness. But as the wise man says praise shouldn't reach the head and make you overconfident, I am keeping my mind calm. I come out of my tent with the sword hanging by my waist and the bow on my shoulder. I see Sumitra feeding the horses and arranging the quivers in the chariot. The orange ball is gradually coming out from behind the eastern hills. The birds' chirp and the cool breeze make the surroundings cheerful. As per the schedule, I reach the meeting point. The elders are already there. Ever handsome twin brothers, the man with the broad chest, the ambidextrous, and the patient mind, all are in one frame. The commander is explaining today's strategy. He wants it to be simple today. The last day's combat was in our favor so the chances are that the foes would strike strong today. There is nobody who can predict the strategy of the grandsire. We are advised to form *Vajra* array once again for today. Again, the positioning of the warriors is set. My father has to lead from the front, uncle Bhima and the twin brothers to form the left and right wing of the array. Uncle Yudhishthira, Ghatotkacha and I are supposed to be in the center with Shikhandin and the commander forming the tail. As instructed, we take our positions and advance towards the center of the field.

The foes' army is already there, and as expected, it is a surprise for all of us. Guru Drona and the mightiest grandsire have transformed the army miraculously. The enthusiasm in the soldiers is filling entire field and the heaven. It looks like several circular structures webbed together to form a large circle, like, *Mandala* array. One elephant followed by seven chariots, one chariot followed by seven horsemen, one horseman followed by seven bowmen, and one bowman with seven swordsmen guarding. This forms one set, and the entire Kaurava army is arrayed in similar sets in hundreds of thousands in numbers. Any soul will be threatened with the Guru's anger and the grandsire's intellect. Bhishma is leading the array today who is in turn surrounded by brave soldiers led by Duryodhana's brother Chitrasena. The soldiers are equipped with scientifically designed hazardous weapons. Each of the warriors is well guarded with thick metal sheets surrounding his chest and shoulders. The strongest soldiers well trained in different war forms, of average age, strong built, who freed themselves from all the worldly desires, are ready for the combat. The array formed by both the groups are proven on the ground and well described in the scriptures and the prowess of the commanders can never be doubted.

The two groups are ready, the energetic soldiers and the spirited animals wait for the signals from the leaders. The first conch blows and in response, many other conches are blown by the army leaders. This is the signal to run and kill. This is a signal to defy the odds, forget the family and start slaughtering without any second thought. The combat starts. As the duty given to brother Ghatotkacha and me, we cover the king and advance towards the opponents. Krishna is rushing my father's chariot with the speed of wind. Father when releases the string of his *Gandiva*, a loud twang fills the strength of all the soldiers. The mighty uncle Bhima is holding his favorite mace, ready to squash the skulls of enemies.

Seeing the vast army approaching towards us, father roars loudly and says, "O Krishna, take me towards one corner of the field and I will destroy the array formed by the grandfather. I will today slay anyone coming towards us in front of you. I will show no mercy today, be it guru, be it the old friend or be it brothers."

Krishna takes the chariot to the right side of field and Arjuna in a blink of eyes showers hundreds of arrows towards the foe's army killing everyone coming in the range of the arrows. Bhima's mace smashes many collars and skulls, painting the earth red. Nakul cut off many heads with his sword and Sahadeva pierces many others with his sharpest arrows. The commander and the king Virat take over Drona, and Shikhandin takes charge against Ashwatthama. The entire scene is beyond explanation. Taking a lead over opponent army gives relief to mind but the merciless killings give pain to heart. The brothers, the uncles, the friends, the mentors, the disciples, and the sires, everybody has forgotten their relations. Compassion is meaningless and the cowardice has no place.

Chitrasena and Vikarana find the way out and their chariots like snake advance towards the king Yudhishthira. I am ready to take control of any situation. I look at the king, fold my hands, and seek his blessings. The king raises his hand with his blessings. Sumitra knows when to command the steeds and as the foes reach in my target range, I release many shafts. Some strike the horsemen; some strike the foot soldiers. Both brothers of Duryodhana are well guarded by the shield-carrying soldiers. It is not easy to break the formation designed by them today. I command my troop to advance towards the opponents and break the hurdles. The soldiers with swords, arrows, spiked maces and javelins in their hands rush towards the army and the fierce combat starts. The sharp metal blades clang, the clubs strikes, the arrows whiz, and the swords swish. The soldiers are unstoppable, and they soon take over the opponents.

Sumitra then commands the steeds and I with Satyaki and Ghatotkacha rush towards Chitrasena. The strike is clear, and the enemy is on target. In one shot, I can remove Chitrasena's head from his shoulder. But I am bound by the oath of uncle Bhima. I am given the task to protect the king, kill the warriors but not the Kaurava brothers. The oath taken years ago becomes shackles today. I turn back and look at the king. He's surrounded and guarded by the soldiers; there's no threat to his life. Satyaki and Ghatotkacha have controlled the other warriors and there is no threat to us too. I then release the arrow to make Chitrasena and Vikarana unconscious. With one strike, they both fell on their chariots. I shout at their charioteers to take them away.

Meanwhile Shikhandin charges towards Ashwatthama, son of Guru Drona. Ashwatthama is decked with a pearl on his forehead. This pearl is the source of energy for him, given to him by his father. He is unbeatable, invincible and ever energetic till the pearl is shining on his forehead. He targets Shikhandin's chariot and in one strike the chariot breaks into pieces. The horses are freed from the ropes and they run for their lives. Shikhandin jumps off the destroyed chariot with his bow and quiver and a sword hanging from his waist. In the second strike, Ashwatthama breaks his bow and then showers many arrows at him. Shikhandin, a skilled sword fighter, at the blink of the eye takes out his sword and starts cutting all the arrows coming towards him. In the fraction of seconds, Ashwatthama releases many venom-soaked arrows but Shikhandin breaks them all and manages to rescue himself from the place.

The same time, Satyaki fights with the prince of the demon clan Alamvusha, who is skilled in creating illusions just like Ghatotkacha. He has created an array of army striking from different directions at the soldiers. Satyaki then calls one of the powerful missiles and releases it towards the Rakshasa destroying the illusions. Alamvusha rushes saving himself from Satyaki's anger. Dhrishtadyumna, commander of our army is in the duel with Duryodhana. Although Duryodhana is a skilled warrior and he knows how to handle multiple weapons but Dhrishtadyumna manages to surround him with the hundreds of arrows, making Duryodhana run back towards his camp. While Duryodhana was rushing towards his camp, Dhrishtadyumna strikes strongly breaking his chariot. Duryodhana then runs barefoot on the ground. The commander takes aim once again on him and as he releases shafts to imprison him, Shakuni comes to his rescue and takes him away in his chariot. One more opportunity goes fruitless. I can hear the frustration in the commander's roar.

Salya is in combat with twin brothers Nakul and Sahadeva. Sahadeva strikes at his maternal uncle with hundreds of arrows covering him all around. Salya replies with a smile seeing the skill of his nephew. He must be proud today. The war-fares which he had taught him in his childhood, is being displayed today on the field.

Nakul and Sahadeva are sons of grandmother Madri, sister of Salya. Their birth is result of the blessings of mantras grandmother Kunti shared. Both of them are handsome, intelligent, skilled warriors and experts in the field of medicine as well. Nakul has the talent to understand the language of animals and he can control any wild horse and tame it. He is an expert in making treaties with his political understandings. On the other hand, Sahadeva is full of worldly wisdom. He is an expert in sensing the true and underlying meaning of the speeches of others. Based on his statistical and strategical skills he can predict the events. But the world is never ready to see the future. The future can be estimated based on the experiences, based on the learnings and based on the wisdom, but the truth can never be altered. The events can be tweaked, but not the truth.

The war between the twin brothers and their maternal uncle is underway. Salya gives his blessings to his nephews and in response to the arrows showered by uncle Sahadeva, he strikes both of them with multiple shafts. The venomous arrows, the shafts, and the javelins are being exchanged. Salya is rigid like a wall and he responds to each strike from the brothers with a stronger attack. He then breaks Nakul's chariot, killing all the horses tied to it. Nakul managed to escape by jumping off the chariot and Sahadeva quickly helps him to ascend his chariot. The two brothers are now on the same chariot striking at their maternal uncle. It is getting tougher for both of them to control Salya's strikes. The teachings of Salya are being used on him only. Both the brothers strike continuously to control the wrath of their uncle but in vain. Salya has response to each strike of the twin brothers. But experienced warriors never give up and the same happens when uncle Sahadeva gets an opportunity to break the bow of Salya. In fraction of second he releases another arrow which pierces Salya's body like Garuda pierces snakes. Salya couldn't bear the impact and falls on his chariot unconscious. His body turns blue and blood oozes out profusely. His charioteer rushes from the spot and takes him away. Salya is unconscious, badly hurt but alive.

Far in the field, *Gandiva's* twang is filling the atmosphere with fear for the opponents. The skilled charioteer Krishna drifts the chariot and skillfully commands the steeds to run in all directions. The reins of horses are safe in the hands of wielder of Sudarshan. The four horses with unbeaten energy and strength run in the field like the waves in the ocean. And, the arrows from Arjuna's bow are like a downpour from the thunderous clouds. The foe's army is being decimated in large numbers and the soldiers can't find their way out to save their lives.

The grandsire, the son of mighty Shantanu sees this and asks his charioteer to move towards father. He reaches near and tries to control the cruising arrows from my father's bow. The overflowing river in the rain needs a rigid dam to get controlled, and Bhishma is that dam today. Grandsire is followed by the big army of Trigartas and other kings. King Yudhishthira asks his three brothers to rush to the point and control the anger of Bhishma. All five brothers are now present there and a lethal combat starts between the sire and the grandsons. Bhishma is uncontrollable and his roar affrights the soldiers.

Shikhandin, who came with Yudhishthira to support Arjuna, gets terrified and tries to flee away. Seeing him getting away from the battlefield, Yudhishthira shouts loudly, and this is the first time in the war, I heard him shouting ragefully. The patient man was frightened after the first day of the war but today he is furious. He couldn't see his key warriors getting afraid and running away. It is important for a leader to ensure that stability in the group is always maintained. There should be nobody in the team afraid of any situation, nobody should be terrified of the adversaries and all are equally empowered.

Uncle Yudhishthira picks his javelin and throws at the grandsire. Bhishma skillfully ducks the attack. The combat is getting tougher, the anger, the frustration, the rage and the wrath are seen everywhere. The grandsire is countering every attack at him. The five brothers are not able to control him. His love for his motherland is above his love for his grandsons. Each strike from each of the Pandava brothers is miniscule in front of the grandsire. Yudhishthira, losing his cool, commands all his brothers and other supporting warriors, "Leave everything and strike the grandsire." Following the command, everybody runs towards the grandsire. Duryodhana sends his other brothers for the support and covers the grandfather. Yudhishthira strikes the Kaurava brothers with his strong bow. He also covers a couple of them with the hundreds of arrows and making them immovable. The grandsire is giving the fitting reply to everyone.

The sun is gradually moving towards the horizon. It seems that the ground is painted with an orange hue. Here the Pandava brothers are combating with Bhishma, the guru on the other side of the ground is taking over the king Virat. Multiple shafts and arrows are being exchanged between the two. Drona attacks Virat with endless arrows breaking his chariot and killing the steeds. Virat, also in return strikes at Drona with blazing arrows. The strikes fill the atmosphere with loud noises. And with a loud thud, Virat's chariot breaks. His son Sankha comes to his rescue and lifts him to his chariot. Virat and Sankha then standing on the same chariot target Drona. But controlling Drona is no less than handling fire with bare hands. Drona releases hundreds of arrows at the father-son duo. One of the most virulent arrows strikes Sankha deep. Sankha couldn't take the attack and falls senseless. His body turns pale and the king Virat rushes him immediately out of the sight of Drona.

King Virat is holding the senseless body of his third son when his other two sons are already dead. He has lost a lot in the war so far. He reaches the camp where the physicians are ready to revive him. I too rush towards the camp. But before I could reach, Sankha's soul leaves his body. I see the teary eyes of the father. The lips are shivering and sweat is dripping from this forehead. His eyes are wide open, but his senses are not under his control.

He is holding the dead body of his third son. In last seven days, he has lost a lot of his soldiers, a group of his close aides and all of his sons.

The sun is becoming invisible in the abode of western hills. The sky is painted orange and the soil red. The war for the day is called off, all the warriors return to their camps. I am standing close to my father-in-law. He is yet not ready to accept that Sankha is dead. His lineage is no more. He looks at me with quest eyes. I know he thinks of his daughter and my wife Uttara. How are we going to reveal to her? I have to do this. I prepare myself and advance towards my tent. Uttara is waiting there for me, innocent and unknown about the tragedy happened today.

I enter the tent. She is preparing garlands for evening prayers. As I enter, she comes close to me. I can see the spark in her eyes. I have no courage to convert the spark into dampness. I suddenly feel like a coward; the words are not coming to my lips. My heartbeat sinks, my hands' shiver. Uttara senses, something is not right. She brings water in a clay pot for me and pats my back. I place my weapons at their place and sit on the mat. In one gulp, I drink the water from the pot. She is now sure; something is really not aligned. She puts aside the clay pot and asks me about the truth.

I, quite literally with heart in my mouth, tell her the truth! "Today in the battlefield Guru Drona was relentlessly striking. His strikes stole many lives and just before the evening he hit brother Sankha. Sankha couldn't take the strike and lost his life."

She listens to me and the tears start rolling from her eyes, the kohl of her eyes has covered the cheeks. She is inconsolable. Her cries pierce my heart. I try to embrace her, but she pushes me. I sense firmness in that soft little girl. A lot has changed since we got married. I married this fragile, innocent and delightful girl a couple of months before. But today this war has converted the fragile girl into a tough woman. She has lost a lot in the war. All her brothers are dead, her father is committed to war and nobody knows his future. I am committed to the king and I don't know which day will be my last. Uttara knows all this better than me.

And her moist eyes say a lot more. I pull her towards me, embrace her.

Pecking her forehead, I wrap her in my arms, "O dear! I understand your pain. But you have to stay strong, for the future of this kingdom. You have to control your agony for the generations to come. You have to stay firm for our child in your womb." And I gently touch her belly with my fingers. The future of my lineage is breathing inside her. She places her fingers on mine. The tears are still rolling from her eyes.

"Look at mother Draupadi, how she controlled her emotions for thirteen long years. The woman, who never stepped out the palace without palanquin, the woman who had hundreds of maids surrounding her round the clock, had lived the life of rags in these years of exile. She has never lost the hope and confidence of coming back and winning over the agonies. You are daughter of Kshatriya clan; the emotions of losing your siblings shouldn't kill the strength. You are the backbone of Pandavas clan, and you are the future.", I continue.

She nods her head to make me feel that I am able to convince her. Only my heart knows how difficult it is for me to share the truth of her brother's death. "The war doesn't benefit anyone", mumbling, I come out with Uttara for the last rites of Sankha and other soldiers.

DAY 8

Chapter 8

THE DEATH OF IRAVAT

The unclenched fist is left with the traces of sand showing the wounds of history

Last night was one of the longest for me. I couldn't control the emotions flowing out of Uttara's eyes. I have never seen her crying so hard before. Apparently, every experience, every incident, every day teaches us more than what a thousand textbooks could have ever taught.

The miseries of a young girl seem to be never-ending. The cheerful moments can sublimate in seconds. The strong survives, the weak perishes, but the time never stops. With the orange hue in the sky, I jump out of my bed and prepare for today's combat. Seven days of the battle have passed, but there is no clear winning side yet. The groups are not losing but the individuals are. The groups are not winning but the individuals are. None of the sides are ready to back out; no side is ready to talk for peace. The desire of kingdom, the desire of materials, or the desire for justice, how does it matter when the desires are surpassing the value of human lives! Greed is above pain; ego is above the dharma and thirst for victory is above humanity. How is this a just world?

We gather at the center of the field. The Kaurava army is already there. They formed a different array today. The entire field is flooded with the soldiers and it seems like the warriors have formed the high and low tides of an ocean. The grandfather, the guru and the Kaurava brothers with hundreds of soldiers on foot, on horses and on chariots are spanned across the field like an ocean forming, *Oormi* array. Guru Kripa covers Duryodhana with his troop consisting of warriors from southern regions. Duryodhana is well protected and guarded. Seeing the large formation, king

Yudhishthira asks his younger Arjuna and the commander Dhrishtadyumna to form the counter array. The waves of the ocean look stronger and we need something which can penetrate the waves and settle the attack. Father comes with the thought of forming an array where the army is grouped in middle and the stronger warriors form the two horns on both sides, to counter the attack from the opponents. It sounds great to everyone and as per the advice of the commander, we position ourselves. Uncle Bhima leads the left horn, Satyaki with his troop becomes the right horn, and my father with his group is positioned in the middle. Behind him, king Yudhishthira and twin uncles stand on their strong chariots. The king Virat, brother Ghatotkacha, son of mother Draupadi, brother Iravat and other warriors form the tail of the formation. The entire formation looks like a water chestnut and as per scriptures, it's called *Sringataka* array.

Iravat is the son of Arjuna and queen of Naga tribe, Ulupi. His war skills are different from us. He has brought special horses with him who can run at the speed of the wind. During the self-imposed exile period, when my father Arjuna reached the land of Nagas, there he met the Naga queen Ulupi. Her husband was killed in the war and she became the childless widow. But when Arjuna came to know about her condition, he reached out to the queen and accepted her as his wife. The Naga queen then gave birth to the handsome and valiant son, namely, Iravat.

Both the groups, ready to attack, are waiting for a conformation from their respective leaders. As the sun's rays become brighter, the commanders of both the armies blow their conches, signaling the troops to advance. The formation charges and the dust cover the entire field with the movement of the huge troops. The foot soldiers with their shields and lances attack their antagonists, the horsemen and the elephant riders counter in their respective capacities. The twangs, the clangs, and the roars in unison shake the entire field. The arrows, the shafts, and the javelins cover the sun. The downpour of the arrows looks like cloudbursts. Grandsire Bhishma covering the Kaurava brothers is leading the line of attack. He starts showering arrows in hundreds killing a large number of soldiers. The killings have started, the chariots become ownerless, the steeds become master-less, and the shoulders become headless. The day once again is filled with the pain and the cries. The quarter is not yet ended, but both the groups are reduced in large numbers. Father Arjuna gives the fitting reply to the foes' attack. Uncle Bhima and Satyaki are guarding the array formed, and the inner layer is protected by the twin brothers.

Brother Iravat and I are countering the attacks on the opposite side of the array. Iravat has come to support us from the land of Nagas. As he joins, our army gets extra boost in their confidence and strength. The king is well guarded. Each warrior in the group is leading the smaller troop, and each troop consists of different skilled soldiers, arms handlers and first aid suppliers. This is the plan of Arjuna to make sure that each side of the big array is protected by smaller groups and in turn, each group is guarded by the other group.

Grandsire Bhishma slaughters the army ruthlessly. Nobody is spared of his attack. He attacks the army like a panther. He is not sparing anyone coming in his way. His wrath is no less than the God of death today. Beholding the situation of our army, father signals uncle Bhima to support him in countering the attacks. Uncle Bhima takes the lead and commands Visoka to move the chariot towards grandsire's troop. He picks his strongest bow and showers multiple arrows in one shot. The downpour of showers from two brothers now control the situation caused by Bhishma. Bhima takes another route to retort Bhishma and the two brothers now stand in one straight line, a couple of meters apart. The grandsire when faces them, it forms a triangle. Bhishma now has to answer the attacks from the two directions. Duryodhana sees that the grandsire is finding it difficult to control the continuous strikes from two brothers and he commands eight of his brothers to support grandsire in the combat. The Kaurava brothers immediately rush towards their commander but in the meantime, Bhima strikes another bunch of arrows killing Bhishma's charioteer. The steeds of his chariot become command less, but as trained they run towards the Kaurava camp taking grandsire with them.

Uncle Bhima is now facing the eight Kaurava brothers, viz, Mahodara, Adityaketu, Sunabha, Vahvasin, Kundadhara, Aparajita, Panditaka, and Visalaksha. All eight brothers are well equipped with metal covers on their shoulders and chests. They carry strong bows and their chariots are filled with hundreds of arrows. All of them are well trained in different war forms and mentored by guru Drona himself. In unison they attack uncle Bhima and father with multiple shafts. Their chariots are running in multiple tracks, not giving space to the Pandava brothers to target them. They strike Bhima with multiple arrows, a couple of arrows pierce Bhima's shoulder and some pierce Arjuna's thighs. Bhima, the slayer of demons, is not willing to take the strikes quietly. He roars aloud shivering the steeds and elephants. He picks his bow, pulls the string and places arrows with multiple heads over it. He targets the Kaurava brothers and in half a blink of eye strikes them with hundreds of arrows. Uncle, capable of crushing the gravels with his bare hands strikes Aparajita and cuts off his head. He then targets Kundadhara with his pointed arrows and releases his soul from his tough body. Strike by strike, Panditaka, Visalaksha, and Mahodara, all are freed from the earthly desires. Their heads are off their shoulders and their blood mixed with the soil creates a gruesome scene. With a loud roar, Bhima then picks up his mace and throws it towards Adityaketu. Before he can react, his skull is crushed with the single strike of Bhima's spiked club, and with another shaft, he pierces Vahvasin. All the eight brothers are dead. Bhima roars like a lion and then blows his conch as a signal of victory.

The second quarter of the day has passed, and the field is filled with moans and cries and shrieks. The lust of winning has made the field a difficult place to stand. There is no stopping to the merciless killings, the senseless bodies are scattered all around. At the command of the king, a large portion of the troop is continuously combating in the formation designed for the day. The attacks are getting brutal and both groups are still fighting with full energy. After the death of another eight brothers, Duryodhana becomes restless. The grief of losing his brothers on the third day is still hounding him and today he lost another eight. His pain is visible in his eyes and his grief is difficult to hide behind the placid face. And when his emotions shower out, his maternal uncle, Shakuni with his five other brothers, decides to avenge the death of his nephews. Shakuni with his brothers forms a small troop and attacks our army from the point where Iravat is positioned.

Iravat is present in the war as per his promise to father. He, well equipped with the finest arrows, is positioned on a strong chariot, driven by fastest steeds on the earth. The six uncles of Duryodhana when attacks us, Iravat, takes charge against them. Shakuni strikes with the number of shafts and arrows and his brothers in harmony release hundreds of arrows killing Iravat's army men in large numbers. Iravat strikes with his pointed arrows which pierce the bodies of soldiers killing them in one shot. The opponents are terrified by the strikes of Iravat and his fighting methods. The uncles of Duryodhana couldn't stand for long against Iravat and when Duryodhana sees the terrible condition of his uncles, he commands the demon Alamvusha to attack Iravat.

Alamvusha, as commanded, creates a lot of illusions generating terror in Iravat's troop. The shower of arrows from different directions, the demonian laughs, and the gory scenes of shattered skulls. Alamvusha has created a parallel battlefield for us. Nobody is sure how to get away from these illusions.

Iravat himself is not aware how to break the illusions. In the virtual world created by Alamvusha, Rakshasas in large numbers attack Iravat. Perplexed Iravat doesn't know which way to strike. He tries to observe the situation but Alamvusha is faster than his thoughts. The continuous strikes from the demon weaken the strong prince of Naga clan and soon his breathe starts holding up. His body is pierced with multiple shafts and lances. Blood fills his chariot and his eyes flake out. The valiant warrior, skilled with various skills, gets trapped in the virtual world of the demon and loses his life. His soulless body pierced with many shafts is lying on his chariot. Ghatotkacha rushes towards his chariot and takes Iravat's body to our camp.

Ghatotkacha's returns to the field with reddened eyes full of rage. He roars like a wounded lion. His heart is pierced to see his brother's dead body and his anger bursts like the black cloud in sky downpouring gallons of water and flooding the lands. The loud shout of Ghatotkacha is enough to shiver the opponent soldiers. His shriek trembles the men with strong shoulders, and the sweat rolls from the affrighted soldiers' foreheads. He starts striking while his huge wagon rushes towards the foe's army. He is equipped with maces, swords, and multiple quivers with deadly arrows hang from his shoulders. Beholding the wrathful *Rakshasa* running towards them, Duryodhana gathers a large troop of ten thousand elephants and commands them to attack in unison. All the army men sitting on the back of humongous elephants run towards Ghatotkacha. Seeing Duryodhana and his army in front of him, Ghatotkacha shouts, "I will today free myself from the debt that I owe to my father and sires. I shall today avenge the injustice happened with my sires. You will have to pay back for the cruelty you did to mother Draupadi. This will be my vengeance and I will free the mother earth from the burden of yours if you don't leave the field."

Duryodhana with his vast army aims Ghatotkacha but the latter is in no mood of showing any mercy. Ghatotkacha crushes the skulls of huge elephants with his bare hands. One strike of his mace breaks the limbs of anyone in the range. He is so huge that his foot can crush the soldiers coming in his way and the single strike of his sword is enough to cut into half, a human or a beast. During his killing spree, he sees Duryodhana's chariot. He takes out the bow from his shoulder, stretches the string and with the power of mantra, calls for one of the deadliest arrows capable of crushing even a mountain. He installs a crescent-shaped arrow on his bow, sufficient to strike off the head in one strike. He releases the arrow towards Duryodhana, but just before it could strike Duryodhana, another warrior from Kaurava camp on his elephant, covers him and the arrow strikes the elephant. In one blow, the huge elephant dies. Duryodhana survives but the warrior couldn't survive the fall from the elephant's top. Seems Iravat's death has shaken this son of uncle Bhima. Iravat was younger to Ghatotkacha and certainly lifting his younger brother's dead body has made his heart tougher and he has become more merciless. Ghatotkacha is not sparing anyone advancing towards him.

Ghatotkacha looks unstoppable. His strikes are punishing the opponents. Duryodhana looks perplexed. He has no clue how to stop this hurricane. I smile within seeing the helplessness of Duryodhana. As a warrior in a battlefield, I shouldn't be mocking at his condition. But as an opponent I enjoy beholding the vulnerable Duryodhana. Grandsire Bhishma observes the trouble of Duryodhana and thus he commands another troop to rush towards him. Warriors like Jayadratha, Bhurisravas, Salya, Vikarana, and Ashwatthama rush to rescue Duryodhana from the death shackles. But Ghatotkacha is in no mood of sparing anyone.

He faces the warriors valiantly. He smites Jayadratha with his arrows. The arrows strike the shoulders, arms, and thighs of the antagonist. He then cuts Jayadratha's bow with one strike of his sword. Targeting Bhurisravas and Salya, he releases multiple shafts which surround the warriors in their respective chariots, making them immovable. He releases lances towards Ashwatthama which relinquish the steeds of the latter's chariot. Vehemence is just a word for him today.

Grandsire Bhishma sees that his warriors are being troubled by Ghatotkacha. The soldiers are being decimated faster. He asks guru Drona to strike Ghatotkacha. The guru takes a large group of well-decked soldiers and advances towards Ghatotkacha. The ocean of soldiers, with different powerful weapons is ready to counter one man. The earth shakes when hundreds of soldiers tap the feet together. The clangs and twangs shiver the entire field. Hearing the loud noise from the direction of Ghatotkacha's position, the worried king Yudhishthira looks at uncle Bhima and me. He says, "The advancement of troops in large numbers seems to be towards Ghatotkacha. He is valiantly combating with the foes since morning but a collection of great warriors including the guru can be a burden on the resplendent warrior. I will never be able to bear the loss of two sons on the same day. O Bhima, the mightiest, delay not a moment and rush towards him. Take the courageous Abhimanyu with you and rescue the son."

Listening to these words of the king, uncle Bhima and I with a large troop rush towards the location where Ghatotkacha is struggling with the vast army. Uncle leads the array formed by six thousand elephants. A large group following us makes huge noise shaking the two worlds. Sumitra commands the steeds and like high waves in the ocean, they run on the field. We reach to the place, Ghatotkacha hasn't given up yet. He and his small troop are surrounded by a large group of opponents. Without causing any delay, Bhima and I smite the opponents with endless arrows.

Ghatotkacha has crushed many skulls and cut hundreds, the dead bodies are piled up. And as we enter the area with the men decked with metal armors and carrying heavy swords and lances in their hands, they strike each other ruthlessly. Arrows are being showered in hundreds and thousands, some cut the weapons, and some cut the skin. The skulls are being smashed, the bones are being cracked, the blood forms a pool, and we stand on the reddish mud. The soldiers, the warriors, the animal, nobody is being spared. The charioteers cut their palms with the continuous pulling of the reins and the robes controlling elephants create numerous wounds to the masters. And in no time the foes army is trapped in our attack. Our group has also suffered a huge loss, but the destruction caused by us is way more! The soldiers start running towards their camp leaving behind their weapons and armory. To ensure the victory, sometimes, one has to narrow down the targets. I had always known that larger goals are achieved through a culmination of tiny successes.

Guru Drona gets agitated with the combined attacks of Ghatotkacha, uncle and me. He is never-give-up master. He calls his son and along with Kripa and Salya targets uncle Bhima. Drona pierces Bhima's chest and he falls unconscious. Seeing his father's condition, Ghatotkacha loses his cool and creates a big illusion on the field. The soldiers are terrified of the attack from endless demons from all sides. I shower arrows on the troops terrifying them further. The army finds it difficult to control and the warriors are also shivering with fear. They all then flee away as they can't stand in midst of the illusions. Ghatotkacha then blows the conch and tries to take away his father from the field. Uncle gains his conscious and denies going away. He is a committed warrior, committed to his duties, committed to his oaths. He ascends to his chariot and with load roar marks his presence.

Meanwhile, father is informed about the death of Iravat and he comes near to us. He looks wrathful and the pain in his eyes is evident. He is standing at the edge of a sword; at one side his fatherhood calls him to go and see his son and the other side his duty towards the country calls him. He rages loudly and asks Krishna, his charioteer, to take the steeds to the western part of the field. Krishna looks at me. Understanding the situation, uncle Bhima and I follow Arjuna's chariot.

The ocean of soldiers with the eight Kaurava brothers, Vyudoroska, Anadhriti, Kundabhedin, Virat, Dirghalochana, Dirghavahu, Suvahu and Kanyakadhyaja wait for us. Bhishma and his close aides, Drona and his skilled troop, Kripa and his clever warriors, all form a huge circle to protect the Kaurava prince. Arjuna takes off the *Gandiva* from his shoulder and releases many deadly arrows at the opponents. The furious son of Indra resembles the God of death. His arrows strike many soldiers; cut off many bows, pierces many shields and penetrates many shoulders. The eight brothers of Duryodhana then surround uncle Bhima. Bhima picks his heaviest mace having the strength of thousands of clubs and jumps off his chariot. He takes on each one of them and frees their souls from the worldly desires. As the angry wolf standing in the center of the herd of deer, makes them its prey, the same way, Bhima treats the Kaurava brothers like terrified deer in front of a lion and kills them.

I deprive many foremost warriors of their souls with my collection of pointed shafts and lances. The lessons learnt during the practice sessions and the scriptures read in the gurukuls seem to be paying off in a great way. With the intelligence and versatility, we are able to penetrate deep inside the formation and have caused huge destruction to the opponents' army.

The day is about to end, the sun gradually moves towards the west. The war is still on, but the strained warriors need some rest now. The final conch blows, and the day's war stops. Both the groups then start towards their respective camps. It was a long day, caused great damage to both sides. Uncle Bhima has killed sixteen Kaurava brothers. My father has killed many key warriors and helped the soldiers in combat by breaking difficult array formation. Grandsire and Guru once again were unshakable, and they decimated Pandava army in huge numbers. I protected the king as expected and the other sons of mother Draupadi had done their bit. It's almost dark now and we have gathered in the camp for the last rites of Iravat.

I see my father sitting near the dead body holding brother Iravat's lifeless head on his lap. The eyes are moist, the fingers shiver as he glides them over Iravat's hair. The strong man, the unbeatable warrior is now an inconsolable father. He looks at Krishna and says, "O dear friend! Many heroes are being slain in these eight days. The visionary Vidura had already warned us about the destruction caused by the war but still, we entered in the combat. The peace treaty was not useful. And this all is happening for the sake of wealth. What wealth is it? Death is better than the possession of such wealth which we get from the slaughter of kinsmen. What will we gain even if we get the entire wealth after this war? This battle is not benefitting anyone. With so many deaths on the field, with the loss of the brave kshatriyas, this battle is obnoxious for me." Saying this he embraces his dead son and the stream of unstoppable tears flow from his eyes.

DAY 9

CHAPTER 9

THE INVINCIBLE BHISHMA

Intelligence and Morality, if decayed, paves the way for destruction

This is the ninth day of the battle. The Sun God once again decorates the soil with its orange hue and the rays hug the earth when dawn kisses the horizon.

Everyday a lot of soldiers die, many get hurt but there is no end to the determination and commitment of the soldiers towards the nation and the love for their motherland. The beating drum signals us to come out of our tents and gather for the daily morning brief. I pick my bow and quivers and prepare to come out of the tent. I look around. Uttara is performing her morning prayers. She finishes the rituals and walks towards me. A tiny smile makes the petals on her face rosier. I always get enthralled with the mesmerizing beauty. She walks closer and rests her head on my chest. I wrap her in my arms. For a moment, it feels my entire world is in my arms. We both float in the ocean of our love when blare of conch hits my ears. I peck on her forehead and walk out of the tent.

The soldiers are already gathered and waiting for the commander. The ostlers are feeding the horses and the charioteers fit the quivers in the chariot. The mahouts cover the elephants with mail and put the palanquin on their back to hold the weapons. I reach to the meeting point, the commander Dhrishtadyumna, my father Arjuna, uncle Krishna and other elders are also gathered. I greet each of them and seek their blessings. The other brothers are also gathered, and we stand in different rows. The leaders of each soldier-group are also present. The leaders are directed to be mandatorily present for all these morning huddles and strategy discussions. The commander stands to face us and talks about the strategy and the subsequent soldiers' positions for today. We are told to form three layers of the array. The king Yudhishthira, with Bhima, Nakul and Sahadeva will be in the first row with their group of soldiers. The second row will be formed by Dhrishtadyumna, King Virat, Shikhandin, Satyaki, Arjuna and Ghatotkacha. This second row will then be covered by a large troop of chariot warriors and elephant riders. The third and last row will be governed by me and king Drupada. The commander orders not to leave the king exposed and uncle Bhima is given the responsibility to guard the king.

The meeting is dispersed and while coming back I overhear some of the soldiers talking about some discussion happened between Duryodhana and the grandsire. I hear them saying that Duryodhana daggered Bhishma with his curse words. He remarked that the grandsire was not using all his potential against the mighty Pandavas and hence each day their army had to face the defeat. The grandsire could not hear the blunt remarks and he promised Duryodhana that he would slay everyone coming in his way.

I'm not surprised to overhear this, as I'm well aware that Duryodhana is a cunning person. His speeches are always well thought and planned. In this case, he targeted the sentiments of the grandsire and provoked him to go on a killing spree! This thought sent shivers down my spine. To my knowledge, no human can slay an angry Bhishma! I'm scared of what we are about to face today! The grandsire has skills to combat with Indra himself and everybody knows that a wounded and angry lion is merciless.

I reach the defined position of the array. Sumitra has placed all the arrows and darts in the chariot carefully. Contemplating the impending disaster, I hang the bow on my left shoulder and ascend the chariot. The ocean like array is now ready and we are waiting for the commander to signal us. The soldiers fit their shields and check the sharpness of the swords and lances. We are ready to combat. I know Bhishma is going to be a tough opponent and we have only Arjuna and Krishna who can sublimate his attacks. As Krishna is not fighting, it becomes the prime responsibility of my father to save us from the grandsire's anger. We reach the center of the battlefield. Another vast group of men decked with arms are already positioned.

Kripa, Shakuni, Dushasana and Bhishma are in the front. Drona, Salya, Bhurisravas in the right. Ashwatthama and other warriors are on the left. The Rakshasa Alamvusha with his troop of demons is at the back and Duryodhana is positioned at the center surrounded by the vast army of Trigartas. It seems that they have formed a square, but actually, the array formation as per the scriptures is called, *Sarvatobhadra*, safe from all sides. Bhishma is also protected by Dushasana and his troops. This looks to be a fitting reply to our formation of a constellation. I'm worried about Bhishma's strategy. If the soldiers whom I overheard were correct, the grandsire will definitely not spare the king today.

The conches blow, it is the signal to run and kill the enemies. The combat starts with the beats of drums and cymbals. The roars, the shouts, the cries and the rush fill the different worlds with terror once again. The Gods must be getting angrier each day seeing the men fighting for materialistic desires, but the greed of men is heavier than the anger of the God. The rage is inflamed, and the rush is impetuous. Who meets whom, who kills whom, who knows? Relationships are sacrificed in the flames of hatred and the friends turn to foes due to lust and worldly desires. Each morning as the orange rays fall on earth from the welkin, the jackals and the vultures, the dogs and the crows make their way towards the ground. For eight days they are feasting on corpses and their noise resembles their happiness. They don't have to hunt any more. They get food each day in plenty. Such an irony of life; A great warrior, well respected, feared, envied, loved when alive, but a mere lump of meat when dead!

Battle of the day starts and grandsire Bhishma targets the area where Yudhishthira is positioned. Bhima and the twin brothers are there to guard him. They try to nullify the attacks from Bhishma. A series of arrows, darts and some powerful missiles create havoc among the troops. Bhima takes guard of the situation and leads the counterattack. Arrows are being exchanged and the endless strike is in progress. The soldiers on foot take on their counterparts and once again mother earth is being flooded with the crushed arms, legs and skulls of her sons. The mud becomes red and animals and men lie on the ground as rocks scattered in an ocean of blood. The strikes are increasing with the sun going to its extreme.

I am using all my potential and the powerful missiles against the enemies. The energy of my arrows consumes the enemies enormously. The darts pierce the human chests, arms and shoulders, and get stuck to the earth, the spears cut the body into two and the arrows strike off the heads. The continuous downpour of the arrows is like a thunderous strike from the clouds. The enemies are terrified and shivering soldiers run for their lives. Beholding the dance of death, Duryodhana commands the Rakshasa Alamvusha to counter my attacks.

The prince of Rakshasa clan is a different kind of fighter. And as directed by the prince Duryodhana, he targets me. His war style is similar to Ghatotkacha's and to counter him I will have to use celestial weapons. I look around; Ghatotkacha isn't in my vicinity and Alamvusha's target is only me. I make myself ready to counter the attacks. I try to read his next move. He strikes repeatedly with his arrows powered by mantras which create a thick cover above the field. The darkness engulfs the sun, and nobody is visible on the field. In that darkness, he strikes soldiers of my troop killing and hurting them in great numbers. The soldiers in my troop find it difficult to fight in the dark and Alamvusha is taking full advantage. I think of the celestial arrow in my quiver with solar energy. The weapon is capable of penetrating the darkness. I take it out from the quiver and release it against the darkness created by the Rakshasa. With the deafening strike, the solar weapon clears the sky, and everything becomes visible. Alamvusha wonders how I countered his strike and within the half blink of an eye, I release multiple shafts at him. Some pierce his body, some his shoulders and some strikes the horses of his chariot. The demon is shocked and trembles with fear. Blood starts oozing out his body and in great agitation, he jumps off his chariot and flees away.

I continue rushing towards the opponents' side killing many soldiers coming on my way. Bhishma sees the furious attacks from me and before I could reach the central part of their array, he strikes at me. He releases hundreds of arrows at a lightning fast speed and blocks my way. I am covered from all sides and my steeds can't move an inch. I want to strike back but there is no space for my arrows to get out of the boundaries created by the grandsire. I try to remember the counter attacks written in the scriptures but in vain. I look around to check if I could call anyone to remove the boundary. My father sees me in distress and rushes towards me. He reaches near my chariot and with his one powerful strike he clears off Bhishma's array. I am freed up and Sumitra immediately commands the steeds to run. Arjuna's chariot is in front of mine and the two *Krishnas* become my guard. My chariot is taken to a safer place and the physicians assigned for my troop immediately takes charge to scan my body. The celestial weapons from Bhishma can cause damage to my cells and the immediate aid is required to heal the wounds in my body.

Krishna drives Arjuna's chariot towards the deeper part of the battlefield and positions it at angle for Arjuna to target the bigger portion of the field. Arjuna showers a huge bunch of arrows at the enemies and the soldiers tremble in fear with the twang of his Gandiva. The ambidextrous kills many in the foe's army. On the other hand, the grandsire and the guru are not sparing anyone coming in their way. They both are furious, energetic and invincible today. The attacks have reached the epitome of cruelty. Arjuna targets Bhishma to control his attack but he is countered by Kripa. Arjuna is surrounded by Bhishma and Kripa. Seeing his mentor in trouble, Satyaki attacks at Kripa. He releases many shafts and lances at Kripa which the later managed with difficulty. Ashwatthama who is engaged in the war at the other section of the field sees Satyaki's attacks at Kripa and to nullify, he counters Satyaki. Ashwatthama is a great warrior, who is no less than his father in the skill of warfare. He attacks at Satyaki and cuts off his bow. Satyaki at the blink of eye picks another bow, and attacks at Ashwatthama. The disciple of Arjuna is overpowering the son of the guru. His pointed arrows pierce Ashwatthama body and he is badly hurt. Satyaki cuts off Ashwatthama's bow and with the speed of light, he strikes multiple arrows at him. Ashwatthama's condition is not good and his chariot fills with blood pouring out of his wounds.

Ashwatthama's charioteer rushes him away from the battlefield and this catches the attention of Drona. Drona roars in anger seeing his son's pierced body. He attacks at Satyaki and releases many venomous arrows at him. Satyaki's body is pierced by the powerful arrows coming from Drona's bow. Drona is getting angrier with each drop of blood coming out of his son's body. Drona strikes with more power at Satyaki and Satyaki now finds it's no easy to control the angry bull. It is Arjuna's turn now to save his disciple. And he strikes Drona with many arrows. Arrows come out of his *Gandiva* in great speed and the bow becomes circular as the string is being pulled continuously. Arjuna releases many pointed darts and different other arrows powered by Mantras to control the guru. The guru Drona calls for the help from the Trigartas army. The Trigartas in large numbers with the drumbeats and cymbals come to rescue the mentor of the Kuru kingdom.

The large numbered army runs in an array. The smacks of elephants, the clangs of metal and the hooves of horses fill the entire battlefield, piercing the eardrums. The soldiers in hundreds surround Arjuna's chariot giving space to Drona to move away from his target. Then Trigartas men in unison attack at Arjuna. Sensing the range of attacks, Arjuna calls for the celestial weapon having the power of wind, and releases towards the large army of Trigartas. The powerful weapon creates a hurricane in the field and the foot soldiers could barely touch the ground. The men and their guards, the swords and the javelins, everything starts flying with the wind powered by the weapon. And then Arjuna releases many other missiles and firearms to kill the Trigartas in large numbers. The chariot warriors, the horsemen, the elephant riders and the foot soldiers, nobody is spared by him. The Trigartas are embarrassed, overpowered and defeated by the warrior. They run in the field clueless to save their lives. The wind generated by Arjuna's weapon root out their entire plan and send them fleeing.

Beholding the defeat of the Trigartas, Drona releases a powerful arrow to counter the wind effect. And the wind gets calmer. Meanwhile, Bhishma with a large troop of elephant warriors advance towards Yudhishthira to surround him. Bhima is present to take control against this charge and in fierce combat Bhima makes sure that nobody reaches near the king. He kills many warriors and numerous animals are hurt with his strikes. The king Yudhishthira is safe from the attacks of the grandsire.

The sun reaches its extreme and is shining just above our heads. The half-day battle is over, but the count of death today is more than any other day. Today, Bhishma's attacks are ruthless and it seems whatever I heard in the morning from the soldiers of my troop proved to be true. The grandsire is provoked by the prince of Kauravas and in love of his motherland, he has become Yama. His wrath and roar tremble the three worlds today.

The physicians have covered my wounds and have fed me a few medicines and I feel energetic after the treatment. I ascend to the chariot and ask Sumitra to take me back to the center of the field. Bhishma's attacks seem to be never-ending. He with his large troops has surrounded our commander Dhrishtadyumna and is crushing the troops like the herd of bulls crush the paddy. The commander is supported by King Virat, Drupada and Shikhandin. But nobody is able to control the grandsire. I reach near the King's place, bowing down to him I ascertain my presence. The king then asks me to join the cavalry with other sons of mother Draupadi and Satyaki to go and support the commander. Bhishma's attacks in the first half of the day have killed lot many soldiers in our group.

With the command of the king, we all rush towards the wall of Hastinapur, Bhishma. The powerful horses decked with golden shields run in the field with the speed of the wind. The elephants carrying the warriors and tons of metal in their back run per the commands of the mahouts. The violence is at its peak. The killings are at its extreme. The Yama's abode is being filled and the souls are in the queue to enter his palace. The master-less animals run all over the field crushing each other. The wounded soldiers deprived of their guards run for the shelter in the open field. The blood flows like the river with the dead combatants as the fishes in the river. The king and Satyaki are releasing series of weapons, killing a large portion of the cavalry. I am in the close vicinity of the king taking guard of the attacks from opposite side. My hands are swiftly releasing arrows in large numbers. The men who come too close to my chariot meet my sword. I am picking my moves carefully not giving chances to foes to react. The celestial weapons with different powers are being released all over the field killing men in thousands. Sometimes it becomes dark, so the other release solar weapon to remove the darkness. When it becomes windy, someone counters with the weapon to hold the wind. When a warrior releases arrows with power of fire, some other nullifies them with the shower of water. Everyone is skilled to counter the attacks and each warrior has his own antagonist. The skills meet loyalty and loyalty sprinkled with hatred results in the recipe of killings.

Chitrasena, brother of Duryodhana, targets the king. My chariot is running very close to the king's and Sumitra is a swift charioteer. At his command, my chariot comes in front of the king. The lances which were released for the king penetrate my chariot. One pointed arrow touches my body. Blood starts pouring out but there is no time to look at the wounds. I immediately smite multiple arrows at Chitrasena. A couple of arrows penetrate his charioteer's chest, and he loses the balance. His chariot is running without the master and he also loses his control. I strike a few more arrows completely dominating him. Seeing his defeat waiting for him, he jumps off his chariot and rushes towards his other brother's chariot and flees away. Meanwhile, Satyaki has reached in the target range of the grandsire. He targets Bhishma and releases many venomous and pointed arrows at him. In return, Bhishma attacks him with more powerful arrows. Satyaki with the speed of light dodges the attack and that celestial weapon with the power of fire God lands on earth creating a huge noise like a meteor strike. My spine shivers to see the blaze and to hear the loud thud! Sweat falls from my forehead on my foot wondering , "what if that arrow would have penetrated the chest of Satyaki."

He regains his control and smites at the grandsire. This time Bhishma cuts his arrow in the air. I am baffled by the skills of the grandfather. At this age also, his energy overpowers any young warrior, the quarter of his age. Bhishma smirks at Satyaki after cutting his dart and then smites him with a couple of arrows. Satyaki falls on his chariot and following the Kshatriya dharma, the grandsire leaves him and moves away.

I rush towards Satyaki. He is bleeding but breathing. I ask his charioteer to immediately take him to camp for proper aid. We are not getting a way out to control the invincible warrior today. The commander shouts loudly to surround the grandsire. The warriors from the Pandava side, as per the instructions of their leader, surround the grandsire. Bhishma counters the attack on him from different sides skillfully. His chariot is his fire-chamber, his bow contains the flames, the arrows, the maces, the shafts are the fuel and he is the fire who can consume the forest of Pandava army. He is the protector of the Kauravas and till his last breath; he is committed to his motherland. He counters all the attacks in half the blink of the eye. His weapons are never-ending and so his attacks. He is a tireless warrior who can control the enemies at his fingertips. The twang of his bowstring can be heard in the entire field. The fierceness can shake the Indra's seat in heaven and tremble the soldiers on the field. That wielder of all weapons has deprived many bodies of their souls today. The valiant soldiers of Pandava side cannot withstand the wrath of the disciple of Parshuram and they run for their lives.

The sun God who witnessed the massacre the entire day is gradually settling in the west. The howls of jackals are increasing as they waited the entire day for their feast to begin. The tired soldiers beg for their lives, the animals are breathing heavily, the blood pool has filled the entire field, the shattered limbs and crushed skulls are scattered. The chariots are deprived of their masters, the horses and the elephants are without their riders, and there are dead men all over the field. In the center of this quagmire, a man stands on his chariot with his bow on his broad shoulders. The white beard can't hide the energy of the warrior and the wrinkles in the skin speak the experience. The man has proved his worth today; the man has proved his strength today. More than fourteen thousand chariot warriors were killed or wounded. Thousands of other soldiers were sent to Yama's palace, but the great sire is standing firm. The sun settles behind his chariot and the day's war is called off.

Today, the Pandava group has faced a massive defeat. All the Pandu sons with other key warriors tried the best of their intelligence and the skills to counter the attacks of Bhishma but in vain. We reach our camp. The wounded soldiers are being treated and the animals are being fed. The tired warriors in the need of rest retire to their tents. The sun is totally hidden and it's dark. The stars cover the sky and the fireflies spread light to penetrate the darkness. I am in my tent cleaning my wounds when the messenger enters the tent and requests to gather near the king's tent. The king has called for the urgent meeting with the key warriors and strategy makers. I affirm my presence and ask the messenger to leave. I dress up for the meeting and walk towards the king's tent. I reach to the place, all the seniors and the group leaders with Krishna are already present. I can see the sadness in uncle Yudhishthira's eyes and tension in his gestures. After all, one old man has distorted the entire plan of the day. There was nobody, except Arjuna who could counter the attacks of the grandsire today.

In his sad voice, the king acknowledges our presence. He turns towards Krishna and with the moist eyes asks for his guidance. He says, "Krishna! I can't bear the killings of innocent people any further. My loyal men and core warriors are being removed from the battlefield like the flies. Is there no way to stop this hurricane?"

"If there is nothing, I would retire to the woods rather than seeing these men die.", he continues.

I have not seen the king so helpless before. The man had tried everything to avoid the war but there was no benefit and now the two groups of the same clan are standing against each other in the desire of kingdom.

Krishna listens to him patiently and then says, "O king, O elder son of Pandu and the keeper of dharma, you are always firm on the path of righteousness. You have faced the injustice thirteen years ago, but you didn't lose your calm. You had to leave the affluence of the palace and lived in the austerity and solitude for years and yet your mind never diverted from the path of dharma. You are surrounded by men of heavenly skills. These slayers of foes, O elder, will slay anyone on your command. You should not get into sorrow."

Krishna takes a deep breath, looks at me and other brothers and continues, "The man in distress loses the ability to respond and thus, O senior among all the Pandu sons, you should leave the sorrow in your heart. Though I had vowed not to pick the weapon in the battle if you desire so, I can challenge the old man in the war. I can slay the grandsire in the middle of the field if you wish so. With my one strike, I can push him off his chariot. I can nullify all the powerful weapons smitten by him. If the throne of Hastinapur is dearer to him, the Pandu sons are dearest to me. Arjuna is my friend, my relative and my disciple. And for the sake of Arjuna and his brothers, I will leave my vow and pick my *Sudarshan*. I will avenge your fear. That which terrifies you, will be petrified. The hands which strike arrows to penetrate the flesh of yours, my *Sudarshan* will cut off those hands. I at your command can slay anyone in the battlefield. O son of Dharma leave the worry and share what is in your mind. I will guard the victory for you."

Listening to the words of Krishna, king Yudhishthira sighs with relief. He knows Krishna is present in the field as the protector, the preceptor and the power. But he cannot undermine the strength of Bhishma. His skills are not copied from the scriptures. His strategies are not just inspired by the books but also pragmatic and learnt from the numbers of wars fought by him since his young age. The grey hair on his head speaks volumes about the experience he has gained over the years. His strengths are known across the three worlds and he is equipped with celestial weapons including universal missiles. The missiles which can mark and kill; the missiles which can penetrate the mountains, the missiles which can reverse the flow of the rivers; the missiles which can erupt volcanoes, and the missiles which are enriched by heavenly powers are the grace of his quivers. Bhishma, the man who vowed to protect the throne for his entire life is standing strong and no weapon is powerful to infiltrate. Everyone knows if the grandsire is standing, the defeat cannot touch Kauravas.

Uncle Yudhishthira looks stress-free listening to the words of mystic Krishna and says, "O dear Krishna, the slayer of demons, the protector of the universe, you have relieved me from the stress with your words. I know I will get what is desired when you are standing at our side. But just because of my glory, I cannot afford the falsification of your vow. I am the follower of dharma; I ask my brothers not to leave the path of righteousness then how can I ask you to forget your words and enter the battle like the warrior. Your hands are to protect and not to kill. I request you to devise a way so that your words will be protected, and I will not be burdened."

A baffled me looks at smiling Krishna. Perplexed me, is ready to ear the next words from the king. It somehow seems to me that Krishna knows what's coming next.

King Yudhishthira folds his hands and says, "Grandsire Bhishma and I had an agreement before the war started. When I went to meet the grandsire for the definition of war rules and to seek his blessings, he promised to counsel me at any point of the war. He said that he would fight for Duryodhana but could aid me with the secrets. I am sure if we go to him and seek his advice, he will keep his words."

Krishna is still smiling, and his head is nodding in an agreement as if he knows what the eldest Pandava is deriving at.

The king continues, "O lotus-eyed Krishna, I feel this is the right time when I, with my other brothers should go to grandsire

Bhishma and ask the secret of his death. And I would want you to come with us."

I shiver as a chill ran through my spine. We have reached to the lowest level of humanity when the sons are going to their father seeking the advice for his own death. The man has protected his sons' generations after generations. And the sons behind the words of seeking counsel are going to ask the secret of his death. My heart is beating faster resulting in a moist forehead, my mouth dries up, and my sight becomes unfocussed. Bewildered, I request permission from the king to go with them and he nods in agreement.

Then, all the Pandava brothers and I with Krishna head towards the tent of Bhishma. We bow before him and Bhishma blesses us all. The strong man in the morning is the mellow grandfather in the evening. He asks us to sit and asks the reason for our visit at this hour of the night. Uncle Yudhishthira joins his hands and mentions the reason for his worries. He asks how the Pandavas can ensure their sovereignty in the battle.

Bhishma says, "Till the time I am standing in the field, there is no way you can win the war."

King Yudhishthira reminds him about his promise of counselling Pandavas in the war.

Bhishma asks, "What is your desire, O son?"

Yudhishthira says, "O son of Ganga, dear grandfather, you are dear to all of us. We want your shadow on us for entire life, but the adversity has pushed us in the war. I know till the time you are standing in the battlefield; the victory can never be ours. I also know that you in your heart want us to win. Father, I request you to tell us the way you can abstain from the war and we then could attain the victory. I can't see the ocean of soldiers being killed by you every day."

Grandfather Bhishma listens to uncle carefully. He smiles and gets up from his seat. Beholding the keenness of his grandsons, he says, "Son Yudhishthira! I am committed to the throne of Hastinapur, but I believe the time has come when I have to get away from this materialistic world and find space in Yama's abode."

"I have learnt the warfare from mighty Parshuram and have been blessed with many weapons which can erode the mankind. Your army consists of many strong warriors who individually can slay many soldiers in the combat. You have mighty Bhima who can root out the mountain like a flower. You have twin brothers Nakul and Sahadeva who possess the skills of many war forms. But Arjuna and Krishna are the only two at your side who can defeat me. Krishna has vowed not to fight in the battle and thus, Arjuna remains the one. However, until I stand on my chariot with my bow and arrows, I will never be smitten by Arjuna."

We all look at him with confused minds. Yudhishthira gets up and reaches near the grandsire. He joins his hands and asks for the way out. He wants to save his countrymen and he doesn't want the grandfather to fight in the battle. Both are possible only when the grandsire decides to put down the weapon and leaves the field.

Grandsire Bhishma continues, "Listen, O Son of Kunti, you have a warrior, viz., Shikhandin, fighting from your side in the battle. Shikhandin was born as the female Shikhandini, but because of her desire of becoming a warrior and to fight in battles, she transformed herself into male and learnt the war forms. She is now a man but for me, he is still female and as per Kshatriya dharma I can never strike a woman. So, if Shikhandini strikes at me I would not counter and then Arjuna from behind can attack at me. I will surrender before Shikhandini. My father had blessed me with the boon of choosing the day of my death. Therefore, I will only be smitten but not die till I choose."

The secret is revealed but the death of grandsire depends on his desire. At least we know how to stop the hurricane of grandfather. We join our hands, bow down before him and ask for his leave. We leave his tent with the mixed feelings. I couldn't believe what just happened. It was very difficult for me to fathom the depths of what was spoken about. How could my father and uncles with Krishna stoop so low?

The rotten desire of winning has reached its zenith. The sons are ready to kill the father and the father's father. The grandsire always dreamt of one kingdom where the brothers can live in harmony. The palace where there is no place for jealousy and hatred, but the time has eaten up all the dreams. The lust for material desires and the thirst for wealth have pushed the human to go and ask the grandfather the secret of his death. Intelligence and morality have decayed and paved the way for our own destruction.

DAY 10

CHAPTER 10

THE FALL OF THE WALL

Capability is undermined when exposed before the ignorant

As the sun rises in the east, the day commences with the usual routine. The only difference today is that our commander knows the secret trick of defeating the grandsire. I am sure that though, grandsire has told the secret of his defeat, he will not leave any stone unturned to defend himself and the nation.

The bell rings and we gather at the meeting location. The commander's eyes are sparkling; the confidence in his voice is evident. He looks at Shikhandin and they both exchange a smile. Shikhandin has been instrumental and an endearing force since the inception of the war. He had led from the front wherever required but today is a different day. Today, he is being given a humongous task. Shikhandin could very possibly be the most crucial factor for our victory. Everyone knows the grandsire will never counter Shikhandin's attack, but we also have to keep in mind that it takes immense courage to aim at him and probably Duryodhana will never allow us to target and slay the grandsire.

The grandfather Bhishma has earned respect from everyone after years of his devotion and unconditional love that he has showered on his kingdom. The devotion towards his father by sacrificing the desire of becoming the king; the devotion towards his brothers by winning the kingdoms for them. The devotion towards his grandsons by mentoring them and the devotion towards his motherland by acting as an unbreakable wall. His presence marks the confidence among his followers, and his words inject energy in his countrymen. His humility separates him from his peers, but his intelligence makes him their master.

Bhishma had learnt the war skills from the greatest of all masters, Parshuram. And with his dedication, Bhishma had earned a multitude of weapons of distinct powers. He had witnessed many wars in his life and applied the theory of war forms in real life. His knowledge is not only limited to the pages of a book, but also pragmatic.

The commander knows the importance of Shikhandin in today's war and hence he asks the two strongest warriors of our group, Bhima and Arjuna to keep guard on Shikhandin. Arjuna's role is equally important today. This will be the test for his affection towards the grandfather against the longing of victory. Among the warriors, he is the only one, who has the caliber to fight against Bhishma. But to ensure Bhishma doesn't counter Arjuna's attacks, the later has to stand behind Shikhandin and target him. This will certainly question his skills. The warrior who can defeat thousands of soldiers' single handedly will have to let go his pride. The world's best archer who once hit the eye of a moving fish with an arrow by just looking at the reflection will have to hit the Grandsire by using Shikhandin as a shield! But to protect the group of men who have gathered to fight for us, to save the lives of soldiers who couldn't stand before the mighty grandsire, my father will have to stand behind Shikhandin and strike.

The commander explains the array formation and shares the strategy for today's war. There is only one strategy today! Not to allow Bhishma to move away from Shikhandin and protect Shikhandin from the attacks of Kauravas. We are asked to position ourselves at respective places and proceed towards the center of the field. Shikhandin is at the front, with the left and right sides guarded by Arjuna and Bhima respectively. Behind his chariot, I am placed with other sons of mother Draupadi. I am then covered by Satyaki and Dhrishtadyumna. They are followed by uncle Yudhishthira and twin uncles on either side of the king. The last row of the array is formed by king Virat and the king Drupada. The other warriors have positioned themselves as commanded. Today is the tenth day of battle but the energy among the soldiers is at its peak. The commitment for the masters and the love for their motherland has not deviated a bit. We reach the center of the battlefield with the sound of conches and drums.

The foes army also comes, with as always, the grandfather leading the array. The remaining sons of Dhritarashtra are positioned behind the grandsire. Duryodhana and Dushasana are standing closest to grandsire Bhishma. They know to ensure their victory the protection of Bhishma is prior to anything else. The Kaurava brothers are then followed by father and son, Guru Drona and Ashwatthama. Then the other leading warriors and soldiers are positioned. They are prepared as equal to us. Their energy is at same level as ours and they are committed as equal to us. They respond to our invitation by blowing their conches. Bhishma blows the final signal and commands the soldiers to strike. Arjuna on our side then signals our warriors to run impetuously. The clash of the two groups begins.

Bhishma initiates the strikes and releases deadly arrows from his powerful bow. He is looking threatening today, no marks of tension on his face, even after disclosing the secret of his defeat. He is not giving space to Shikhandin to strike and his arrows are keeping Arjuna and Bhima busy. The brothers of Duryodhana, led by Dushasana is making sure that nobody reaches near Bhishma. It's very well planned and scripted! They don't know that the grandsire has revealed the secret of his death, but they know the importance of his presence on the field.

I come forward and take charge against the Kaurava brothers. Brother Ghatotkacha takes on other warriors including the demon Alamvusha. The twin uncles Nakul and Sahadeva are countering the attack of guru Drona and his son. The king Yudhishthira is charging against the other brothers of Duryodhana. The slaughter has no end, and once again, the motionless bodies start piling up. The furious volcano spurts the gory of violence. Father, not getting any way out to strike Bhishma. He, then urges to Shikhandin to move ahead towards grandsire Bhishma.

He says, "Shikhandin! Worry not of the fury of grandsire. Move ahead as the commander instructed you. I will root out the foes coming in your way."

Grandsire will never lift the weapon against Shikhandin and that will be the time when my father will strike him. To fulfil the desire of the king and to follow the command of the leader, Shikhandin asks his charioteer to move towards Bhishma's position. I also ask Sumitra to move towards opponents. If not Bhishma, the others will take no time in striking Shikhandin and we need a backup to support these warriors.

Bhishma, as per his promise to Duryodhana, had slain thousands of soldiers each day. The past nine days, every day, he had fulfilled his vow before retiring each day and today he looks more furious than ever. The anger on the calm face resembles the calm ocean full of tides. He is fighting like he was indebted all these years and today he wants to come out of the shackles. As if he wants to sleep after the years of struggle, the struggle to lead the kingdom without being king, the struggle to not beget the sons but treat the sons of his brothers as his own, the struggle to win the land and wealth and materials for the king, and the struggle of being silent even after witnessing the injustice. The old man has witnessed many folds of life but always stood like a wall for the dynasty, protecting everyone from any external forces. But today, his soul wants to overcome the desire of materials, his mind wants calmness and his heart certainly wants peace.

Our army, as commanded then proceeds towards Bhishma's cavalry. The opponents, comprised of Drona, Ashwatthama and other Duryodhana brothers with Dushasana as head, also proceed towards Bhishma with the desire to protect him. It's a paradox that the grandfather is dear to both the groups, but one group wants to kill him and the other wants to protect. The group which wants to slay him desires to defeat injustice, while the group which is protecting him desires to defend the injustice. It's so complex!

The presence of an old man in the middle of the field will define the future of justice. Both the groups rush against each other, the earth trembles and the welkin shivers. The sound of drums, conches, metal clangs, the twang of bows, the swish of arrows, the rattle of chariots, the hooves of steeds, and the thump of elephants fills the welkin. We rush towards Bhishma following

Shikhandin. The brothers of Duryodhana with Dushasana as their lead advance towards Shikhandin and Arjuna with the desire to kill both of them.

Dushasana reaches near Shikhandin's chariot. The other Kaurava brothers surround my father. Bhurisravas targets uncle Bhima. There is no way out for the Pandu sons, Shikhandin is on target of Dushasana and he releases the crescent moon shaped arrow from his bow. Shikhandin wants to cut the dart but his arrow misses the opponent's and Dushasana's arrow strikes Shikhandin's shoulder. The noise of penetration into Shikhandin's armor attracts my attention. I immediately pull the string of my bow and release an arrow striking Dushasana. In the blink of an eye, I release a couple of more arrows piercing his body at many places. In pain, he cries aloud calling for help. His brother Duryodhana turns and excited with wrath, he rushes to help his younger. I see the furious Duryodhana coming and his target is me. Before I could realize, his arrow touches my shoulder and whiz away. I pick the javelin and throw it at Duryodhana's chariot and before Duryodhana could safeguard himself from the iron rod I released the couple of arrows which strikes him. Duryodhana gets more furious. He can't take that a young boy's arrows have touched his body. He shouts in rage. The roar shivers the steeds of his chariot. I cover chariots of two Kaurava brothers making them immovable. This gives an opportunity to Shikhandin to target Bhishma. Father seeing Shikhandin advancing towards Bhishma asks Krishna to move the chariot with Shikhandin's but the other brothers of Duryodhana don't allow him to move an inch. I'm now free from Duryodhana's attack and hence, rush towards father's place and counter the other brothers. Krishna immediately commands the steeds to rush towards Bhishma's.

Shikhandin and Arjuna are in the range of Bhishma. As decided in the morning, Shikhandin is at the front and Arjuna protects himself from the target area of Bhishma. Shikhandin strikes Bhishma with ten arrows and per his vow, Bhishma doesn't strike back. The arrow pierces him deep. The tense muscles and twisted eyebrows speak the intensity of his pain. Father finds this an opportunity to strike grandsire and releases arrows to strike him down. But the old man is still left with energy. He picks his sword and cuts down the arrows released from *Gandiva.* Duryodhana, still in the cover of my arrows, commands a large troop to counter Arjuna. The large group of charioteers and horsemen rush towards my father in the desire to surround him. But he releases arrows in great numbers to consume the warriors coming towards him. The fire emitting arrows burn the soldiers like insects. The entire field seems engulfed in fire and smoke.

Recovering from the strikes of Shikhandin, Bhishma rises up to fight. He pulls the string of his bow makes it circular and releases many arrows and shafts on the soldiers on the field. Many foot soldiers, chariot warriors, horsemen and the elephant warriors are killed with the strikes. Thousands of Kshatriyas are lying motionless on the ground and the furious Bhishma licks his lips in rage. His eyes are red, the sweat is dripping from his forehead but there is no sign of exertion on his face. He calls for the celestial weapon and targets my father. Shikhandin sees this and quickly ascends on Arjuna's chariot covering him. Bhishma is left with no choice than dropping the weapon. Shikhandin sees this as an opportunity and strikes Bhishma again. The arrow pierces Bhishma's body deeper. It penetrates into his heart and blood starts pouring out of the body.

Father sees the bleeding sire, his hands' shivers. Before he loses his control over the mind, he strikes multiple shafts on grandsire. The arrows penetrate Bhishma's body at multiple points. Strikes by strike, the arrows continue piercing his body. Arjuna and Shikhandin are on the same chariot and there is no chance for Bhishma to counter the attacks of Arjuna. Shikhandin cleverly manages to strike Bhishma and save Arjuna at the same time. Is it intelligence of Shikhandin or his opportunism? Arjuna continues striking with multiple arrows endlessly. The attack breaks the bow of Bhishma, and he gets no chance to lift another. Seeing the attack of Arjuna, the brothers of Duryodhana comes to rescue the grandsire but Bhima and I are standing to counter anyone coming in between Arjuna and Bhishma.

With every arrow that strikes Bhishma, a teardrop rolls down slowly from the eyes of father. The two generations are standing against each other. The old man is being targeted at vital parts of the body and the shafts from the *Gandiva* are hitting him repeatedly.

The grandsire is now weapon-less and motionless but still standing. Tears are rolling from his eyes. Tears of sadness or happiness? Well, I can't judge, but judging from the faint smile on his face, it seemed as if he was waiting for this day for long. The gentle smile on his face appreciates the skills of his grandson Arjuna, and tears from his eyes bless him for the victory in the battle. Such an irony!

Each arrow is like a messenger of death, but his soul is in his command. It cannot leave his body till he desires. Hundreds of arrows have penetrated his body not leaving a finger's breadth of space in his body. Arjuna's strikes are not stopping, the Kaurava brothers want to intervene but we have left no space for them to come in between the grandfather and the grandson.

Seems the sun God also couldn't tolerate the gory attacks and mellows down its hue. The sunlight reaches the west and with the sun approaching the horizon, the grandsire fells from his chariot. He is lying on the bed of arrows with his head hanging towards the east. He needs a pillow to support his neck. There is silence on the field. The warriors have stopped fighting with the fall of Bhishma from his chariot. The old man is a couple of feet above the ground with no support to his head. A couple of soldiers pick the seats of chariots to put them below his head, but he refuses. The full body of the mighty warrior is pierced. The tears are rolling down from everyone's eyes. The grandsire asks Arjuna to provide support to his neck. Arjuna then strikes three more arrows piercing the earth to support his head. We gather near him, some crying, some praising the grandsire's efforts for these many years, some cursing Shikhandin for being the reason of the fall of the wall, and some cursing Arjuna for striking from behind Shikhandin questioning his prowess. There are always mixed emotions with every event. There are supporters and then there are opponents. Arjuna who has proved his skills many times in the past, who has acquired the weapons from the Gods, who has defeated many warriors in combat, is today being criticized. The people who criticize the efforts haven't received any feat in the war but yet they question the caliber of Arjuna.

The grandsire listens to all this and he asks for water. The water can be brought in the vessels, but the old man says he doesn't want to use any materials anymore. He calls Arjuna and asks if he can quench his thirst. My father capable of bringing the storm with the power of his arrows, having the caliber to stop the flow of ocean with the strikes of his bow, once again pulls the string of his bow and with a powerful strike pierces the earth near Bhishma. The soil shifts and a jet of water comes out of the earth. The water, as pure as Ganga, as sweet as nectar comes out and quenches the thirst of the grandsire.

The grandsire drinks water, but to me, it's pretty clear that it is the answer to critics who questioned Arjuna's prowess. Bhishma's intention was to show everyone around that my father is not a coward hiding behind Shikhandin, rather he's more skilled than anyone present in the battlefield.

Capability is undermined when exposed before the ignorant.

The grandsire is lying on a bed of arrows, his head is resting on the pillow made of arrows and the sun's hue is gradually diminishing. The war is halted, and the warriors have gathered around. Everyone bows down with respect and the grandsire responds to each one's salutation. Seeing the prowess of Arjuna, Bhishma appreciates him in front of everyone. He admires his skills and compares his skills to *Vishnu* Himself. He then urges Duryodhana to call for the peace. He wishes with his death the peace should be installed among the brothers. The Pandavas should get half of the kingdom and rule Indraprastha. The wealth should be distributed equally, and both the kingdoms should live in harmony. He also mentions that many times in past Arjuna has proved his skills and there is no benefit in fighting with Arjuna, as he is invincible. The dying man wishes for the peace for the motherland he drenched with his sweat and blood. The man opines that the coming generations should remember the two clans for their love and brotherhood and not the hatred. The capability of each of the Pandu sons can't be challenged and before Yudhishthira loses his cool; before Bhima becomes vengeful; before Nakul and Sahadeva use their skills at its highest; and before the warrior of the warriors Arjuna ends up killing everyone, the grandsire wishes the peace to be established.

The mother earth who has witnessed the killings of thousands of warriors per day from the hands of this old man is today holding her son on a bed of arrows. The motherland which Bhishma has protected for many years, is today embracing him. The son of the soil, the great warrior, the mentor of generations is lying in front of us. The tears are rolling from thousands of eyes, and many others are inconsolable. The four-generation warriors, the gurus, the commanders, the leaders and many other soldiers who came on the invitation of two groups of Kuru clan are standing and praising the lord of Kuru dynasty. The man who has defeated death himself many times, by his strength and by his good deeds, is lying on the deathbed, but the soul is still in his command. He hasn't allowed the soul to leave his body yet. The orange hue in the sky is gradually diminishing, the hearts are cheerless, animals are howling, the earth seems to be trembling, and the clouds seem to be getting thicker. The pores in my body contracts and the spine shivers to see the great wall of the Kuru dynasty lying in front of our eyes. The powerful man endowed with endless energy is today tied with the arrows. The grandson tied those arms on which he played in his childhood.

The twilight thickens, the moon comes out. It's time to retire to the tents. All soldiers start returning to their respective camps. The closed ones of the grandsire are unwilling to move. The darkness covers the field, the fire in the camp is lightened, the dim lights in the tents are glowing and the great man is lying with his eyes closed. His heart is pumping slowly, the breathing is calm. The pain is evitable, the blood is still pouring out from his wounds. The physicians have covered the wounds with the healing paste and to avoid any insects coming near the wounds. Each drop of the blood from his body explains the pain of years. The pain of emotions is always more than the pain of wounds.

The night is knocking, and the grandsire asks us to go to our tents. He wants to be alone; he wants to experience each pierced arrow and wants to memorize the years of struggle he has lived with. As per his wish, we stand up and decide to move back to our respective camps. On the way back, we are crossing through the bloodsheds and shipwrecked bodies, some without hands, some without legs, some without heads. The ornaments of the soldiers are lying in the field, the shields and weapons are left unattended. In the mid of these ornaments, I notice a glistening bracelet. I think I have seen this before. I get closer to observe the ornament, to my utter dismay, I realize that it belongs to the *Matsya* kingdom, the ruling region of my father-in-law. "The king Virat is alive but his sons are already dead, then to whom it belongs to I don't know.", I mutter and my heart sinks. I could think of only one name, Satanika, brother of King Virat. O Lord, what am I going to witness! Haphazardly, I rush to the ground in search of the owner of the ornament.

Not able to locate, my heart beats faster. Hundreds of emotions run through my mind. I am still trying to come out of the pain of Bhishma's fall and now this! The moist eyes try to locate the person, and the mind tries to console the heart. And then I see what I don't want to see. The body of Satanika with an arrow pierced in the chest. I know the owner of this arrow. This arrow belongs to grandsire. The grandfather, before being knocked out had done the damage, enough damage for me. My wife Uttara is still recovering from the death of her three brothers and now one more news for her. I certainly don't want to reveal this by myself. I believe the king Virat also doesn't know about his loss. A couple of minutes before, I was consoling the pain of Bhishma and now I am pierced with a number of similar arrows. The only difference is his pain the world can see but not mine. The heart cries and the eyes comprehend. I pick his body in my arms and start walking towards my tent.

The pyres are set for the martyred, thousands of soldiers were killed by the grandsire alone today and among those dead men, I place Satanika's body. The last rites are being performed and it will take hours for the fire to engulf thousands of martyrs. The pain is at its extreme. One fire is burning before the eyes and one nobody could see. There is a lot more left in the war. The son of the sun yet to show his strength. The guru yet to surprise the world with his intelligence and the rules are yet to be broken. The fire burns, the heart melts, but the desires are yet to be met. A lot yet to be seen, the preponderance yet to be shown…

DAY 11

CHAPTER 11

THE NEW COMMANDER

Skills and Perseverance when shake hands; Success is assured

The tenth night in the battlefield is over. The man who nurtured the Kuru dynasty with his blood, sweat and tears is now lying motionless, waiting for his soul to leave his body. The grandsire, as promised to Yudhishthira didn't lift any weapon against Shikhandin and Arjuna left no space in his body without an arrow. The wall of Hastinapur has fallen and the protector of throne is lying on the field. The glory and triumph of years are silent but will be remembered for the years to come.

The sun once again rises in the east and the rays fall on the field. The sun's rays falling on the armor of the grandsire reflect back on the field as his blessings on us. The bell rings and it's a signal for us to gather before the commander for today's strategy. The commander Dhrishtadyumna with Arjuna, Bhima and other brothers and warriors are standing outside our camp. We all gradually reach the meeting point and then the commander first expresses his grief for the loss of the Kuru dynasty and then praises Arjuna for being a relentless warrior yesterday. The king and other elders applaud my father and in one voice second the words of the commander. The commander starts speaking about the strategy for today and we are advised to form the crane like array, called *Krauncha* array, to protect the king and counter the attacks of Kauravas. After the retirement of the grandsire from the war, we are not sure who will be the next commander for them and what will be the attack strategy. But, Karna's entry into the battlefield is certain.

Karna, the best friend of Duryodhana, is son of a charioteer as told by my father, but he possesses skills of Kshatriyas and is a great warrior. The man with golden armor on his body, well versed in different war forms, a learnt scholar and owner of multiple deadly weapons and missiles, will enter the war zone today. Karna used to learn archery with Kuru sons in his childhood but left the school of Drona because of his bigger aspirations. He went to Guru Parshuram to learn the weapon handling skills and various war skills. When he returned, Duryodhana garnered him as the king of Anga, a small kingdom in the outer vicinity of Hastinapur.

Duryodhana was always aware that he could stand against any of the Pandu sons except Arjuna, as among all his brothers there was nobody who could counter Arjuna in archery. And when Karna came back after learning the various war skills, Duryodhana immediately befriended him, sworn him as the king of his extended kingdom, Anga, and decorated him as close ally. Karna who was filled with competitive jealousy against Arjuna accepted the offer and vowed to uproot the Pandavas whenever the opportunity given. It was Duryodhana's assumption that with the help of Karna, he could possible defeat Arjuna.

Karna's lineage is of a charioteer but because of his interest in being a warrior, he learnt the skills from the great mentors of the time. I know lineage doesn't decide the destiny, learnings ensure the future. Therefore, I have a lot of respect for him. This man has learnt beating the odds. I don't know about his envy with my father but certainly his life journey inspires many.

The grandsire on the other hand never accepted him as a warrior because his learnings were always incomplete. He left Drona's school in middle and was expelled from Parshuram's gurukul as well. Karna went to different gurukuls to pursue his aspirations but unfortunately, couldn't graduate from any institute. For the grandsire, he was a half warrior and I am sure that was the reason grandsire asked Karna to stay away from the war until he was standing as the protector of the Kuru kingdom. He felt insulted and vowed that if Bhishma manages to kill the Pandu sons, he would retire to the woods, but if the Pandavas manage to defeat or kill Bhishma, he would single-handedly slay all the Pandu sons.

And today when Bhishma is slain, Karna will be entering the battlefield with his golden armor. This is known to the commander that Karna will lead the large group of soldiers, but it is still not revealed that who will be the commander of the Kaurava army.

We are ready for the upcoming challenges; the soldiers are fearless, and the warriors are prepared. After all, we are governed by the firmness, intelligence and virtue of uncle Yudhishthira. We are protected by the man with the strength of hundred elephants, Bhima. And we are mentored by the son of Indra, Arjuna, whose enormous strength, invincible war forms and undefeatable strategies are known to the world. If this is not enough, we are guarded by the twin brothers who resemble the God of death himself and we are blessed with slayer of demons, the mystic, the god in the form of human, Krishna. There's probably not a single sane human being who would want to raise his weapon against us. With this thought in my mind and energy in my blood, I ask Sumitra to advance the chariot towards the center of the field along with other soldiers. We reach to the place and see that the opponents are yet to come. Arjuna blows his conch to invite the foes for today's combat.

A large troop with cheerless hearts is seen to be advancing from the west. The soldiers are advancing as if a commander is not decided for them. A leaderless army is like a boat without the helmsman. They approach towards us and then stop at some distance. We could see the large troop like the ocean of guards but not sure about their plans. Suddenly, I hear the rattle of chariot wheels and the hooves of steeds. A man with a shining armor dispersing the dirt on the field is advancing towards us. The sound increases as the chariot reaches near the Kaurava army. I get awestruck seeing the man with golden armor in the battlefield.

Karna enters the field. As Karna approaches, a new level of energy storms into the soldiers. The cheerless hearts jump with joy and the blowing conches and drums show the high-spirited souls. Karna enters with sixteen quivers filled with powerful arrows which resemble fire and are as poisonous as the venom of *Vasuki*. His golden armor shines brightly in the sunlight and his headgear shines like effulgence of the sun. The chariot is filled with maces, darts, shafts and the horses of his chariot are capable of running at the speed of the wind. The mighty bow with prowess equal to *Gandiva* is hanging on his right shoulder and a mighty sword capable of gulping the blood of thousands is decked in his waist. Anybody can be mesmerized with the presence of the mighty warrior with valor equal to Arjuna. Duryodhana roars loudly and expresses his happiness seeing Karna on the field.

I could see Duryodhana talking with Karna and Drona. Seems they are strategizing for today's combat or identifying the leader for the army. Nothing is audible from here and like me, the commander of our army is also confused. As per the rules defined, we can't attack till they respond to our invitation by blowing the conches and beating the cymbals. The bemused commander sends a spy towards the foes' army. We are now waiting for either the return of our spy or the acceptance for today's combat. Minutes later, the spy returns and the story which he shared disturbed the king. He asks Arjuna to stay in his close vicinity. He also asks the commander to rearrange the array and let Arjuna lead the combat. If Arjuna is the protector, no arrow can touch the king. The spy told us about the declaration of Drona as commander. He told that Karna suggested Duryodhana control the strength of warriors and to suppress the egos of powerful soldiers they needed an experienced warrior who had proved his valor in multiple occasions. Although Duryodhana wanted Karna to lead the combatants it was Karna's intelligence which directed him to nominate the guru Drona as the commander.

This impresses me. One should know when and how to use his prowess and how to make sure that the warrior of a higher caliber is satisfied. If Karna would have accepted the offer of Duryodhana in presence of Drona, many Drona's supporters would have backed off including the great archer and son of Drona, Ashwatthama. All of them are necessary to fight against us and if they win the battle, Duryodhana will definitely need the support of these warriors to support his kingdom. Karna has indeed proved his mastery and foresightedness.

Drona is paid for his skills, loyalty and perseverance. The skills of learnt Brahmana had imparted him the employment in the Kuru dynasty. He treated all his disciples equally but Arjuna was his favorite. Arjuna, with the hunger of learning, had overwhelmed the guru and Drona taught Arjuna all the skills known to him. Arjuna in return had cleared all the hurdles imposed on him. Be it shooting the metal bird hanging from the tree, be it showing prowess on the graduation day or be it capturing the King Drupada on the orders of the guru, Arjuna seized every event.

Drona is an intelligent strategy maker and skilled warrior. He was born into a poor Brahmana family, but he had aspirations to live the King's life. He worked hard under the mentorship of Guru Parashuram and earned the weapons from him. He learnt weapon handling skills and war strategies from him and left the place with the promise not to teach anyone outside Brahmana community. But his poverty provoked him to break the promise and his greed pushed him to the Kuru clan. The grandsire wanted the best mentor for his dynasty and Dronacharya was the best fit. He was given the role of chief mentor for all the princes and had the responsibility to train the future of Kuru dynasty.

I was lost in my thoughts of Guru Drona and Karna when I see the tense faces of the King and the commander. The spy told us that Duryodhana asked the commander to capture the king and not kill him. When Duryodhana expressed his desire, the new commander asked the reason for it as he could kill Yudhishthira and end the war. Duryodhana then explained that the moment Yudhishthira is killed, the next moment will be the last for everyone on the field because my father Arjuna would not accept the death of his elder brother and he would slay all the warriors. Hence, he wanted king Yudhishthira to be captured and the seized king would then be forced for another dice game. He knows Yudhishthira can never win against Shakuni and he can then enforce another exile on all the brothers. I was mesmerized at the level of political intelligence the Kauravas possessed! Though I always hated them, upon listening to their strategies, I couldn't help but admire the skills of Duryodhana, however vile his ideas might have been. This was the masterstroke from Duryodhana, and the loyal Guru is trapped in it. At the same time, this filled my heart with spite. I was appalled at the thought of how low someone could stoop for the desire of material possessions. Duryodhana wanted everything and nothing less than everything will satisfy him!

We were listening to the spy when the conch from the foes side is blown. This is the acceptance of our invitation and signal for the warriors to advance towards each other. Drona is leading the command of the foe's army. The determined Drona is approaching towards the king. Arjuna and Dhrishtadyumna are ready to counter the attacks. The shouts of *Check Drona! slay Drona!* is being heard on the field. Within a moment, the guru starts slaying the soldiers coming on his way. Nobody is spared from the wrath of Drona. The inflamed eyes are ready to consume the vast army. The chariot warriors, the elephant riders, the horsemen and the foot soldiers, all are surrounded by the mighty arrows of the guru. The venomous arrows smite the soldiers leaving a gory sight on the field. Each released arrow resembles Yama for the soldiers in the vicinity of the guru. The scattered arrows, the shafts and the lances on every side have covered the field and except blood, nothing can be seen. Killing thousands of soldiers and beheading many warriors, Drona attacks uncle Yudhishthira. Satyaki saves Yudhishthira from Guru's attack. The grinding forces of Drona are then seized by Arjuna.

When Drona enters deep inside our array formation; the army, from all the sides who are headed by different leaders, attack to control him. Drona is surrounded by Bhima, Arjuna, Satyaki, King Drupada, the twin brothers and me. We all have managed to control the unstoppable Guru. Seeing the Guru surrounded, combatants from the foe's army in large numbers rush towards us. The shower of arrows is continuous and there is no time for us to capture Drona. Shakuni and his troop have attacked from the west and uncle Sahadeva is the target.

Sahadeva's charioteer is hit by multiple shafts, and the control to steeds is lost. The horses run away breaking the reins, leaving

Sahadeva in middle of the ground. Sahadeva in return fires multiple shafts towards Shakuni breaking the latter's chariot. Shakuni picks up the mace and jumps off the chariot. Sahadeva also jumps off with his powerful club. The two warriors without their chariots but both having maces in hands stand against each other like the crest of hills. The maces strike, the sound resonates across the field.

Meantime, Drona attacks King Drupada. Both of them are struggling with their past and trying to hide the emotions of their childhood friendship behind the shower of arrows. Uncle Bhima takes on against Duryodhana's brother Vivinsati. The duel starts between them with the arrows. Vivinsati kills the horses and cut off the bow of Bhima. A couple of arrows pass through the shoulders of Bhima. Bhima roars in pain and jumps off his chariot with his strong mace. He runs towards Vivinsati and with one strike he breaks his chariot. The steeds fell on the ground and the standard of the chariot is broken. Vivinsati has no choice than to jump off the chariot. He picks his sword and shield, and rushes towards Bhima. The two angry lions both deprived of their chariots fight on the ground.

Salya fights against his dear nephew Nakul, but his love for Nakul doesn't allow him to be tough on his nephew. Nakul easily breaks Salya's chariot and frees the steeds. Salya jumps off the chariot and is rescued by the other warrior. Satyaki, the disciple of Arjuna, is fighting against Kritavarman and both target each other keen shafts. Satyaki's dexterity is similar to Arjuna's and seems he has observed Arjuna keenly. In midst of all these warriors, the two warriors of Rakshasa clan, Ghatotkacha and Alamvusha face each other. Both are of equal caliber in creating the illusions and the strategy of both the warriors is similar. The desire of slaying each other is clearly visible in the wrathful faces of *Rakshasas.*

I am standing in the close proximity of the king. As per the king's advice, Arjuna and I are not moving much today. We have to keep a watch on Drona's counters and if spy's words are true, Drona will keep no stone unturned in capturing the king. If the king is seized, the war is over. Suddenly I hear the hooves and rattle of chariot advancing towards us. I look at left and to my surprise king Paurava has entered into the closed vicinity of the king. He has cleared the outer layer and his next target is certainly us. He is the ruler of a neighboring kingdom of Sindhu, and a good friend of.

As the rattle of chariot increases, Paurava releases multiple arrows towards us. I quickly counter the attack cutting down the arrows coming towards me. Then I strike Paurava cutting down his bow. I release seven more arrows towards Paurava, the couple of them strike the steeds tied to his chariot, killing them there only. His chariot goes out of control and then I fix an arrow on the string of my bow with the target to slay Paurava. I was about to release the arrow when with the speed of the wind, Paurava smote back and cut off my bow. My arrow and bow both are wrecked and I am on Paurava's target. Quickly, I pick my sword and shield. I whirl the sword cutting the arrows coming towards me and the shield on my other hand protects me from the arrows. I jump, I whirl, and I bend to duck all the arrows coming towards me. And in the course, I advance towards Paurava and quickly ascends to his chariot. I kick his waist bending him down. I pull his hair, and he shrieks in pain.

I put my sword aside and raise him up. He is in my clench just like a snake in *Garuda's* beak. He is prostrated and hanging high from the ground on my two hands, deprived of his senses. Paurava's life is on my mercy now. I can break his spine; I can tear him apart or I can throw him high in the sky cutting him into two pieces. I then hear the loud leonine like roar from the right side. The King of Sindhu and brother-in-law of Duryodhana, Jayadratha, in the desire of protecting his dear friend is advancing towards me with sword and shield in his hand. He summons me for the duel and shouts for Paurava's life. I leave Paurava aside and jump off his chariot with sword and shield in my hand. I rush like a tiger towards the huge elephant-like Jayadratha. The metal clangs and the shields strike as soon as I reach near him. The dirt spreads all over our bodies when we touch the earth.

The tap of the feet and friction of the bodies generate a lot of chaos on the ground. We both are covered in mud and we attack each other like the lion attacks with the claws. The whiz of the sword and the clang of the metal pierce the ears and then Jayadratha with full of his strength, attacks at me with his sword. I place my metal shield in front of me, the sword pierces the shield and gets stuck to it. He pulls harder but I twist the shield breaking his sword into two. His sword is half stuck in my shield and half is in his hand. I quickly strike from my sword and cut off the remaining portion of his sword. Seeing his broken sword, he moves back a couple of steps and ascends to his chariot. A feeling of pride broadens my shoulder with the swollen chest. I smile and mount on my chariot. Both Paurava and Jayadratha are out of sight and I resume my position to protect the king.

I was engrossed in the pride of winning against Jayadratha, when I sense the trembling earth. A loud noise of chariots' wheels with hooves and clangs is approaching towards us. I see Salya in his chariot equipped with diverse weapons and grouped by a large troop of warriors is advancing. In a blink of an eye, I am surrounded by a large force and a fierce dart pierces my chariot. I see Salya laughing when the dart ignites a portion of my chariot. I quickly seize the flames and in next very moment release multiple arrows towards Salya giving him no time to react. The arrows pierce his armor and some pass through his shoulder and penetrate the earth behind him. I release multiple shafts towards the other soldiers and chariot warriors came with Salya. All of them are being greeted by the keen shafts released from my bow. I have learnt to hold the bow in both of my shoulders and like my father I can release the arrows from both my hands. The bow turns into semi-circle when I release the arrow and the foes get soaked in blood when the arrow pierces it. The other warriors from my troop including Satyaki, uncles Nakul and Sahadeva join me in combating with this troop headed by Salya. The shower of arrows from both the groups is non-stop. A fierce combat is being fought until the range; eyes can witness. The blood, the cracked bones, the crushed skulls, the displaced gears, the masterless chariots, the headless warriors and affrighted animals are all around.

The sun is at its full strength, the war is intense but there is no sign of tiredness in the warriors. The warriors sublimate the foes army as the camphor melts away as soon as it comes in fire's contact. Seeing the great number of deaths in Kaurava army, Salya releases many arrows towards my troop and a lot of soldiers lose their lives. In turn, I release an igniting arrow towards him. The arrow strikes at his chariot and it starts burning. Saving his life, angry Salya jumps off his chariot with mace in his hand. He rushes towards me, and I with plentiful energy invite him for the mace duel. I have never seen his mace fighting skills, but I have learnt mace fighting. I am confident I will be able to counter his attacks.

I jump off my chariot with mace in my hand and advance towards him. Seeing me running on the field with my mace towards Salya, Bhima picks his huge mace and jumps off his chariot. Bhima runs towards me and shouts to stay aside. Listening to his command, I stand aside giving him the way. Bhima reaches near Salya and the two warriors then stand to face each other like two immovable hills. The two mighty warriors, both skilled in mace fighting, having their powerful maces on their shoulders are ready to strike each other. The two fighters' course in circles and look into each other's souls like a hungry tiger looks at its prey. The maces strike, the clang pierces the ears. The lightning flashes on the ground as the strings decked in the maces rub each other during the strike. The two warriors, no less than each other, push their foes and try to control the other. The strikes seem never ending. On one hand Salya hits Bhima with his powerful mace, in return Bhima responds with even harder strike. The two warriors fight like the angry elephants claiming their possession in the jungle. I thank Bhima in my heart as he has asked me to stay aside. I have never witnessed Salya in mace fighting. Though I had defeated him with my arrows but with mace certainly he would have grounded me.

I am saved by Bhima or else it would have resulted in a disaster for me. I had practiced mace fighting with Bhima during pre-battle training sessions, but Salya has more experience and enormous strength, which is required for club fighting. The war between the two mace masters is continuing for long now. The mud mixed with sweat is rubbed on both of them. The two fighters look like angry bulls fight in the mud pond. The blood is pouring out, the limbs are wounded but nobody is ready to give up. The powerful strike from Salya and the tactic defense from Bhima. The maces get tangled and the two warriors roar like angry lions. The twist of the mace with expert use of an arm and Salya loses the control of his mace. Bhima quickly kicks on his chest and Salya moves back by six steps and his club leaves him. In another hit, Bhima can crush Salya's skull. He runs towards him whirling his mace but Salya runs faster and quickly ascends to Kritavarman's chariot and they both go out of sight. Bhima roars wrathfully and summons Salya for the war but he has already gone away in the ground.

Drona is far from king Yudhishthira and we have covered him well. I am sure we can protect the king till the day's war ends. I look up, the sun god is still shinning but the energy is diminishing with his presence in the western part of the field. The war on the eleventh day will end soon. The King asks his troop to put greatest possible energy in the final hours of the day and the soldiers on his command rush towards the Kaurava army shouting and roaring. The hurt soldiers become more merciless and the attacks become intense. The massive combat starts among the foot soldiers, with swords, maces, lances, javelins and other pointed weapons. Our soldiers start slaughtering the antagonists brutally. They know the day is about to end and if they dominate the opponents, the day will be declared on their side. The other key warriors of Kaurava camp are already hurt and Drona is struggling with the warriors on a different side of the field. The soldiers start running to save their lives as the Pandava camp is full of energy and they are uncontrollable. The sound of conches, cymbals and drums are mixed with the whiz of swords and clang of metals and the entire field is filled with the noise of winning hearts. Seeing the mangled soldiers of his side, Drona uses a powerful weapon against the warriors combating with him, making them immovable, and rush towards the king.

With anger in his eyes, desire in his mind and hatred in his heart, he penetrates into the middle of our army. As he enters, he shoots Shikhandin with twelve arrows, uncle Nakul with five, and uncle Sahadeva with seven and more than ten on me. The king also receives multiple arrows shot from Drona's bow and in less than half blink of the eye, the situation turns favorable towards them. The cheerless Kaurava army suddenly becomes joyous and they start shouting with their heart out. They know Drona can slay anyone coming in his way and they all are protected.

We hit back Drona with multiple arrows, but Drona knows the tricks. He has taught the warriors and only his best disciple can counter him. Our attacks on Drona seem useless as he clears them off easily. We look naive before him. Drona is furious, he is faster than wind and his dexterity of handling the bow and arrows is remarkable. He is proving that he is the Guru of the warriors of the Kuru dynasty and his skills on the field proves his authority. He is near to the king and to stop him is a mammoth task for us.

The twin brothers, the king, other sons of mother Draupadi and I, all are controlled by the single man and we have no answers for his strikes. His speed increases as the sun wants to settle down in the western hills. The red steeds of his chariot are running faster than the wind and the arrows from his bow resemble the downpour from the clouds. We start covering the king just to ensure his arrows should not reach near to Yudhishthira. The soldiers form a wall around the king, the chaos is all around, but Drona is unstoppable. He reaches in the range of the king and releases an arrow towards the king, and before we could react, another powerful arrow strikes it and there's a blast in the sky. The smoke covers the welkin, the earth shakes, the men on the ground shivers, the Guru is amazed and before the eye could blink again, a series of arrows forming a net covers Drona. Arjuna enters the vicinity of Drona. The soldiers surrounding the king jump with joy, as the protector is here. Everyone knows, till the time Arjuna is standing firm on the battlefield, nobody can reach the king.

It was too early for Kaurava camp to fill with joy and presume the victory was theirs. It was also too early for us to get panic stricken.

Father breaks the soldiers' array formed by Drona, killing thousands of them. The carnage fills the field with fresh blood and the slaughter fill the field with soldiers deprived of their souls. The soldiers of our army rush towards the opponents and make them run away from the field. A different level of energy rushes the adrenaline. The opponents run for their lives and the guru shouts in anger. Drona's desire of seizing the king is killed and the sun sets in the western hills. The day ends, the conches blow, and people start chanting for Arjuna. He saved the king and has once again proved his authority on the field. The war has not ended but we have been successful to send spine chilling fears to the Kauravas. It was Arjuna's day, a proud moment for Pandavas. The master must be elated seeing the disciple's fortitude. And somewhere in the sky, the lord must be exalting.

DAY 12

Chapter 12

THE TRAP FOR ARJUNA

Darkness of desire consumes the light of humility

Day eleven ended with the valor of Arjuna. The information gathered by the spy was correct; Drona was ruthless as his main target was to capture the king. He is loyal to the Kuru dynasty. Drona found his first employment in Kuru kingdom when the grandsire judged his ability and installed him as the chief mentor for all the princes. Once teacher to all the Kuru princes, today he is the greatest foe of the Pandavas. He taught both the groups with the same sincerity but sided with the Kauravas in the war. Was it because he got what he desired for long when he was honored with the responsibility of being the caretaker of the Indraprastha kingdom for thirteen years? He always wanted to see his son as the ruler of a throne and when the Pandavas were thrown into exile, his dream was fulfilled by Duryodhana. He gave Indraprastha to the father-son duo to maintain and rule. The desire was fed. And hence greed was born. I feel so giddy in my stomach that such learnt people will stoop so low, kill thousands of people to feed their hunger, the material desires! It's so despicable.

We witness the rising sun for the twelfth time on the field. The assembly bell rings, and we are called for the morning gathering. Though Arjuna has fought brilliantly yesterday, Drona's strategy can't be undermined. The king knows it well and his tense face says it all. The commander, Dhrishtadyumna, is walking with the bow in his hand and a confused smile on his face. He not only has to defeat Drona but also has to avenge the insult of his father, king Drupada. That happened when Drona seized the kingdom of Drupada with the help of his disciples including

Arjuna and forced Drupada to leave half of his kingdom to save his life.

The story goes back to the time when Drona and Drupada were friends in their childhood and the teenagers promised each other that whatever they would earn in life would divide equally. Later, Drupada, after completing the education became the king of Panchal and Drona was left in the rags. The years passed and Drona begot Ashwatthama. He was living in distress when one day he couldn't see his hungry son and went to Drupada and asked for half of the kingdom. Drupada declined and in turn offered him a cow which can help feed his son. Drona got angry and vowed to deprive Drupada of his kingdom, as Drupada broke his promise.

This makes me wonder, is it ethical for King Drupada to give half of his kingdom just because he promised his friend in teenage? The promise made in the teenage can be relooked as the maturity grows. A kingdom is earned, and an empire is built which can't be given in alms to anyone because of some immature promise made under the influence of emotions. Drupada had to think of his country and countrymen, while Drona was considering his son only. And when Drupada declined the demand of Drona, the furious Drona vowed to return with the army of best warriors and deprive the king of Panchal of his kingdom. He did what he vowed, and the cycle of revenge started with the first generation to next. Dhrishtadyumna, the son of Drupada, is living with the emotion of same revenge and today when Drona is decimating his combatants, his heart bleeds to save his troop and avenge for his father's wish.

The commander calls all of us and starts sharing the plan for today. We are listening to the strategist when a messenger from the Kaurava camp comes. He comes with a shock to the king. Guru Drona has played his masterstroke. The messenger tells that the Trigartas with ten thousand soldiers of their cavalry, combined with other twenty thousand soldiers from different parts of the country have summoned Arjuna for the battle in the southern part of the field. They all have vowed to either slay Arjuna or get slain today itself.

The Trigartas have their personal envy against Arjuna. They always feel that Arjuna never respected their skills which they believe is superior to all. The messenger goes back after reading their summon for Arjuna. Their plan is clear to everyone, keep father away from the core battlefield and seize king Yudhishthira, as nobody else in the field can control Drona's fire. Everyone looks at Arjuna as he must respond to their summon. If he doesn't go, the question of his valor will get tagged to his entire life and if he goes, there will be the threat to King's life in today's battle. The warrior has to choose. He takes a deep breath and speaks, "Protecting my brother from the foes is my utmost responsibility but responding to the summon is my Kshatriya dharma. My love for my brother wants me to stay in the field but my dharma wants me to go and face Trigartas. I am standing on the edge of the sword, one side of which is my family and the other side is my duty. The generations to come will remember the decision I will make today. And I will never want that the next generation of Kuru dynasty remembers their ancestor as cowards. I will respond to the summon and will go alone to face the thousands of Trigartas soldiers."

Listening to Arjuna's decision, Krishna smiles and the king gets tensed. King Yudhishthira says that he respects Arjuna's decision, but he should also make some arrangement to avoid any untoward incident during the day's war. Arjuna then nominates Satyajit, brother of Dhrishtadyumna, as the protector of Yudhishthira. Satyajit's prowess is known to all and he is as skilled as the commander. The two brothers together have won several battles in past and have proved their authority many times. Satyajit has not participated much in this war until today but his skills are undoubtedly superb. He can penetrate any array formation and is skilled in different weapons handling. Satyajit happily accepts the responsibility and Arjuna passes the baton to him. The warrior then climbs his chariot with ape image flag hoisted and rushes towards the southern part of the field with Krishna. As they go, we proceed towards the center of the field.

We reach and are welcomed by the laughing Kaurava brothers. Their trick of keeping Arjuna away from the field has worked. They believe the battle is half won with Arjuna not present in the core battle area. The loud noise of conches, the drums, and the horns show the cheerful hearts. They are arranged in the *Garuda* array, with Drona standing at the mouth of it. The head of the Garuda is formed by other Kaurava brothers. The other great warriors and the large troop of soldiers form the different parts of the array and each segment is protected by the strong force of elephant riders and mighty chariot warriors. The entire formation looks aggressive and Karna's presence in the tail of the array does the icing. The loud roar mixed with joy is audible as they have already gained the victory. The confidence in the soldiers is at its epitome. When the leader is cheerful, the followers gain enormous confidence. When the leader is confident, the acolytes are certain. And the same is happening with Kaurava camp today. Drona is confident that with no Arjuna in the opponent, he would be able to control our army and his confidence is doubled by the cheerful troops.

Seeing the array formed by Drona, Yudhishthira turns to Dhrishtadyumna to form an array which can protect us from the fury of preceptor. The commander assures king that he will counter Drona and will not let him fulfil his desire. The king is covered from all the directions. The two Panchal brothers, the twin brothers, mighty Bhima and, I with other brothers have surrounded the king with hundreds of soldiers. The conches blow, it's the signal to attack. The soldiers in unison shout loudly and rush towards the opponents. The chariot riders decked with the specialized weapons and carrying heavy bows on their shoulders target the opponents with a downpour of arrows. The elephant riders with javelins in their hands pierce the chest of opponents and the horse riders with swords cut the foes heads. The entire field is filled with chaos and the soldiers with their bodies covered with armor and mud run to kill the others.

The massacre has no end. Dhrishtadyumna rushes towards Drona with his large troop. Drona is supported by Duryodhana's brother Durmukha and his army. Durmukha counters the attack of our commander and gives way to Drona to escape the attack and target for king Yudhishthira. Dhrishtadyumna is surrounded by Durmukha and his army. Drona finds his way out and rushes towards Yudhishthira. Beholding the raging preceptor advancing towards the king, the protector Satyajit gets alert. He roars like a young tiger which runs for its first prey. He releases a powerful weapon with pointed arrows and pierces Drona at multiple places invoking Guru's anger. Satyajit then quickly releases multiple other shafts which kill the steeds of Guru's chariot. The preceptor's charioteer is also hurt and soon he loses his senses.

Drona's chariot goes out of control. With the speed of light, Guru controls his chariot and puts it on hold. Drona, the crushers of foes, doesn't want to feel belittled in front of the son of his old friend. His raging face turns red. With bloodshot eyes he picks his most powerful bow, mounts the crescent-shaped arrow on its string and releases it towards Satyajit. Satyajit doesn't get an opportunity and his head lands on the earth with the arrow. His body shakes and a bloodstream releases like a fountain from his neck. The mighty son of Drupada fought brilliantly to save the king, but controlling an angry preceptor was out of his caliber. The headless body falls on the earth. The spine of the soldiers in his troop shivers and they run away to save their lives. Satyajit, the valiant warrior of Panchal is dead. Drona quickly rushes to another chariot and mounts on it. He then targets the warriors of Matsya, Kekayas and many other kingdoms. Whoever tries to counter him loses his life. Many others flee saving their lives. He has so far defeated almost every group which came against him. The soldiers are terrified of the massacre caused by the single man.

Drona, the mightiest, the great bowman has installed fears in the minds of every soldier present in the field. The twang of his bowstring is no less than thunderbolt and the whiz of the arrows resemble the hiss of the poisonous snakes. The clangs resemble the lightning flashes and the Brahmana learnt in all war fares like a Kshatriya is standing in the mid of the field like mountain crest. He is outrageous and causing great damage to our troops. There is nobody who can control the high tides created by Drona. The killings are at extreme and the river of dead men seems to be flowing towards Yama's palace.

Uncle Bhima takes charge and with his troop targets the preceptor. The brave soldiers surround Drona backed by the warriors with powerful weapons. The large array of troops belonging to different kingdoms from remote areas surround him to counter the attacks of the guru, but nobody can achieve the feat. The Guru is at a different level today, his energy, his dexterity, his intellect, nothing can be countered. A large number of arrows are being released with every blink of eye, the foot soldiers are killing their antagonists and the elephant riders are making the other elephants master-less, but Drona is invincible. The shout of *"Kill Drona! Slay him! Attack!"* fills the surrounding, but Drona continues mangling and crushing the soldiers like elephant crushes the dry grass while walking in the forest.

The arrows released by the warriors towards Drona are being cut in the air, the ones which manage to reach near the preceptor are cut down by his mighty sword. Couple of them succeed to pierce his body but are unable to pull him down. The havoc caused by Drona since morning continues. We are at the mid of the day, but Drona hasn't given a single moment to the opponents to breathe patiently. So far, the king is protected by the large group of warriors of our side. I, with twin uncles Nakul and Sahadeva, am managing the attacks from the brothers of Duryodhana from one side but the other side of the field is completely engulfed by Drona and his troop.

Arjuna is still fighting with Trigartas supported by the other warriors. He is probably facing soldiers in thousands. I'm very worried about father as I can't see anything from my position and moreover, I don't know whether he'll at all return! The day is at its extreme and Drona knows if Arjuna remains away, he would be able to seize uncle Yudhishthira.

With the desire of capturing the Pandava king, Drona on his chariot finds the way and rushes towards the place where Yudhishthira is positioned. There is no rule being followed, the only target is to seize the king. The foot soldiers who reach too near to Drona are being crushed by his chariot wheels or his javelin pierce them. The chariot warriors are being pierced by the arrows. Those who come too close to Drona are either slain with the sword or get crushed with Drona's powerful mace. The elephant riders are being killed with multiple shafts. The hurricane of death trembles everyone and Drona resembles the God of death today. There's no regard for anyone, be it young, be it old, or be it peer. For Drona, the target is Yudhishthira and anyone coming in the way is being slain.

The pool of blood-soaked limbs and skulls are seen everywhere. The blood of horses, the blood of elephants, the blood of soldiers can't be separated. The animals tremble with fear and so do the men. Not a single person can stand him. He is rushing like a storm gulping everyone coming on the way. The sons call their fathers, the disciples remember their teachers but there is no clue to anyone on how to save their lives. The foul smell of the dead is mixed in the air making it difficult to breathe. I can see the storm created by Drona but can't control it, as I am surrounded by thousands of other soldiers. My sword has licked the blood of countless enemies and my arrows have pierced numerous bodies. There is an ocean of army all around and the soldiers of both the camps fight for their lives.

I have released many powerful missiles, some of which are countered, some of which have destroyed. The arrows, the shafts, the lances, there is no end to attack and there is no end to the killing. The combatants run for safety, but there is no safety. The soldiers on foot fight with swords, if the sword is broken, they use shields as their weapon and if the shield is broken, they use their fists to strike others. The elephants crush the skulls of dead soldiers and the horses break the bones of lying bodies while running on the field. The chariot wheels run over the dead. The sun is changing its hue, but one thing is constant, killing. This unreasonable spree of butchering has emptied the lap of many mothers, has left many fatherless, has devoid many of their brothers; but who cares.

The last hour of the day's fight, the sand is filling the lower glass fast. There is still no sign of Arjuna's return. The soldiers are killed in large numbers, and many thousands are hurt and deprived of their body parts, the remaining are tired. The energy is drained out, the mouths are dry, the faces are strained, the shoulders pain but there is no end to this war. The warriors lick their lips with their tongues and wipe the sweat from the foreheads. A lack of rain has made the warzone extremely dry. The dust covers the entire field and the armies are all grounded. In the midst of the clouds of dust, the horse hooves and the rattle advances towards us. With the sound of whiz, an arrow passes adjacent to my ear, this was Drona's arrow. I look around, Drona, Karna and Ashwatthama with their troops are approaching me. Uncle Bhima is fighting with other Kaurava brothers deep inside the opponents' area. Satyaki is handling Salya and the commander is busy combating with Kripa. This area is under my charge after the death of Satyajit in the morning. The twin brothers are also with me encompassing the king to protect him from any untoward incident. Drona and others are very near to us. Karna charges against uncles Nakul and Sahadeva. Ashwatthama targets me. The twang of the bowstrings and the swish of swords can be heard from all the sides. The thunderous strikes generate the flashing lights capable of making eyes blind.

While we are engaged with Karna and Ashwatthama, Drona gets the opportunity to advance towards the king. Drona is getting lethal and his skills overpower everyone present in the ground. He releases his arrows in the desire to surround the king, the arrows in great numbers start making a wall around Yudhishthira, another arrow turns into the rope and bind the charioteer. The steeds are immovable. The king doesn't get time to counter Drona's attack. His bow doesn't follow his command, his hands don't reach near his javelin and his feet are standstill. Drona has surrounded the king from all sides. The sun is setting, and the dusk is knocking. Few more minutes, if Drona manages to capture the king, all the efforts of past days will be in vain. The heart sinks, the breathing becomes heavy, the mouth becomes dry and when the darkness surrounds, the faint cry of hope is heard from the distance pleading for life. The sound of moving chariot coming through the clouds of dirt and dust mixed with the twang of mighty bow generates an unknown energy in the nerves. This is the twang of *Gandiva.*

The warrior, Arjuna, the slayer of foes with the owner of this universe, is coming and before we could see him coming out of the thick cloud, an arrow advances towards the king breaking the wall around him. Having crossed many large lakes filled with the blood of the soldiers and having slain large troop of thousands of Trigartas soldiers, Arjuna marks his presence in the center of the field. The protector is here. We jump with joy; a new energy is injected into our bodies. The presence of Arjuna and Krishna is enough to affright the foes.

And as soon as he arrives, the merciless *Gandiva* releases arrows in hundreds and thousands, killing the Kauravas' soldiers. The foes are mute spectators. Arjuna gives no chance to anyone on the field to strike back. The smile on Krishna's face removes all the pain from the wounded soul. I pick my other strong bow, *Raudra*, mount the string with multiple pointed shafts and release it against the foes. Ashwatthama and his army are badly hurt with the strikes. I look at father, he looks back at me and nods his head. As if he acknowledges my way of fighting. The sound of "Help!" and "Save!" is being heard on the ground and the soldiers call for help. They run hither and thither to save their lives. There is blazing fire all around and a thick smoke has covered the entire field. There is nothing visible on the field and the continuous downpour from Arjuna's bow increases the problems of the foes' soldiers. Arjuna signals the king to move away from the field ensuring his safety. The sons of mother Draupadi surrounds him and takes him far away from Drona's attack.

Drona and Karna try to stop Yudhishthira but father, twin uncles and I counter the attacks making sure the safe exit of the king from the danger zone. The king is safe, and father Arjuna is back and the sun changes its hue and tries to settle in the abode of western hills. This is the end of the day, the conch blows signaling the end of the combat for the day and the soldiers start moving back to their respective tents.

The entire field is filled with the motionless bodies, few with cut limbs, few without heads, and few without armors. The red slush on the ground makes it difficult to move. A large number of elephants and horses are killed, and the vultures are seen flying above the ground in the desire of feeding on those carcasses. Drona's vow is not fulfilled, and the king is protected. The warrior with immeasurable prowess, Arjuna, has successfully managed his dharma and his responsibility. Arjuna has paved the way for today's victory over Kauravas. The Guru mustn't be happy, and he will certainly be back with more strength and vengeance in his heart, but today is our day. Arjuna is being praised by the king and I feel proud, after all, I am Arjuna's son.

The evening turns darker and the blanket of stars cover the clear sky. The cool breeze touches the wounds and reminds me the events happened during the day. The physicians are working tirelessly to ensure the hurt soldiers get the treatment faster. It was Arjuna's idea to divide the entire army into multiple smaller groups and each group will have its own group leader, physician and weapon supplier. This way, the commander doesn't have to supervise the entire army if hundreds of thousands of soldiers and the supply would not be affected. I visit the soldiers of my group, few hurt, few with sloshed arms, few plastered, and few died. I take the help of the medico to heal my wounds and then move to my tent. The loud cry of pain from both sides of the camp can be heard clearly in the ground.

Finishing off my evening ablutions, I retire to my bed. I try to sleep but the eyes are wide open. I look at Uttara, she is in her deep thoughts. Looking at the roof, her right palm is on her belly. As if she is trying to make our unborn sleep. The war has robbed her family. The entire generation is just wiped out. Her moist eyes share her heart's stories. This is not only her story, but this is every soldier's story. There are many who didn't even meet their loved ones after committing to this war. And many more died without meeting their kin. My soul haunts to imagine the situation once the war will get over. Will anyone survive? The noise of insects and howling of jackals confirm the night is at its darkest. Not just dark because of the absence of light, the night is darkened with the absence of humanity, with the absence of the light in the hearts of people. Darkness of desire has consumed all. Who's right, who's wrong? What's the purpose of killing, butchering so many people? When will it all end? I am still turning on the bed, thinking of today's circumstances.

Uttara is fast asleep; her placid face is a stark contrast to the incidents on the field. Immersed in thoughts, I wonder that today, my father came just at right time. What if he wouldn't have managed to come back? What if Drona was successful in his desire of seizing the king? The events of the past haunt the future and the present shakes.

DAY 13

CHAPTER 13

THE CHAKRAVYUH

Situations persuade decisions and the decisions determine actions

The orange ball comes over the eastern hills once again and the sky turns crimson. The dawn knocks on our doors signaling a new day and a fresh start. The pain of yesterday should not hound the progress of today, but alas, can we really forget the past?

The Sun God showers his blessings on the immortals of the earth. The flower blooms, the sand on the soil shines like millions of pearls and the water droplets on the tree leaves reflect the colors of different hues. The morning bell rings, it is time for the daily gathering. The emotions of last night are over and I, filled with great energy, start towards the meeting place.

I look at Uttara, she sees me. She holds my hand and her eyes don't want me to leave today. A tiny tear droplet on her cheek looks like the dew droplet on a lotus petal. The pink face is mixed with the kohl of her eyes. She runs and blocks my way trying to plead me to stay, her moist eyes are louder than any word. She picks my bow and to hide it, rests her waist on it. Her bosoms are drenched with the tears rolling from her eyes. She comes near to me, looks at me with the teary eyes. I lift her hand; the henna in her palm smells fresh. She moves closer and rests her head on my chest. I embrace her, my arms surround her slender waist. I give a peck on her head. Her head rests on my chest, I lift her chin and try to console her. I blink my eyes, nod my head, lick my lips, but I can't say anything. The two pairs of eyes meet again. She embraces me, the touch of her lips on mine feels like a nimble fresh rose petal on my lips. Her eyes are closed, and the tears are rolling ceaselessly. I put my hands on her shoulder, squeezing them a bit. She moves back leaving me, she knows there is no way I can stay back. She wipes her tears with the edge of cloth on her loin. A young girl with moist eyes suddenly becomes a mature woman. She is part of Kshatriya clan and call of duty is prime for the Kshatriyas. She hands over my bow to me and with a forced smile on her face sends me off to another day of carnage.

I come out of the tent while wiping the dampness of my eyes; a Kshatriya is not bound to any emotions, when on battlefield. I stretch my arms, put my bow on my shoulder and walk towards the meeting point. I see the tense face of the commander and the smiling face of Krishna. No matter what the situation, the calmness on Krishna's face doesn't go away. He is a mystic and his acts mysterious. His presence consoles the grieving hearts and his speech directs the confused minds. He knows the secrets of life and no wonder why father picked him and not his army for the war. He vowed not to pick any weapon in the war against the Kauravas, but father knew his guidance and intelligence can turn the dice at any time. Krishna doesn't need to lift a weapon, as his mind is the sharpest weapon on this planet.

I look at the king, the follower of dharma, uncle Yudhishthira. He is Kshatriya by birth but has lived the ascetic life always. He enjoys the company of learnt Brahmanas and though he is in the war, his mind always thinks of the safety of his countrymen and friends. I see Bhima, the man like a mountain. His strong arms had crushed many skulls on the field in past days. An expert mace fighter who can knock down an elephant with one strike, uncle Bhima, is also a soft-hearted and most lovable human being. He adores his family more than any other brother and his love for the sons of all Pandu sons is above any other commitments.

The twin brothers, Nakul and Sahadeva, handsome like Ashwin brothers, intelligent policymakers, clever negotiators and skilled warriors are also standing beside the king. I see father standing near his chariot, fixing his quivers and arranging his bows, swords, maces and other keen arrows. The shafts, lances, pointed darts in numbers of hundreds and thousands are being loaded on his chariot.

He is directing the helpers to arrange all the weapons so that he could reach out to them easily. His chariot is mounted with a high ape-bannered flag. I nod my head looking at him, he nods his head and raises his hand to give his blessings. I pause for a second before him, but he waves his hand asking me to join the commander and other elders to listen to today's strategy. I once again nod my head and move towards the place where others are gathered.

I reach to the place and it doesn't take more than a minute to understand what Drona is going for today. Once again, Trigartas in numbers of sixty thousand soldiers have summoned father for a battle. Yesterday, father defeated the group of thirty thousand soldiers and killed Drona's desire in the single day. Today, they doubled their strength and invited him again. The Kshatriya dharma is again calling but when we know the arrangement is intended for a definite death, is it right to intentionally dip the head into the well of filth? When we know the clear intentions of Drona, why, father is being sent again today? The dharma doesn't say that one should leave his countrymen bewildered, just because, some other clever group is politically correct. A Kshatriya once invited by an individual or a group for the war, as per the rules, doesn't deny the summon. An incorrect decision is once a mistake; but twice it's a blunder. Are we heading towards the blunder? The situations persuade the decisions and the decisions determine actions. Arjuna is forced into a situation and his decision will determine our actions.

Krishna drives him away, to the same southern region where thousands of soldiers are ready to slay him. Trigartas are committed but Arjuna is merciless. We are sure he will be back unhurt; his weapons can engulf an ocean of soldiers; but what will happen to this part of the field until the time he comes back, nobody knows. We are committed to the king but Arjuna's absence will discourage the soldiers. As he goes, the commander takes the center stage and makes Bhima as the leader of the army for today. Satyaki, Nakul, Sahadeva and I are assigned to protect the king and the other warriors are asked to support us. The King of Panchal, the sons of mother Draupadi, the king of Matsya,

Ghatotkacha, Shikhandin and many other soldiers are positioned surrounding us. We look protected and the array resplendent. The commander asks us to move towards the center of the field. We reach the battlefield and then the scene on the field is enough to shake the firmament. The soldiers look terrified and the body hair stands straight till the end. The array formed by Drona for today is beyond our thoughts.

The soldiers decked with red banners, red armors, red robes stand by one another. The first layer is moving, and the second layer is moving reverse with the same number of warriors having the power of solar effulgence. They are protected by Jayadratha, son-in-law of Dhritarashtra. The third layer is formed by brothers of Duryodhana and their troops. Behind the Kaurava brothers are standing the mighty warriors, Karna, Kripa, Dushasana, Ashwatthama, Shakuni, Kritavarman and Drona himself. The next layer of the array is formed by sons of Duryodhana and Dushasana. And in the midst of the array, stands Duryodhana.

All the layers form a giant circle with no gap to reach to the Kaurava prince. The preceptor has formed the great circular array. Drona has formed the CHAKRAVYUH! The array is unbreakable, protected and well renowned in various scriptures. No battle in the distant history was fought with such array and thus, only a few warriors, the greatest of the great warriors know how to penetrate, destroy and come out of this Chakravyuh. Seeing the large array of Kauravas, the soldiers in my troop tremble with fear. Most of them have never seen such an arrangement in their lives and only few of them might have just read about it in scriptures. Drona has used his trump card today and we don't have an answer to it.

The excited Kaurava army blows the conches inviting us for the combat. The bells, the drums, the horns are creating a huge noise shaking the earth and shivering the welkin. Dhrishtadyumna responds to the invitation and commands the army to advance towards the foes. The valiant son of Bhardwaj, one born out of a pot, the great teacher, Drona, commands his army to release the arrows in great numbers. The first layer of their array protects the attack from our side and the soldiers behind them leave no opportunity to counter us. Like the high tides of ocean break the rocks on the shore, the soldiers of Drona's army break the array formed by us. The soldiers run for their lives and the warriors don't find any way to control the furious Drona. The soldiers ask for mercy from the king and the king helplessly looks at them. Arjuna is not around and nobody else can break and destroy this giant circular array.

King Yudhishthira looks at me and says, "Son! There is nobody in this earth except Arjuna, Krishna and Pradyumna who can penetrate and destroy this array. But you are the only fourth person who knows the science behind this array. This is the time to repay the debt of your sires."

"O Valiant Abhimanyu! take this responsibility of destroying this array and reproving us all. For a family, a son can be sacrificed, for a village a family, for a country a village and for one's soul this whole earth can be sacrificed. This is not about one family or one country; this is about the truth and justice. This is for the redemption of the soul and to prove the significance of one's birth on this earth. O Braveheart! Take up your arms and destroy this array of Drona", he continues.

Everybody knows the worth of Arjuna's presence on the field and now when he is away, we feel dependent. The presence of a warrior, a leader, a commander makes the entire troop cheerful and the king jubilant. But today, the story is quite different. Standing on the chariot, I bow down to the king after listening to his desires. I have been taught to penetrate and enter this kind of array, but I didn't get a chance to learn how to come out of this array. "I shall not be able to rescue myself if the danger overtakes me.", I tell him with a tinge of apprehension in my voice.

King knows there is no other way to stop the hurricane and there should be someone who should break this array. He asks me to break the array and make the passage for other warriors to enter. And then uncle Bhima also agrees to the plan of someone making way to enter the array. Once the soldiers are inside the array, they will get the chance to counter the attacks and stop the continuous striking.

This sounds like it'll work, we have a strategy to attack and the backup to support me. I pick the heaviest bow in length equal to six cubits, arrange the arrows and ask Sumitra to rush towards the array.

"I am confident of killing anyone coming on my way and making my sires proud today." I tell Sumitra.

Sumitra knows me very well. He is observing my fighting skills from the first day of the war. He asks me "O sire, what is CHAKRAVYUH?".

I explain to him "This is an array of oscillatory motion. The soldiers are moving clockwise and counterclockwise in seven layers. The Guru has presented his best skill today with just one motive, to capture the king. The outer layer is formed by a group of strong soldiers and the inner layers with even stronger warriors. There is no way to escape the death. It is spinning on the field ready to consume everything like a grinding machine."

This is enough to affright any soul on the earth. And Sumitra is baffled by my explanation. With a perplexed face he asks, "If it's so complex, how do we get in?".

I further elaborate, "The seven layers each moving in counter direction to each other has just one small opening, guarded by many strong soldiers. There is certainly no easy way to enter and there is no way to escape at all. We will have to move with the flow of soldiers to sustain the attacks for a very long time with great perseverance and tenacity. We must be patient and focused."

Even after listening to everything, Sumitra seems to be still in doubt and with all his regards for me, he says, "O dear! You are the blessed one. You are a great warrior who can fight with hundreds of soldiers single-handedly. You judge the situation and then react, but today, as your charioteer, as a friend, I want you to ascertain whether you would be able to counter the preceptor's fury. O, great bowman! I want you to judge the gravity of the situation and then react. Your confidence should not become your arrogance. The wit shouldn't meet the destruction."

I listened to him, and with the pride of being Arjuna's son and Krishna's nephew I tell him that there is nobody in this field who can install fear in my heart. I have been invincible in the field all the days, no arrow can break my confidence, and no sword can stop my way. I am unstoppable, I am fearless, I am Arjuna's son!

On my command, Sumitra makes the steeds run with speed of wind towards the array. I strike continuously killing any soldier coming in the way. The Pandavas are following me as per the plan to enter the array as soon as I make a passage for them. Drona commands his soldiers to counter my attacks. I ask Sumitra to keep on moving and I release the arrows in hundreds and thousands. The arrows strike the soldiers, cutting them. Few lose their heads, few their hands, and many other vital parts. The soldiers are well decked with the armor, but I know where to strike to cause the maximum damage. The blood is flowing all over the ground.

Sumitra is cruising with the highest velocity and with a similar speed, I strike the arrows. Observing the speed with which I am advancing towards the array, Duryodhana shouts and commands his troops to slay me. I am determined to break the array and make the passage for Pandava army. I am lucky today to face the cruel prince of Kaurava who has directed this war. The man whose actions resulted into the disharmony among the brothers of the same clan, who had cast away the righteousness and is responsible for all the killing happening for past thirteen days is my target today. I release my arrows towards the place where Duryodhana is positioned but he is quite far and well protected by Drona. My arrows couldn't reach him but if my chariot rushes at the top speed, I will definitely find some spot to target Duryodhana.

Drona sends his top skilled warriors to cover Duryodhana and to stop me. Karna, Salya, Kripa, Ashwatthama and Drona himself start smiting. The arrows are being showered covering me all around. Many arrows strike my armor, many more pierce my chariot. I look at Sumitra. He is safe and he knows how to protect himself. He is a skilled charioteer. The striking is continuous and many of them pierce different parts of my body. But they cannot discourage me today. I pick the weapons given to me by my father and uncle. With those powerful arrows, I strike back piercing these warriors in great numbers. I target the unarmored body parts of my foes as they have undermined my capability of identifying the vital parts inside the armor.

First, I hit Karna. The arrow hits his arm, and he loses his control. In pain, he sits on his chariot giving me the opportunity to strike Salya. With one smite, Salya faints and falls on his chariot. Salya's brother comes to rescue him and covers him from my attacks. But my confidence is at its extreme. I see nobody as an obstacle today, be it sire, be it normal soldier, be it a great warrior, or be it the charioteer. For me all are antagonists, all are the same weal filth!

I strike Salya's brother and cut off his head. His chariot's wheels, the pole on his chariot, the banner, the steeds and charioteer, all are cut off. Like a young cub, I am hurling towards the herd of elephants. Dushasana sees me and then sees hurt Karna and Salya. Filling with rage, he utters a loud roar and smites arrows towards me. He is an expert chariot fighter and knows his moves well. Sumitra commands the steeds to run in the circle, saving both of us from the strikes.

I strike back with the venomous arrows which hit Dushasana's shoulders and penetrates his body. He loses his senses and falls on his chariot. His charioteer takes him away from the field. Then, Kripa and Drona try to strike me down. They have shot many arrows towards me. I am continuously running towards the array in a hope to find the loose end. Like vulture looks for its prey, I look for the spot to hit and smash the array. Bhima, Shikhandin and Satyaki are following me. They provide me backup and counter the attacks from Kaurava army.

I look around, target the point, pick my heaviest bow, *Raudra*, mount the most powerful arrow on it. I pull the string making the ends of the bow touching my body and with the speed of light, I release the arrow. As the arrow strikes the ground, it explodes. The strike felt like the sun exploding and igniting everything around it and burning everything in its range. The soldiers run for their lives leaving the barriers. I then release multiple other shafts covering the heaven. The arrows strike the soldiers as the rain falls from the thick black clouds. The thick shower of arrows trembles the soldiers and before Drona could react, Sumitra commands the steeds to jump over the first barrier. *CHAKRAVYUH* breaks.

I blow my conch, signaling the Pandavas army to advance and attack. My arrows consume the foes and my chariot penetrates into the array like a *Makara* enters the ocean. Mangling the steeds, the chariots, the elephants, the elephant riders, and the foot soldiers, I keep on moving deeper and deeper into the array. The first layer is destroyed, and the passage is clear for uncle Bhima and his troop to enter the array. I look behind, uncle Bhima, Shikhandin, Satyaki, and many other warriors are not far.

"I am sure they will make their way inside the array" I mutter and continue towards the center of the array.

The speed of my young steeds is uncontrollable, and the skills of my charioteer are unmatchable. The foes' army run helter-skelter and I don't pause the striking. I look back again; the Pandu sons are at the edge of the passage. And as Bhima's chariot is about to enter the array, the passage is closed by the thick wall of arrows. And in front of the wall stands, the ruler of Sindhu, *Jayadratha*. I feel terror the first time. If the Pandavas army can't enter the array, I know the result. I look at Sumitra, his face pales. I smile and nods my head. I close my eyes and remember my father. I am the son of Arjuna, a Kshatriya, mentored by Krishna for years. The fear can't evaporate my determination.

Jayadratha is a learnt warrior and he has upscaled his skills to control any number of warriors for one day. He is blessed with many celestial weapons which can counter the attacks of any warrior on this earth, except Arjuna. And today, Arjuna is not present in this battlefield. I can hear the twang of his bowstring and the whiz of his arrows, the cries of affrighted troops and the leonine roar of that warrior. I can neither stop nor return. My present is in the array and my destiny is in arrows. I can kill and win, or I can die and lose but the day is mine, By now, Jayadratha has already filled all the gaps created by me and there is no passage left for Pandavas to enter the Chakravyuh. I am on my own. Seeing no option left, I lift my bow and continue striking. The arrows cut off the bows, the arms and the heads of the enemies. I am ready with my sword and mace whoever comes close to my chariot.

My mace crushes many skulls and my sword shatters many limbs, but nobody can stop me. Arrow by arrow, whiz by whiz, clang by clang, I am moving swiftly towards Duryodhana. I know there is nobody to back me today, there is nobody to cover me today. I am on my own. My win or my defeat is in my hands. If I conquer, I will be remembered. If I die, I will make sure the generations will be proud.

Rukmaratha, son of Salya, and Vasatiya, a ruler from some remote region and their hundred soldiers make a strategic move towards me on the command of Drona. The arrows, the keen-pointed shafts, swords and many other weapons are being used by those warriors. Those arrows cover me, and Sumitra finds no way to move the steeds. "We are stuck", shouts Sumitra.

Finding no option, I think of *Gandharva*, a weapon which could create illusions. Father gave this to me and taught me the usage. I mount the weapon on my bowstring and release it in the sky. In a matter of seconds, the entire area is filled with water flowing down from the wall created by arrows. The next second, it creates hundred more Abhimanyu striking from different directions. A hundred warriors now face hundred lookalikes. The trick worked and I get an opportunity to shoot all the warriors, making their path towards Yama's palace. The God of death must be busy today. This is just the beginning and I move further.

The soldiers running on the field make the dirt clouds. The eyes are not able to find the target but the ears direct with the sound of weapons. Suddenly, I receive an arrow on my left hand. It brushes my hand and lands on earth behind me. Clearing the dirt, a chariot pulled by four white steeds comes towards me. This is Lakshmana, son of Duryodhana, an invincible warrior. I remember I spared his life on the fifth day of the war when he became weaponless. He was lying senseless on his chariot and was on my target but as per the rules of the war, I spared his life and then he was taken away by his charioteer. I hear his loud voice.

He is inviting me to the combat, "O son of Arjuna! I am here to avenge my defeat on the fifth day. When I became weaponless, you smote me. If I wouldn't be rescued, I would have died. Today, I will not give you an opportunity. It's between you and me now."

A smile comes to my face. How people misjudge and misinterpret? When you are full of hatred, even the positive done by the opponents are censored. Only I know that I didn't kill him despite him being on my target but why should I explain. He is my enemy. Today he is decked with the weapons which will be answered by mine. He strikes me with tens of shafts. My body is now experiencing no pain, be it any number of arrows striking it. The goal now is not to protect self but to somehow reach the Kaurava prince and turn him down. I release a couple of arrows in response to Lakshmana's attack. The arrows strike him, his body bleeds. I don't have much time left and the journey is long. I mount a crescent-shaped arrow on my bow and release with full energy towards him. Within the blink of an eye, his headless body falls on the earth releasing the fountain of blood. His head mounted on the crescent-shaped arrow touches the soil behind his chariot. Lakshmana is no more.

Seeing his dead son, Duryodhana roars loudly and I smirk at him. He commands his close aides to fight back and the six warriors run towards me. I tell Sumitra not to stop and rush towards those six warriors. The time has come, I will disburden this earth today from the cruelty. I will free myself with the debt I owe to my sires and Krishna. I will today avenge the injustice happened years ago.

Pulling the string of *Raudra* and creating a great twang I summon all of them. I release the arrows in hundreds with every blink of my eye, I have become ambidextrous. The nimbleness of my hands allows me to strike the foes in great numbers. The arrows thus released, hit Drona, Kritavarman, Karna and Kripa. The warriors who are advancing towards me are all hit by my arrows. In turn, I am completely covered with arrows released by them. My entire body is pierced with multiple arrows and the blood is all around my chariot. My armor is drenched with blood and my body looks like a porcupine. A close friend of Duryodhana then picks his sword and rushes towards me. I strike him down from his chariot and quickly release multiple shafts. The shafts deprive him of his soul. Thousands of his soldiers run away, seeing the senseless body of their master.

No count to how many soldiers, I have slain since morning. My quivers are emptying up. There is no way for further supply of the weapons, and I have to fight with the remaining ammunition. The mace, the sword and the few arrows left in the quivers are my protectors now. There is no way out anywhere near. The ocean of soldiers has checked all the exits and I don't have any powerful arrow left which can ignite and create the passage. I was busy with the planning in my mind, then an arrow strikes my chariot. The standard and one wheel of my chariot break. In very next moment, a couple of arrows strike the horses, killing all of them on the spot. My four-legged friends are dead.

The arrows strike Sumitra as well and I didn't get a chance to save him as well. A tiny tear rolled out of my eye, seeing my dear friend dying in front of my very eyes. With no choice left, with the sword and shield I jump off the chariot. I am now surrounded by the great warriors of Kaurava army. Like hunters surround a cub, they have encompassed me leaving no space for me to move out. The next strike from Drona cuts off my sword and shield. I am standing weaponless. They rush towards me with their swords and maces in hands. I see the second wheel of my chariot. I pull it out and with both my hands I lift it making it my weapon.

I protect myself from the arrows coming towards me with the wheel. But another strike from Karna and the wheel smashes. I rush towards my chariot looking for a weapon. I see a mace, the last option in my deck. I pick it and like an angry tiger I walk on the field whirling the mace in the air. Blood is oozing from my wounds and my breathing is slow, but the momentum is high, the commitment is higher, and the determination is highest. I rush towards them with only one thought, kill whoever comes in front, be it, man, be it animal. I jump and strike Ashwatthama's steeds, all are dead. Ashwatthama jumps off his chariot with his sword.

I strike elephants and horses and any other soldiers and warriors coming towards me. The blood is the only thing which can be seen on the ground. Ruthless me is standing in the midst of the sea of blood, also drenched in maroon.

Shakuni's brother with his acolytes surrounds me. They all are equipped with maces and swords. I am surrounded like a young cub by a pack of wolves. I whirl my mace and strike without any second thought. I can only hear the sound of cracking bones and crushing skulls. Shakuni's brother dies with his followers and I roar with full of my strength. I look up at the sky, this is the first time of the day I checked the position of the sun. The Sun God is very near to the western hills trying to settle down. I look around, the soldiers are in hundreds and thousands. My breath is continuously slowing down, my eyesight is becoming blurred and the blood from the wounds is not stopping, the pain is numbing my thoughts. I rise once again, with a loud voice summoning the foes, I break the chariot of Durmasena, son of Dushasana. He jumps off his chariot with his mace. I rotate my mace and strike at him. He counters the attack and kicks me back. I hit him on his shoulder, and he hit my back. I strike again and in turn, he kicks my waist. And before I could react, he strikes my head with full strength. With a loud thud, I collapse on the ground with my broken skull.

My eyes won't open as I lay motionless with no energy left to lift myself. I look up at the sky, the clouds are scattered giving way to the sun's rays to spread across the skyline making it crimson. The cool breeze touches my wounds trying to soothe the pain, the mind is calm, the heart wants to stop pumping and the soul wants to leave the body. I clench my fist to pause the time, but the unclenched fist is left with the traces of sand and memories of the injustice. The Kaurava warriors with their superior weapons are standing near me and want to suck out the last drop of blood from my body. The power has killed the wisdom, the land which was irrigated with the love and harmony for years is today drenched with hatred. I want to stand one more time, want to raise my arm and hold my bow high, want to pull the string and mount the arrow, but for what? The story which was started years ago is not yet ended but a chapter is getting closed. The desire has killed the humility and the cynicism have rotten the wisdom. Power is being exploited for worldly benefits and the justice had died years ago. The masters fight against disciples, the sons against the fathers and the friends turn foes, but for what? Only greed! Human greed has paved the way for the destruction of humankind. The stone-hearts and ignorance decimate the glory of mankind. My mind wants to wake me up, but my heart asks, for what? When blood becomes enemy and thirst becomes the desire, and when the fear has killed the light of hope, I don't want to rise again.

I will rise when knowledge will be supreme, when the masters will get their glory, and the elders will get the due respect. I will come back to the world when humility will be chosen over desire and the wisdom over terror. When the wish to live for the country will be more than the belief of killing for the land, when the warriors will not fight for the loyalty but for the liberty, I will come back. I will breathe my last breath today, the last drop of blood will pour out, the soul will be freed, the mind will leave with no desire and the body will have no senses, but I dream for the world when humanity will prevail. I dream of oneness and fraternity, I dream of the land with space for everyone with no boundaries, and I dream of one world one home.

To be continued...

ACKNOWLEDGEMENTS

This book, in its entirety, in many ways is a collective effort of different minds working together. I am inspired by various research works based on the epic MAHABHARATA in the past, by many intellectual writers, gurus and guides. This book is an adaption of the epic which has been glorified in different versions by different people. The work couldn't be a reality without the support and efforts of my friend *Suranjan Paul,* who has guided, corrected and edited the book at different stages. I thank him for his endless support throughout the journey.

The book can never be completed without reading the prose translation of the epic by *Kisari Mohan Ganguli* and retelling of the story by *C. Rajagopalachari.* The modern retelling of Mahabharata by *Carole Satyamurti* left a firm impression too. Last but not the least; the endless articles and theories on the epic which are the expressions, opinions, perspectives of various esteemed writers in time have been a source of inspiration to dig deeper into the story.

Lastly, a big thank you to my wife, *Varuna* for her continuous words of encouragement which has kept the pace going till the last word.

www.ingramcontent.com/pod-product-compliance
Lightning Source LLC
Chambersburg PA
CBHW031342230926
51848CB00002B/343

* 9 7 8 8 1 9 3 6 6 0 2 8 7 *